## A MARRIAGE
## MADE IN MYSTERY . . .

Raising her head, she froze and listened. Someone was unlocking both locks. She heard the door open and shut. Heavy muffled steps went along the entrance hall and then came closer as they moved up the circular carpeted staircase.

Lori moistened her lips and tried to form some kind of question or protest. "Who is it?"

No one answered.

Flinging her purse aside, she got to her feet as he came into view. As he paused and deliberately looked her up and down, an expression of disdain settled on his face as if she represented something very repugnant to him. Then he gave a short laugh that had no mirth in it.

"So my new wife has arrived," he said. "Welcome home, Mrs. Brandon."

# THE HOUSE-SITTER

## LEE KARR

AVON
PUBLISHERS OF BARD, CAMELOT AND DISCUS BOOKS

THE HOUSESITTER is an original publication of Avon Books. This work has never before appeared in book form.

AVON BOOKS
A division of
The Hearst Corporation
959 Eighth Avenue
New York, New York 10019

Copyright © 1980 by Leona C. Karr
Published by arrangement with the author
Library of Congress Catalog Card Number: 80-67441
ISBN: 0-380-76364-8

First Avon Printing, October, 1980

AVON TRADEMARK REG. U.S. PAT. OFF. AND IN
OTHER COUNTRIES, MARCA REGISTRADA, HECHO EN
U.S.A.

Printed in the U.S.A.

*To Marshall,*
*who shares my joy.*

# One

"This is it, lady," said her taxi driver as he set two heavy suitcases on the ground. Then he opened the back door for her and waited for her to get out.

Lori hesitated, checking once more the address on a mailbox with the one on her paper. They were the same: Dr. and Mrs. Philip Brandon, 9801 E. Packard Road. This was the place she was supposed to house-sit for the summer.

Even though she was always nervous on a new assignment, getting acquainted with a strange house and any dogs, cats, raccoons, and, on the last job, a pet snake, she had never experienced this hesitation, this sudden sense of uneasiness that kept her from stepping out of the cab and walking confidently up the steps of her new home.

She was not familiar with this part of Denver. In the five years that she had been gone, the city had sprawled out in every direction. This area was sparsely populated, and only a few isolated houses dotted some rocky bluffs that ran in jagged patterns to the south.

The house was new. That's it, thought Lori, peering out the open car door. That was it. It was too new!

The kind of mess workmen leave around a new house was still there—scrap lumber, clumps of hard mortar, bits of wire, and paint cans. The sprawling house didn't look as if even one coat of stain had been put on the wood siding. No landscaping of any kind was evident, and only some wild bushes and tasseled squirrel grass softened the rocky slopes surrounding it.

Undoubtedly the house had been designed to fit into the landscape, but to Lori, as she stared up at it, the dwelling resembled a monstrous insect, squatting against

7

the hill, staring at her with glazed, triangular eyes of glass. The style of the house was ultra-modern in design. It had a rising and falling roof line that accented triangular-shaped windows that slanted forward at sharp angles. A sundeck stuck out in front of two large glass doors which loomed over the driveway where Lori stood. Four stone fireplace chimneys jutted into the air above the irregular roof, looking like black appendages in the darkening afternoon sky.

"That'll be twelve fifty, lady." The driver's bluntness was an obvious effort to get her out of his cab and off his hands as soon as possible. He shifted his gaunt frame impatiently. "This is 9801 East Packard Road. That's the address you gave me," he insisted.

"Yes, that's what it says here." She read the slip once more. There was nothing she could do but get out of his cab and pay him the fare.

"I guess I'll need help up the stairs with those bags," she said apologetically and added another dollar to her tip. She hadn't planned on spending this much on taxi fare, but then she had no way of knowing this address was so far out of the city. Trying to still a nervous fluttering in the pit of her stomach, she put her shoulder bag on one arm and a bulging tote bag on the other. She turned and followed the driver up an unpaved driveway to some stairs between the house and an empty three-car garage.

Grunting, the cabbie lumbered up a dozen steep wooden steps, which Lori guessed must lead up to a back door. The staircase leaned against the rocky hillside as if its stability and strength were only tenuous and it might collapse at any moment.

He let the suitcases fall with a thud and a muttered swear word. His thin arms and legs didn't look as if they were used to much exercise.

"Thank you," she gasped, breathing heavily herself.

"Have to be a damn mountain goat," he said disgustedly and shook his head as if there were no accounting for the stupidity of some people. Then with a slight touch to his hat, he went back down the steps without volunteering to see her inside. His fare didn't include bellhop duties. Muttering as much to himself, he folded his long legs under the steering wheel and without another glance upward slammed the car door and then screeched away.

Lowering her tote bag, Lori let her gaze follow the taxi out of sight, realizing too late that she might well need a twelve-dollar trip back. She should have made him wait until she checked out the house.

"Well, too late for that," she said aloud, startling herself with her own voice. Instinctively she glanced around to see if anyone had heard her talking to herself. As she did so, she caught sight of a small green Triumph with a bent bicycle rack on the back of it. It was parked farther down the driveway at the foot of the hill that circled the house.

Letting out a long breath, she relaxed visibly. Someone was here after all. Briskly she knocked on the door and replaced her bag on her shoulder.

Almost immediately the door opened. An attractive Oriental woman of about forty smiled warmly at Lori. "Hello."

Lori returned the smile. "Mrs. Brandon?" she asked.

"Oh, no. I'm Mrs. Holmes. Come in. I'm the cleaning lady. Just finishing up." She opened the door and before Lori could introduce herself, she picked up a suitcase and the tote bag. Lori took the other bag and followed her in. "I'm Lori Martin, the house-sitter. Have Dr. and Mrs. Brandon already gone?"

"I think so. Nobody's been here all day." She led the way through a utility room, into a large open area that was a combination kitchen and family room with a two-way fireplace in the middle. Without pausing, she took Lori up a flight of stairs into a huge irregularly shaped living room with two large triangular windows that opened onto the sun deck.

On another day, at a different time, the western scene from the windows might have been dramatic, but right then either smog or twilight had blotted out the scene and Lori could only see a grayness that seemed to be seeping up the hill into the shadowy room.

Mrs. Holmes must have felt it too. After she set down the bags and motioned for Lori to do the same, she turned on an elaborate swag lamp which, because of the

9

color of its shade, seemed to give off a greenish light. All of the furniture was modern, massive, and organized in several conversational groupings, like an elite hotel lobby.

"The bedrooms are on this level. There are two off a balcony overlooking the lower floor and there are two more off an inside hall. I made them all up so you can have your choice." Then very quickly she launched into a brief description of the floor plan, which made no sense to Lori. Some of her bewilderment must have shown on her face, for Mrs. Holmes added quickly, "But you'll have time to explore everything at your own leisure. I know you're tired and I really must get on home too."

She must work as efficiently as she talks, thought Lori, for Mrs. Holmes's dark slacks and white blouse hardly seemed mussed. But perhaps she had just changed from her working clothes, contemplated Lori, while she said rather apologetically, "I'm supposed to locate the fuse boxes and become familiar with the security system. All house-sitters hired through the agency are instructed in some basic precautions—a routine, so to speak."

"Of course. This way." But her smile was a little less ready as she took Lori back down to the utility area.

As they moved through the beautifully furnished house, with its open beam ceilings, thick carpets, and heavy drapes, Lori saw that everything was immaculate. A modernistic dining room could be seen through an arched doorway, the furniture all chrome and glass. Huge planters hung on chains from the high ceilings, but the greenery in them was artificial.

Everything was arranged too precisely. It was almost as if the place were one of those false sets used by movie companies. The sets looked real enough, but behind their elaborate fronts there was nothing more than empty darkness.

"Have the Brandons lived here very long?" Usually Lori became acquainted with the residents before they left her in charge of their house and belongings. It was important for them to feel secure, satisfied that everything would be in good hands while they were away. In fact, the owners usually bombarded her with so many detailed instructions that she prayed for them to hurry up and leave.

But now she wished someone besides an impersonal cleaning lady were here to fill her in on the personality of the people and the personality of the house—for all homes had one. Except this one! The thought kept nagging at her. There was no real evidence that anyone had ever lived here to make the house feel like a home. She repeated her question as Mrs. Holmes led her back to the living room.

"I really don't know. The agency just sent me out with a list of things to do. But it's a brand-new house. Lovely, isn't it?" She smiled at Lori the way a proud parent might.

"Yes, well, I guess so."

Mrs. Holmes waited, the smile still on her face. Lori shrugged, giving a nervous laugh, furious with herself for acting like a schoolgirl in front of the competent woman. "I guess it's a bit grand for me. Somehow it seems like a furniture store display—you know, the kind where they set up rooms to show off every piece to—best advantage."

Mrs. Holmes laughed. "Well, I'm sure, Miss Martin, that you'll move a few things around to make it more homey. How long are you going to baby-sit—I mean house-sit?"

"Most of the summer, I believe. Mrs. Wallace, the lady who runs the Association, wrote on my assignment that the family was going abroad until late August." As Lori heard the words in her own ears, she thought, My God! Can I stand being alone in this place that long? When she had accepted the Colorado job, she had pictured one of those delightful mountain homes, perhaps on the road to Aspen or Vail. She had spent her winters in Kansas City, teaching in a small high school. All of her other house-sitting jobs had been near there. She had welcomed this Denver assignment because she hadn't been back to the mile-high city since she graduated from the University of Denver nearly five years ago. But as Mrs. Holmes began to take her leave, Lori's feelings were definitely of a different timbre. "How about the telephone? I don't think I noticed—"

"There are several in the house and a jack for one in

every room. There's one in the hall." She motioned toward the bedrooms. "Would you like to check it before I leave?"

Lori nodded, deciding to keep Mrs. Holmes around until she was certain everything was in order. In the hall when she lifted a small white princess phone and heard a reassuring dial tone, she called, "It's working," and then replaced the receiver.

"Bye, then," responded Mrs. Holmes, her voice floating up from the lower level. And then the front door banged shut.

Lori leaned over the balcony that ran along one wall above the kitchen-family room area but she couldn't see the front hall from there. "Wait! Just a minute—" She ran along the carpeted hall and down some circular steps. She spun around the corner into the foyer and opened the front door just as the green Triumph pulled away, and continued around the house until it was gone.

Chilly night breezes that keep Coloradans under blankets ten months out of the year made her shiver and she turned back into the house. Shutting the door firmly and slipping a dead-bolt lock into place, she said aloud, "Well, that's that." Her voice seemed thin and bounded away from her into deepening shadows in the unlit house. "I guess I'll turn on some lights in this place."

She really should stop this habit of talking to herself, she thought, as she went back up the stairs to the spacious living room. It came from being alone too much. She knew she had never done it when she had been living with Kyle. They hadn't spent much time talking anyway, she mused, and for a moment the chill was gone and she wasn't standing in the middle of a huge room, trembling slightly, but was back in a cozy apartment with the sound of someone's stereo coming through the wall as Kyle drew her to him.

Then she pushed the reverie away. "No more of that." She moved her lips but only let the words come out in a whisper. It would never be like that again. "But does it always have to be like this?"

Loneliness as strong as a physical ache rose up, and she tightened every muscle in her body against it. She was just tired, anxious, but she was over her grief. Kyle was gone forever. She knew it and had accepted it. She was making a new life for herself. It was going to be a good life too. She jutted her chin out slightly.

Blinking back the start of tears, she went over to her luggage. This house was luxury, pure luxury. She would choose the fanciest bedroom and soak in the most elegant bathtub with soap bubbles up to her ears. Enough of this senseless apprehension and mooning over the past.

She reached down to pick up her things, and froze with a start. Her brown shoulder purse, which she had flung on top of her bags, wasn't there. It was as if watery eyes were blurring her vision, and she brushed a hand across her face. A purse lay on top of her tote bag, but it didn't even resemble her own. This one was made of a tapestry cloth and had two short plastic handles. Certain that her own purse was in the pile somewhere, she moved all her suitcases and even went down on her knees to look under a nearby chair and end table.

She sat down on the couch, her expression one of irritated puzzlement. Could Mrs. Holmes have taken her purse by mistake? But that was ridiculous! Every woman knew her own purse. Still, the cleaning lady was the only one who could have taken it—by mistake or otherwise. "If she took it for money," said Lori aloud, "she's in for a surprise." Less than five dollars remained in her wallet. She was broke until her school district sent out her June check. That would take time because it would be forwarded to her from her Kansas City apartment. Only her credit cards and driver's license were of value.

Angry to think she had been the victim of a petty robbery, Lori opened up the strange purse and rummaged around in it until she found a lady's wallet. It must have been a mistake, thought Lori, and not a deliberate switch. The wallet was as full of cards as hers was and there was a lot more money in it. Not interested enough in the green bills to count them, she opened up a plastic filler and looked at the first pocket, which contained a driver's license.

She expected to see Mrs. Holmes in the identification photo, but the unfamiliar face took a second to come into focus. It certainly wasn't a picture of Mrs. Holmes. The woman was young, with tawny streaked hair a little

13

lighter and longer than Lori's own light brown hair. In a more artistic photograph, she might have been pretty, but the overexposed picture made her features vague and rather flat. Lori quickly read the vital statistics alongside the photo. Mrs. Lois Brandon. Age: 34. Hair: Blonde. Eyes: Blue. Weight: 115. Height: 5'6".

"What in the—" swore Lori, losing her feelings of indignation to something akin to anxiety. "I don't believe it!" She said it again loudly. "I don't believe it. Why do I have Mrs. Brandon's purse instead of my own?" As her thoughts whirled in confusion, all hope of comprehending the weird situation eluded her.

Later, she would wonder how much longer she would have sat there, searching for the thread that would unravel a meaningful explanation. Her mental gymnastics were brought to an abrupt halt by sounds below her at the front door.

Raising her head, she froze and listened. They were not *furtive* sounds. Someone was unlocking both locks with the clatter of trying to find the right key. She heard the door open and shut. Heavy, muffled steps went along the entrance hall and then came closer as they moved up the circular carpeted staircase.

Lori moistened her lips and tried to form some kind of question or protest. For someone who was always talking aloud, her squeaky "Who is it?" was pathetic.

No one answered.

Flinging the purse aside, she got to her feet as he came into view. In the dim light, his short gray hair made her misjudge his age; she thought him to be an older man. Then as he came toward her, she could see that his face was tan and youthful, and she realized that he must be only about thirty-five years old. He moved in an easy, confident manner and wore the kind of casual slacks and shirt shown on TV by leading sportsmen.

He paused and deliberately looked her up and down, and an expression of disdain settled on his face as if she represented something very repugnant to him. Then he gave a short laugh that had no mirth in it. "So my new wife has arrived," he said. "Welcome home, Mrs. Brandon."

# Two

Instinctively she began backing up. He must be mad! As his sardonic grin stiffened, she wondered if she had spoken the words aloud. "I'm not Mrs. Brandon." She forced a laugh. "But you know your own wife. I'm Lori Martin, the house-sitter. I just got here. Mrs. Holmes—"

"Shut up!"

His words were like a physical blow and her knees gave way as she sat back down on the couch. The billfold was under her, and as she retrieved it he ordered, "Give me that." He glared down at her and his hazel eyes changed from green to a shade of gray as cold as iced pewter.

It was a mistake to try and hold on to the billfold. It wasn't hers, and God knows she didn't want it. But as her heartbeat thumped loudly in her ears, she tried to think. Her grip was like an iron vise around the soft leather.

"I said, give it to me." He spoke softer than before. Somehow this tone was more threatening.

"It isn't mine. I don't know what happened. I just got here in a taxi. The fare was twelve dollars and there weren't many bills left, so my purse wasn't worth stealing. Then Mrs. Holmes left and my shoulder bag—"

"Will you shut up? I hope to God you don't always run off at the mouth, *Mrs. Brandon.*" He flipped open the wallet and stared at the driver's license. "You must have been having a bad day when you had that picture taken."

"That is *not* my picture. You can tell by just looking at it. Only our coloring is the same—besides, I'm not that old!"

He laughed openly as if really amused and tossed the wallet back on her lap. "Trust a woman to sift out the important things. Well, don't worry about a few years'

15

difference. It's hard to be sure of a woman's age—especially my wife's."

"Where is your wife, Dr. Brandon?"

At the swiftness of her question, he raised one eyebrow, which remained jet black despite the early graying of his hair. Then he lowered himself into a pillowlike chair that was part of a cozy grouping around a glass-top coffee table. He crossed a pair of long legs in front of him. "You might say she's dead—but not quite." There was a ghoulish mirth in his chuckle. "She has been briefly reborn in you, Miss Martin."

"Then—then you know who I am! You knew it all along." Angrily she lashed out at him. "I don't care for your sense of humor, Doctor. I fail to find your little joke anything but cruel."

"It's no joke, I assure you. You might as well get used to your new identity. It's the only one you're going to have for a while."

"You are crazy! I came here on an assignment to house-sit. My boss knows I'm here, and I'm sure she'll understand when I tell her I've changed my mind." She got to her feet and tried not to let the shakiness of her legs get into her voice. "Now I'll call a taxi and catch the next flight back to Kansas City." She picked up the wallet. "I'll use this money to cover my expenses." Taking out the bills she tossed the wallet back down.

As she moved away, she glanced sideways at him, expecting to see him make some angry retort or physical protest. But he didn't move and only a sardonic smile crossed his face.

"Whatever you think, Lori, but it would be a tragedy if Kyle lost his life because you refused to cooperate."

She stopped, as he knew she would. Turning around slowly, she stared wide-eyed. "What did you say?" She must not have heard him correctly.

"Why don't you come back, Lori, and sit down. Then we'll talk about how you can save Kyle's life." He was lighting a cigarette and not even looking at her, as if he were sure there was no question about her trying to escape.

Kyle? Kyle! But there had been no word from him in nearly three years. When the POWs were being returned she had prayed every time she read a list that his name would be on it. And then, in those last days when everyone was scrambling to get out of Vietnam, she knew he would have made it if he had still been alive. Finally, she accepted the fact that she was one of those who would never really know what happened to a loved one in that deadly military fiasco. It was her imagination that this abrupt stranger had just spoken Kyle's name as if he were very much alive. With nothing else at the front of her mind except a soaring hope, she sat back down, her eyes never leaving his contemptuous face. It was obvious he viewed her as some unpleasant demand on his time, and he was enjoying her utter bewilderment. Like a cat watching a mouse wiggle in its deadly claws, the doctor offered no further enlightenment.

She broke the heightened moment with a rather inane statement. "You know Kyle."

"Obviously," he returned impatiently. "You *are* a wizard in deduction."

His jeering comment just washed over her. "How is he? Where is he?"

"I'll answer the first question. He's fine . . . at the moment. That might change if you refuse to cooperate in this very simple matter. But perhaps your feelings about Kyle aren't the same." He watched her from under half-closed lids. "Maybe they've changed."

Even in her bewilderment, she felt that he was much more interested in her reply than his casual tone indicated. If she had been more artful, more on top of the situation, she could have strung him along. But she couldn't think. She played right into his hands. How could she deny that aching longing that surged up in her young body at just the sound of his name? God, how she still cared. "Kyle . . . how do I know? How do I know he's still alive?" Her words were coated with a plea to prove to her that this was not another cruel joke of his.

As if he appreciated some indication of intelligence from her, he nodded. "A very good question." Then reaching in his pocket, he drew out a rather crushed envelope. He tossed it to her.

Her fingers were thick and clumsy as she tried to break the seal, finally ripping it in an uneven line. Inside was a picture and a small slip of paper. The photograph was familiar. It was one of Kyle and herself sitting upon a stone wall on the D.U. campus. One of their friends had taken it just before Kyle had left so that he would have a picture of both of them together. There was only one line written on the paper. "Do what they say. K." It was his hand-writing and warm tears blurred the words as she recognized it.

"Yes, I can see that you still care," said her tormentor, and there was unmasked disgust in his voice. "So let's talk about saving your precious Kyle's skin."

"What do you want me to do?" Her question was simple, indicating complete capitulation.

"Just what I told you. You are Mrs. Philip Brandon. That's it. You will live in this place and play house—with me." A flicker of a smile twisted up his lips. "Doesn't that appeal to a maiden lady like yourself?" There was open derision in his tone.

"Why? I don't understand." Her mouth was dry. Her concerns still centered on Kyle's safety. Her own danger in the charade had not come to full realization yet . . . nor what might happen to her once it was over.

"It's really very simple. Mrs. Brandon is going to receive something and you are going to be here to get it. Once that happens, you give it to me and there will be no more need for Mrs. Brandon."

Or for me, added Lori silently and then ignored the warning. "And what about Kyle?"

He shrugged. "He'll be free to come back—if he wants to."

"How can I be sure?"

His laugh was a mockery. "You can't."

She cut short his laughter. *"What happened to your real wife?"*

Again, her question seemed to startle him. He sat up and smashed his cigarette in a brass ashtray. "She was killed in a freak accident—quickly and anonymously. We'll have several months before the public knows."

"I can see you're choked up about her death," taunted Lori, the first real flicker of hatred sending warmth through her leaden body. Instead of responding fearfully to the obvious murder, some instinct for self-survival had led her into an attack.

"Lois wasn't the kind of woman who endeared any mourners. Anyone who might be slightly interested in her demise can wait a few months for news of it."

"A few months! You're insane. How could I keep up a foolish pretense of being another woman for that long? There must be plenty of people who knew her."

"Not here—in Denver—not this place. You see, the Brandons have never lived here."

Then the truth hit her like clanging brass cymbals two inches from her ears. "You're not Dr. Brandon. He's dead! You've killed him, too!" Fear like a snarling dog bit into her and she cringed back in the cushions.

"My name is Philip Allen Brandon." His steady cold look dared her to deny it. Then he curved his lips upward. "But you may call me Bud."

She shivered as he got to his feet.

"Where is the liquor kept in this place? I want a drink." He pulled her to her feet. "Come on, Miss Martin. Let's find the booze." As they went down the steps he said, "Why would anyone build a barn like this?"

At least their taste in houses was the same. She gave a hysterical giggle as she stumbled along beside him. They found a liquor cabinet in the family room—well stocked.

"A martini all right with you?" he asked as if this were a normal social moment instead of a hideous nightmare. "I'm hungry," he added without waiting for her answer. "See what's in the kitchen, Marty," he commanded.

At least he hadn't called her Lois. The last strand of her self-control would have snapped if he had. As her muddled brain tried to sort out its recent intake of bizzarre information, she found the refrigerator. It was filled with delicatessen items: salads, cold meats, beer, milk, and cheese. The refrigerator, like the liquor cabinet, offered a wide variety.

Lori took a loaded tray around the dividing fireplace and set it down on a round oak table that had six modernistic captain chairs around it.

"Who is Mrs. Holmes?" she asked bluntly. No ordinary cleaning lady saw to a larder of food and drink like this one. They didn't drive expensive cars like the Triumph, either. She should have realized that the minute she saw it. From the first the trim, attractive Mrs. Holmes had not fit her role, and Lori had ignored some inner naggings and had accepted her at face value.

"One of us," he answered simply as he handed her a fragile stemmed martini glass. "To the success of our mission." Clinking her glass lightly, he gave a pleased kind of grunt as he took a sip. "Just right. I hope it is not too dry for you." The smile was solicitous.

Without raising her drink, Lori continued to stare at it. The reflecting glass and clear liquid gave back a blurred image of her face like the one in the license photo. Feeling her own identity slipping, she gave herself a mental shake. She knew who she was. Even though the aunt who had raised her was no longer alive, Lori had followed the lifestyle that Aunt Adele had mapped out for her. She had gone ahead and completed her education at the University of Denver and had become a teacher at the same high school where Aunt Adele had been a formidable institution for so many years. Except for her brief romantic interlude with Kyle she had displayed a backbone nearly as stiff as her aunt's. There had not been much open affection displayed between the two of them, but after Aunt Adele's death Lori realized how empty life was going to be without the forceful, dominating lady who had always called a spade a spade and had maintained that two and two made four, no matter how modern-day morality tried to make five out of it.

She knew how Aunt Adele would have felt about her moving into an apartment with Kyle during her last year at college. Even though they hadn't talked definitely of marriage, Lori was certain everything would have worked out to Aunt Adele's sense of values if the draft hadn't interfered. If Kyle were alive . . .

She swirled the liquid around in her glass and then raised it slowly and deliberately. "To Kyle," she said, "and his safe return." Her gaze was steady and then began to waver as she suddenly wondered how many months it would be before anyone missed her—if they ever did.

# Three

The telephone ringing by her bed woke her up the next morning. At least it was morning, she thought, as weighted eyelids flickered open and she saw a large bedroom flooded with light. Last night she had arbitrarily chosen the first balcony bedroom because its position in the house seemed less confined than those in the inner hall.

She had paused at the bedroom door, looking down at the impostor doctor sprawled in front of the television, apparently not interested in her quick exit.

The food she had brought out from the kitchen had choked her, bringing such a rising nausea to her stomach that she quickly sought out a bathroom. She had never been able to tolerate gin, and the way she had gulped down the martini, combined with her emotional upset, had made the drink act like an emetic.

Weak and slightly dizzy, she had decided against going back down to the family room and had struggled with her suitcases, managing to bring them into the bedroom. Grateful that there was a doorknob with a push-in lock, she had turned it purposefully, as if this feeble precaution could keep her pretend husband outside her bedroom.

She had given little attention to the luxurious queen-size bed, matching Mediterranean dresser and bureau, deep pile fuschia carpet, and swag drapes. As quickly as her shaky legs could move, she went through a small dressing room that was as elegant as the bedroom and that adjoined a large bathroom done in white marble with black accessories. There was another door at the end of the bathroom which Lori determined opened into the second balcony bedroom.

Again she turned a lock to prevent the sharing of the

bathroom with any occupant in the other bedroom. Pushing aside the feeling that her efforts were only token gestures, she stripped for bed and took a quick shower that left her more exhausted than refreshed. She knew that there was little reason to believe a couple of locked doors would keep Bud out if he decided to come in. Still, there was some kind of reassurance in having gone through the motions.

She tried to hold on to a feeling of reassurance as she lay stiffly in the huge bed listening for sounds that would warn her of his approach. She had no idea how far he intended to carry this husband-wife pretense.

"Kyle, Kyle," she whispered, closing her eyes and trying to recapture the elation she had felt when she learned that he was still alive. Although she tried to caution herself that his silence these last few years might be of his own choosing, hope made butterflies in her stomach. "Where are you?" she whispered. "Where have you been all this time?" She had read the slip of paper over and over again. He must be in more danger than she was. He wouldn't put her in this kind of situation unless he had no choice.

As she lay there wrestling with her thoughts, she realized there were a dozen questions she should have asked immediately. She didn't even know if Kyle was in the States or not. Tomorrow she would find out. Tomorrow . . . She would insist upon some answers. Tomorrow . . . Finally, a restless sleep came to her taut body and no one disturbed her—until the telephone woke her up.

Automatically she reached for it and lifted up the receiver before she was fully awake.

"Hello," she croaked, her voice heavy with sleep.

"This is Oriental Nursery. We are calling about a delivery. Is this Mrs. Brandon?"

She let the caller wait in silence while her fuzzy brain tried to shake off its cloudiness. "No," she began, "this is—" And then the reality of the moment came flooding back. She sat up in bed. "Yes—yes, it is," she stammered.

"Mrs. Brandon?" Now the male voice seemed to hesitate.

Wetting her lips, she said, "Yes," in a very firm fashion. Maybe this was the expected package. Thank God this masquerade might be nearly over. "Yes, this is Mrs. Brandon. What is it?" she stammered.

"I was checking to see if we can make a delivery this morning. Will you be at home?"

"Yes, yes, I will. Who did you say this was? Mr.—"

But he didn't follow through with her lead. "Oriental Nursery. Thank you, Mrs. Brandon. Good-bye."

Lori stared at the humming receiver before replacing it in its cradle. A nursery? It didn't sound like anything mysterious but it might be a front. Bud hadn't indicated anything definite—just that Mrs. Brandon was going to receive "something." He had said it as if he wasn't quite sure himself.

Choosing her new beige jump suit because it was the easiest thing to slip into, she forgot how she had picked it out with such anticipated pleasure for her Colorado vacation. Now she gave little attention to how she looked in it as she dressed and then tied a striped orange and tan scarf around her light brown hair.

She had never taken much pleasure in looking at herself in the mirror. She would have preferred a fuller face and a nose that people called "cute." Aunt Adele had always said that her facial bone structure was the kind that would hold its beauty into old age, but Lori had never been concerned about such preservation and continued to think her cheek bones too high and her nose too slim. Her eyebrows were three shades darker than her tawny hair, which Aunt Adele called honey-colored and Lori termed "dishwater."

She automatically touched perfume to her earlobes with other thoughts swirling uppermost in her mind. Then she slowed to a snail's pace as she gingerly opened her door and stepped out.

Looking down into the family room and the kitchen area not hidden by the large center fireplace, she saw that everything was in as perfect order as it had been on her arrival. All the mess of last night's snack was gone—and so was her pretend husband.

She strained to hear any kind of movement in the multilevel house but there was none. An odor of perked coffee made her aware of an empty and growling stomach. Taking a deep breath to relax taut muscles, she went through the lobbylike living room, down the stairs, and into the kitchen.

By a glass coffee maker there was an opened package of breakfast rolls. She expected to be interrupted any minute by Bud's unwelcome presence and hastily poured a mug of coffee, took a roll, and then went back upstairs.

Balancing her breakfast, she managed to open a glass door and step out onto a wooden deck built outside the funny shaped living room. There were two metal chairs and a chaise longue. Lori ignored the furniture and went over to the solid railing.

The beautiful Colorado morning began to ease away the mounting tension and anxiety she had felt inside the house. The jagged Rocky Mountains looked as if they were cut from purple and blue paper and pasted against a water-spotted, pale blue sky. At their foot, the city of Denver lay under a green mantle of foliage, its buildings hidden from view, except for tall skyscrapers in the city's center, making the heavily populated valley look, from this distance, motionless and peaceful in the crisp, clear air of a western morning.

Lori set her coffee cup down on the ledge and leaned against it as she munched her roll. Just below her was an outcropping of limestone boulders. Somewhere there, on a rocky shelf, a meadow lark trilled a song while two raucous crows, like boisterous children, darted about in a clump of scrub oak.

As soothing as any medication, the setting provided the balm she needed to restore her confidence.

She would cope! Whatever the day brought, she would manage. "I can do it," she said aloud, pleased with the steady timbre of her voice. When the package arrived, she would handle things so that she was quickly out of this charade, and Kyle would be safely on his way home —to her!

And, as if her resolution was made just in time to be put to the test, a yellow panel truck came into view below her on the curved driveway of the house. It looked like any delivery truck except there was no printing on either side of it.

As she watched, a curly-headed fellow with longish blond hair climbed out of the truck's cab.

"Hello," Lori called, moving along the deck as far as she could. "Hello, I'm up here." She waved. "Up here."

Tilting his head way back he looked up and saw her, grinned broadly, and returned her wave.

"You have something for me?" she called eagerly.

"Sure do, Mrs. Brandon."

The personable messenger wasn't at all what she had expected, but he fitted in with her newly found optimism that all would be well very shortly. "I'll be right down."

There were stairs on one side of the deck that went down to a balcony on the second level. The balcony ran along in front of some more triangular windows and then went around the side of the house to connect with the back porch deck. Like someone traversing ladders outside an Indian pueblo, she made her way down to the driveway.

At the bottom she passed the three-car garage and noticed that it was empty. Bud must have taken his car somewhere.

Her visitor was leaning back against the front fender of the truck, watching her journey downward and obviously enjoying the tight cut of her jump suit as she came toward him.

Smiling appreciatively, he said, "No wonder you're in such good shape. I'm not sure I could manage all those stairs very many times a day."

"Me either," she confessed, a little out of breath. She glanced up to see where she had been when she called down to him.

"I bet you're a terrific mountain climber," he said.

"No, I'm not." And for some reason she shivered. A fall over any of those railings would plunge the victim down upon rocks as treacherous as any rocky slope in the mountains. "I don't like heights very much."

"But I bet you ski. No one lives in this part of the country without getting bit by that snow bug. I'm a ski bum myself."

His confession drew her attention away from the treacherous heights to the important delivery. She studied him then, trying to see beyond his sun-bleached hair, pale blue eyes, and well-toned body. He did resemble those attractive young men who made skiing a way of life. She and Kyle had known plenty of them when they were in college. A good percentage of D.U.'s student body had chosen that particular school because of the famous nearby ski resorts. Getting an education was often secondary to spending energy on the ski slopes. Some students dropped out of school completely and gave up any pretense of doing anything else. Those without funds worked periodically to provide a minimum subsistence and the most important budgetary item, tow tickets. Apparently this fellow was one of those, thought Lori. Yesterday she would have accepted him at face value, someone with a summer job to earn money for his winter love.

As if her scrutiny demanded a response, he straightened up. Changing the flirtatious twinkling in his eyes, he settled his gaze a little beyond her and focused on something over her shoulder.

"What's your name?" she asked.

"Folks call me Rex—it means king, you know." There was a hint of boyish pride in the way he said it, even though Lori judged him to be at least twenty-five.

"King of what?" she prodded, so intent upon analyzing him and the situation that she forgot to ease the moment with a smile instead of a demanding stare.

Her abruptness took away his friendliness. "I don't think you'd be interested, Mrs. Brandon. If you'll direct me to the solarium, I'll get unloaded." He started around to the back of the truck.

"Solarium?" she repeated blankly.

"Yes. That's where you want these, isn't it?" He opened up the back doors, revealing rows and rows of green flowering plants.

"Is that all—is that all you're delivering?"

"I work for a nursery and greenhouse, Mrs. Brandon. Plants are what they sell." He looked at her now as if she was the biggest fruitcake he had ever met. "Now, where is the solarium?"

"I don't know—" she voiced the answer as she thought it.

Rex's startled look told her she had been thinking aloud again.

"You don't know? You are Mrs. Brandon, aren't you. Did I get the wrong address?"

Her warm sense of confidence was all gone now, dissipated in her disappointment and confusion. But her hope that he had the important delivery would not die. Maybe he was just testing her, to make sure she was Mrs. Brandon before he turned over that important thing to her. Hope made her acuity sharpen.

"Of course, I'm Mrs. Brandon," she flung back her head with assumed indignation. "I just started to say that I don't know whether the solarium is ready for plants or not. The contractors have been so slow—you can see their mess is still around. I just arrived last night and I haven't had time to check the whole house yet." It was feeble, very thin, but the only explanation that came to mind. "We discussed various places to put the solarium. You know how important the right sunlight is. Probably the east or south exposure is really the best—" As she blabbered, really thinking aloud, her mind skirted about. Where could it be? She had not noticed any structure outside the house. "Go ahead and unload. I'll check to see if I can get things ready for you to bring them in."

Without waiting for his reply, she started toward the house, her eyes searching the outside for a clue. Solarium? Lots of windows, probably the south side, probably— Damn! Why hadn't she listened closer to Mrs. Holmes when she was going over the floor plan? Not on the third level . . . bedrooms, living room, and deck; second . . . family room, kitchen, dining room, utility area. The family room had windows on the east side. Looking up she saw huge triangular windows jutting out on the south in a funny fashion. She had walked by them on her way down from the deck. Now she stopped with her first foot on the back steps. That must be it!

Quickly she retraced her steps up the staircase and along the outside second-floor balcony. She was right. Peering in through the large windows she saw wrought-iron stands, tables, and some empty hanging baskets. The door beside the windows wouldn't open.

"It's locked," she called back down to Rex who stood

with arms folded, leaning back against the car in his usual position, having watched her trip back up. "I'll open it from the inside. You can start bringing the plants up here. It will be easier than carrying them through the house."

Even though she was feeling pretty satisfied with herself, irritation settled upon the missing Bud. Where in the hell (sorry, Auntie) was he? Why had he left her alone to carry off the masquerade? She had forgotten how relieved she had been to find him gone. Now she was cursing his absence. If Rex didn't believe she was the real Mrs. Brandon, he might leave without putting an end to this growing nightmare. She must do a better job of acting. He must be convinced that she was truly Lois Brandon.

Each time he brought up a crate of plants, she met him smiling and with enthusiasm. She didn't have to fake any love of plants. She was in gardening heaven as Rex brought in ferns, bright leaved coleus, fuzzy pink and lavender violets, and even blooming gardenia and orchid plants. Every time he appeared with a new armful, she gave a squeal of delight.

Companionably they placed the plants in flower stands and on wrought-iron tables as Rex volunteered information about sunlight and watering. Apparently growing plants was his second love, and he acted like an adoption agency placing some loved offsprings in a new home.

"Not too much water—let the soil get bone dry on these and then soak them good. More plants are drowned than die from dryness," he warned. "Now these like an acid soil.'" He pointed to the gardenias and hydrangeas. "Use this kind of fertilizer on them." He grinned. "I guess that's the last bunch." Then as he saw her fingering a pink-tipped white orchid, he chuckled. "And don't be afraid to pick blooms.. It makes most plants keep flowering." As if to verify his words, he broke off the orchid and handed it to her. "A lovely flower for a lovely lady," he said tritely.

And for the first time she smiled back at him as if there were no charade to be acted out. The companionship they had shared the last hour had been a reprieve. Worried lines in her face eased away. The immediate task of handling and placing all the plants had dulled the anxiety of her impersonation. And because the mantle of deceit had slipped away from the front of her consciousness, his question jolted her like a quick shot of electricity.

"Mrs. Brandon, do you ski?"

"Ski?"

He was still smiling at her but his penetrating gaze was deadly serious. Was it a casual question or was he testing her authenticity? Did he know whether or not the real Mrs. Brandon was a skier? If he hadn't used the false name, she would have answered truthfully that she was fair on the slopes, but now she hesitated.

"What do you think?" she parried, her relaxed expression gone. And as he studied her, she panicked. He's trying to decide whether or not to give me "it." "Doesn't everyone in Colorado ski?" she asked brightly and then glanced down at the orchid so he couldn't see that there was no lightness in her eyes. "I guess I'm like everybody else."

"I'm not so sure," he said quietly, but he reached into his back pocket as if there were nothing more to be said.

She had convinced him! He was going to deliver the package or whatever it was. For the first time she wondered how he fitted into a murderous deception. But her interest was only superficial. All she cared about was ending this impersonation, getting Kyle freed, and escaping before she joined the Brandons in the obituary column. She really didn't care what the "something" was she was about to receive.

Rex handed her the paper, and in the heightened moment she barely breathed a "Thank you."

"Will you sign it?"

"What—"

"The invoice for the plants."

"Invoice? It's just an invoice?"

"That's the usual procedure," he said wearily, as if he were suddenly tired of trying to understand such a dingbat. He handed her a pen. "Just sign your name here, Mrs. Brandon."

Bitter disappointment and new fear kept her staring at the paper. Was it another trick? Did he want to compare signatures? How could she forge Lois Brandon's name when she had never seen her writing?

"I'll sign it," said a brisk voice from the doorway. Bud strolled in from the family room.

Instant relief made her greeting quite warm and sincere. "You're back!"

"Obviously, darling," he responded in a light, teasing tone as he took the pen and invoice from her. Quickly he scribbled a couple of initials on the proper line. Lori wondered if he had been practicing the signature or if he hoped the scribbled initials would pass. He obviously felt more comfortable in his impersonation than she did in hers. "I've been giving the old golf clubs a workout this morning," he said amicably. "You have to tee off early to get a spot. Very popular sport with us not-so-young guys." As he handed the paper back to Rex, his look expressed an appreciation of the young man's physique.

"I'm a skier myself," responded Rex with a hint of a boast.

"Really? Never had the courage myself. Guess I've seen too many busted knees and collarbones."

How can he do it, thought Lori. Stand there and exchange pleasantries as if he were just what he seems. There was no doubt that he could pass for a professional man. He held himself with just the right amount of formal dignity, and his impeccable, expensive golf outfit denoted a man of taste. He made a good-looking doctor, thought Lori, wondering who he really was and how he had gotten into this intrigue.

"What's your specialty, Doctor?"

"I'm a surgeon," said Bud blithely. "I've been practicing in San Francisco and decided to take a little vacation before I set up practice here."

"Great place, Denver," agreed Rex warmly. "In fact, Colorado just can't be beat."

"I know we'll like it very much. In fact, we do already. Don't we, honey?" He put his arm around her and pulled her firmly to his side. His eyes were more green than gray as he gazed down at her. There was only a slight tic at the corner of his lip that indicated his smile was false.

"Well, thank you, folks," said Rex, picking up a couple

of empty crates. "Enjoy the flowers, Mrs. Brandon." And with a slight wave, he turned and left.

As his figure went past the large windows, Lori had an impulse to call him back. The arm around her waist brought back last night's terror. She did not want to be alone with this impostor. She sensed a fury within him that was barely under control. As if to verify the impression, the minute Rex was out of sight, he swung on her. "Who ordered this stuff?"

"I—I don't know. They didn't say. I—"

"Where did it come from? The invoice said Oriental Nursery."

She nodded. "They called and asked if I was Mrs. Brandon. I thought—I thought it might be what you were waiting for. I tried to say the right things." Tears were forming at the corner of her eyes. Had she blown it? Was Rex the right one?

"Did he believe you?"

"I don't know," she said, blinking rapidly. "I thought so —after I found the solarium. Why didn't you show me around so I would know the house?" she lashed out at him.

"Mrs. Holmes was supposed to do that. No wonder he didn't believe you. My God, what an idiot!" His exasperated look drove away her tearfulness.

She grasped the orchid stem tightly. "I did the best I could. And I think he bought it. But he didn't give me anything. Did Mrs. Brandon ski?"

His thundering look froze for a minute as if he considered her question completely asinine.

"Did she?" Lori insisted.

"A little—what in the—?"

"He asked me and I thought maybe he knew the right answer."

"Ridiculous. I told you she lived in San Francisco."

"No, you didn't. You said she had never lived in Colorado," she countered smugly, delighted to have tripped him up.

But her satisfaction was short-lived. Before her startled gaze he grabbed the nearest pot of flowers, which happened to be the white orchid plant, and with sudden fury crashed it down on the floor, sending dirt, flowers, and clay pieces in every direction.

"No, no," screamed Lori. "That was a fifty-dollar plant."

He gave her an angry shove backward. "You fool." Then he reached for a large hydrangea planter. "It's three million that your empty head will cost." And with that he brought a ceramic pot down against the edge of a black table.

"Stop it!" Lori lunged at him but his expression was so crazed that she pulled back. As he grabbed a copper planter with both hands, Lori thought he was going to bring it crashing down upon her head. Backing away, she screamed and then ran through the balcony door as the sound of shattering clay and glass followed her.

# *Four*

Lori fled down the outside staircase, not knowing where she was going, only intent upon getting away from the crazed man destroying flowers and containers with fiendish abandonment.

She saw his car, a bronze Matador, parked in the driveway. Apparently he had been disturbed when he drove in and saw the panel truck. Lori saw that he had left the keys in the ignition. His story about playing golf must have been true. A golf bag was on the back seat.

She expected to see Bud charge down after her any second. She panicked as she tried to start the car and flooded it.

"Damn," she swore, mentally apologizing to Aunt Adele as her eyes darted to every doorway. Then the motor kicked over and she was out of the driveway with a squeal of tires.

She fought the strange car, wavering slightly on the road until she began to judge her distance and timing. The road was narrow, running along the north side of Cherry Creek. Until she reached Denver's city limits, there was little traffic on the road; the early morning rush from suburbs to the city was apparently over. The open fields gave way to high-rise condominiums and town houses; the quiet, peaceful city hidden that morning by spreads of green foliage emerged now as glaring concrete buildings and a myriad of streets that were seething with people and noise. Growling machines and thundering jets roaring overhead combined to make a mockery of the quiet confidence she had felt earlier in the morning. Her eyes narrowed as a throbbing inside her head matched the clamor of honking cars and the screeching of tires on hot pavement.

She didn't know where she was going. No purse—no money—no purpose, except that of fleeing from a situation that had been building in nightmarish proportions since her arrival.

Automatically, it seemed, she headed south on Colorado Boulevard and then right on Evans to University Boulevard. Three blocks farther and she had turned into a familiar parking space before she really gave full attention to where she was. Then her eyes went automatically upward, to a pair of second-story windows in a white stucco apartment house.

She remembered what a joyous occasion it had been when she and Kyle had found this apartment so close to the University and within their combined school budgets. Both of them were attending the University of Denver on scholarships. Her Aunt had left a small inheritance, and Lori struggled to stretch it to meet the ever-rising college costs. Kyle's father owned a small garage, so Kyle was trying to make do with savings he had made as a summer gas jockey and some help from home.

In the midst of affluent students who often had as many as three different kinds of cars for extracurricular pursuits, Lori and Kyle had recognized kindred spirits in each other when they met in the student center over an evening meal of Cokes and hamburgers.

Whatever the attraction, physical or otherwise, it had been there for Lori the first time the dark-haired youth gave her a slightly crooked smile and eased his lanky frame into a seat beside her.

As these memories came flooding back, Lori opened the car door and quickly walked into the red foyer of the Lotus Gardens Apartments. Her eyes fell upon the second mailbox from the left, and for some ridiculous reason she was jarred to read unfamiliar names there. Joe Harrison and Judy Waits. Double names were common at the Gardens, denoting unwed roommates. This was one of the reasons a friend of Kyle's, Pete Rossi, had told them about it. He and Connie Walters had rented apartment 204 and had alerted Kyle about 205 when it was vacant. They had made a companionable foursome for the eight months they had lived there.

As Lori stared at the mailboxes, she sensed a presence

behind her and swung around to see a large woman with dyed black hair standing there holding a carpet sweeper.

"Hello, Mrs. Perkins," said Lori. "Remember me?"

Rose Perkins squinted. Unruly eyebrows rose. She was obviously having a hard time placing the slender, pale woman. These young ones came and went so fast, she thought, and changed partners every other week, how was she supposed to remember anyone? She had long ago quit trying to keep up with them. She had enough trouble just collecting rents, let alone trying to establish a personal relationship with her young tenants. Still, there was something that nagged her about this one.

"Lori Martin. About four years ago? I had 205 with Kyle Connors."

"Oh, yes—205. That good-looking Mr. Connors." She remembered now. They had made such a striking couple, him so dark and laughing all the time, and her so shy and pale. She set down her sweeper. "How have you been?" Not very well, thought Rose, answering her own question. The girl's face was pinched and drawn, like she had been sick or something. "Looking for an apartment? Sorry, 205 is taken, but 206, next door, is vacant now. Had to do the whole apartment over. Never have seen such a mess. Some people are just pigs. No other way to look at it. But 206 is nice now. Come, I'll show you. Put a light blue paint on the walls instead of white. It looks real nice."

Hesitating to tell Rose she had no intention of renting an apartment, Lori let the moment slip away. Instead of answering, she followed Rose's square body through the foyer door into a courtyard with three floors of apartments rising around it. She needed desperately to reach back into the past in order to gain a firmer hold on the present. In these surroundings she could bring Kyle back. In this place where she had known love and protection perhaps she could shed the cold shivers that gave her goose pimples all over her body, and block out the memories of a crazed man about to shatter her skull with a copper pot.

The small courtyard looked the same. A swimming pool took up nearly half of the enclosed area, and small patches of green grass and lawn furniture took up the rest. Except for one rather large female sunbather, the courtyard was empty. Black wrought-iron staircases and balconies ran along each floor in front of apartment doors. As Lori followed Rose's heavy body up to the second floor, they passed a couple coming down, a very dark black man and a white girl with bleached hair. Mixed couples were also the rule rather than the exception here at the Gardens.

A stereo was blaring out hard rock in a marathon of music that went on twenty-four hours a day.

Lori paused at the top of the second floor stairs and looked over the balcony, down into the swimming pool. She remembered one Sunday afternoon when Kyle and Pete had drunk a few beers before climbing up on the railing, and wavering there a few seconds before diving off into the water below. Even now Lori remembered how fearful she had been that they might break their necks in such a silly stunt.

As Rose went by 205 and began unlocking 206, Lori stopped in front of the door that had been theirs. She could almost feel Kyle's breath upon her neck and hear the shifting of grocery sacks as he stood behind her, waiting for her to unlock the door. And then it was gone, and without the memory she felt stupid standing there staring at a closed door.

All the apartments were alike, even the furnished appliances and the cheap furniture. She and Kyle had made the walls personal with some favorite prints and two hanging baskets. As she followed Rose into 206, it looked very much like their apartment had looked the first time they saw it. In fact, Rose launched into the very same prerental speech she had given them. "Water's furnished but that's no reason to waste it. You pay your own utilities. Rent is due—"

Lori remembered how Kyle's eyes had caught hers in a wink as he assured Rose that they understood the arrangements. Then he had deftly eased Rose out of the apartment, locking the door firmly behind her before he turned and opened his arms to enfold Lori in them. Even now her body felt flushed as she remembered the way passion had sprung up in her and how brazenly she had responded to Kyle's demands. Rose's speech triggered a series of intimate memories. Lori stood in the center of the room with her eyes half closed.

"Are you all right? You haven't got an ounce of color in your face." Rose grabbed her arm. "You ain't gonna faint on me?"

"No, no. I'm fine," Lori stammered, suddenly jerked out of her reverie.

"What's the matter with you, girl? You got eyes like a pet dog that's about to be shot."

"No—I'm fine," she repeated. "I—I was just remembering."

Rose was about to respond to that bit of foolishness, when an irate tenant showed up at the door.

"Mrs. Perkins. Mrs. Perkins—"

"Yeah?" Rose waddled over to the door. "Whatcha want now?"

"The sink! It's stopped up again! Water all over the place. I tell you there's something in it."

"It's your damn hair," retaliated Rose. "I told you there was a matted mass of it the last time. You gotta clean the trap." Rose went out, calling over her shoulder to Lori. "Be back in a minute, Miss— Rest yourself a bit." Her muttering faded away and ended in the slamming of a door.

As stillness settled upon the vacant apartment, it no longer seemed familiar to Lori. The spell had been broken. She became aware of the freshly painted blue walls and a strange shag rug of muted browns and golds. Only the hum of a small refrigerator greeted her ears as something left over from a long ago love nest.

She moved to the window. Here familiarity met her gaze. The campus was a block away and green lawns stretched between new and old buildings. She remembered what it looked like covered with snow and dotted with bundled-up students scurrying to classes with frosted breath.

Their apartment had been a favorite stop for Kyle's friends when they had time between classes. As Lori stared out the window she could visualize a half dozen fellows sprawled around the room behind her. Some drinking, some smoking, and all talking. She had been on the rim of their conversation but had enjoyed being a part of Kyle's life, having no real friends of her own.

They had talked about the Vietnam war—even participated in some protests against it, but in the end Kyle had gone voluntarily. It had been his father's death that ended everything. When Kyle returned from the funeral, he told Lori there was no more money. He would have to drop out of D.U. Without his college deferment, he would be drafted, so he decided to enlist. "That way, I'll get a better break."

As they lay together for the last time, she had cried against his bare chest, "There must be another way!" But if there was, Kyle didn't find it. In a matter of weeks she was back in a crowded dorm, and Kyle was on his way to California and then overseas.

The first year his letters came quite regularly. As their optimistic tone changed into disillusionment and bitterness, they became less frequent and finally stopped altogether. It had been three years since the last one. Lori had continued to write and her letters were never returned —but never answered. She had written to a brother of Kyle's asking for information but he had never replied.

Nothing—until last night. "Do as they say. K." She leaned her forehead against the pane of glass. Kyle, Kyle. Every sense that she possessed seemed to reach out for his presence. Longing like a pain tore through her. A clatter behind her jerked her eyes open, and for a second she was suspended between now and then.

"You should of seen that mess," bellowed Rose. "Damn hair! Just like I said. Take a week to dry out that rug."

Lori turned around. Rose set down a wet mop and pail. "It's hard, keeping a place up, but I try. How do you like the blue walls? Nice, huh? Well, what do you think? Rent has gone up fifty a month—what with inflation and all," she said defensively. "But you won't find anything better." When Lori still didn't answer, she repeated, "Well, have you made up your mind?"

"Yes, I have," said Lori quietly, "and I'm afraid I don't have any need for an apartment right now—maybe later. You see, I'm married. My name is Mrs. Philip Brandon."

# *Five*

"That was a fool thing to do!" Bud lashed out at her. Apparently he had been watching for the car from the third-floor deck because he met her in the kitchen as she came in the back door.

"I had to get away to think."

"Well, I'm glad to see your thinking made some sense. You could blow the whole thing running off like that."

"I'm back, so save the lecture," she said testily.

"Have some lunch." He was being sociable again. His way of switching from the bizarre to the mundane was frightening. He didn't even look like the same crazy man she had left in the solarium. Only a psychopath could switch back and forth as readily as he did.

He motioned for her to join him at the table where he had placed a tray of sandwiches. "You need to eat more," he said.

"Worried about my health, Doctor?" The last word dripped with sarcasm. She knew she was foolish to taunt him back into another rage, but she couldn't help herself. Somehow his solicitous pose frightened her more than his open anger.

"Can't stand sick people." There was a twinkle in his eye when he looked at her.

She stiffened. "Didn't you have enough pots to break?" His good mood was like a red flag to her.

He sat down and took a sandwich. "Well, that wasn't too profitable. There wasn't anything hidden in any of them. Maybe you can save some of the plants—repot them or something."

"You thought—you were looking for—something?"

"Everything that comes into this house has to be examined."

39

"Why didn't you tell me? I mean, how can I cooperate if I don't even know what I'm expecting?"

"Anything that comes for Mrs. Brandon is important. Do you think I'm going to trust you with any more information than that? You could run off to the authorities and foul up everything for me—and for Kyle."

"All right, but I have some questions about Kyle that I want answered. Unless I'm positive that he really is in danger—that what I do really matters—I'm not going on with this charade." She was surprised at the firmness of her voice.

Bud looked at her differently. He set down his coffee cup, pausing a moment before he spoke. "That seems reasonable. Maybe I can answer a few more questions."

"Where is Kyle? This very minute?"

"Bangkok."

"Bangkok?"

He laughed at her puzzlement. "Why, Miss Martin, a teacher like yourself and you're not quite sure where Bangkok is."

"I know it's in Thailand, but what—? How? Why is Kyle in Bangkok?"

"Waiting for you to get him out."

"But how?"

"How are you going to get him out? By pretending to be Mrs. Brandon until we get what we want."

"Who's we?"

"Ah, now you're getting into the no-comment area. You see, I have something at stake too. You have Kyle and I have—"

"Three million dollars," she spat.

"You think Kyle is worth that much?"

"Much more—to me."

"As much as your life?" he asked with deadly disdain.

She ignored a cold shuddering feeling. "I want to make sure that if you get your money, Kyle and I will be safe."

"You have my word, as a doctor." The twinkle was back and Lori was furious that he was making light of her demands.

"And you have my word, Doctor, that unless I have messages from Kyle—in his own voice—this whole fiasco is going down the drain—for everyone!" She bit into a sandwich as if she were holding him in her hands.

"I'm not sure that will be possible."

"In your profession—whatever it is—you must have heard of cassette tapes. I want one—from Kyle. I want to hear his own voice telling me that what I am doing is right. That little note isn't enough for me. It's been too long for me to be sure he wrote it. You want me to play your game? All right, I'll do it—if I hear Kyle telling me to."

He was silent and Lori sipped her coffee nervously. Maybe she had pushed too hard. What if he refused? Could she take a chance on Kyle's life by refusing to go on?

"We may have misjudged you, Marty." He was openly studying her. "Your backbone seems a little more rigid than we were led to believe. I'll see what I can do. In the meantime, on with the show!" He took out his wallet. "I don't intend to dine on delicatessen items at every meal. Here's some money. You have the keys to my car. So buy some groceries. What kind of a cook are you anyway? I rather enjoy a good cuisine."

"Then why don't you plan on eating out!"

He raised one eyebrow. "Now how would that look, darling? Don't you know that happily married people usually eat together. However, if you prefer to dine out—"

"No!" She rejected the picture of a public performance. It was hard enough to endure his presence when no one was around to comment on it. She picked up the money. "Okay. But I refuse to do all the cooking. If you are such a gourmet, you can damn well fix your own meals."

"In that case I'll make you a list of things I need. Unless, of course, you'd like me to come along—"

She knew he was laughing at her again. "No. I'll manage without your company." Then she remembered. "But I don't have a driver's license."

"Yes, you do." He went over to a bookcase and picked up the wallet that belonged to Mrs. Brandon. "Just make sure you don't need to use it."

Her indignation stayed with her the rest of the afternoon. She drove back into the city again, stopping at a shopping center just off Packard Road and Monaco Avenue. Half the condiments she bought off the spice rack she had never heard of before. She didn't know whether he was pulling her leg or if he really knew how to use all of them. Although she had enjoyed trying out new recipes now and then, cooking for one person had not developed her culinary talents very far. When she had been living with Kyle, there had been little time or money for anything but the simplest fare. With some vindictiveness she spent seventy dollars at the grocery, liquor, and cheese stores. Then she bought a new purse and put all new paraphernalia in it except for the borrowed wallet. The back of the Matador was filled with sacks when she returned to the house.

Tired, she carried up one sack and set it down with a thump on a kitchen counter. Then she went into the family room where Bud was watching a late afternoon talk show. "The rest of the stuff is in the car. I'm going to take a shower. If you want supper, you can cook it."

"Just like home sweet home, isn't it, my love? This marital bliss is really getting to me."

"Me, too!" she snapped.

A nice tepid bath soothed her taut nerves. She lay across her bed in her dressing gown, and her mind seemed to be less in a confused whirl than it had been most of the day. She was sure she had done the right thing demanding to hear from Kyle. Visiting the apartment had swept away the years they had been apart. As she lay there she could feel his warm body beside her and she murmured, "Kyle . . . how I miss you!" Her face lost its rigid lines, and she looked as if she were once more sleeping in her lover's arms. As the dream sped away, she was not in their apartment bed but in the mountains . . . snuggled together in the high, crisp altitude of the Rockies.

It was true that she could ski a little. Because of Kyle's popularity, they had spent several weekends and some holiday breaks in Aspen, Colorado, at the McPhee's condominium. The first time Kyle had relayed an invitation, Lori had stammered, "Bertie who? Never heard of him."

"Not him. Her! Bertie McPhee. You know—the girl I've been working with as a lab partner. Her father's a senator from back east and they own a condominium in Aspen. She's having a bunch up there for a weekend. First time I've been included." He gave her one of his special grins. "We've been included."

"Are you sure? I don't even know who she is. What does she look like?"

"Bertie? Short, dark hair, long and loose. Tries to act cool all the time. Never have seen her in anything but expensive pants and sweaters. Guess her old man can afford D.U. and all the extras. Should be fun. I told her we'd come."

"But we can't afford it," she protested, a little irked that asking her about the invitation had been an empty gesture. Neither one had ski equipment. She knew that tow tickets would cost a week's groceries.

"Bertie said the weekend was on her. Besides, I'm sick of sackcloth and ashes. We deserve to live it up a little. Don't scowl like that! It'll be all right. We'll manage." And then he began to kiss away the frown lines on her face, with light, tickling kisses around her eyes and mouth. "That's better," he murmured as her face softened and her lips parted to meet his.

So they had gone—not once, but often. Kyle was a welcome addition to any group. He had a quick wit that set an easy, light tone to every social gathering. As always, Lori was proud of her handsome escort. His popularity shed a halo effect over her, and even though she knew she was included only because Kyle would not go without her, she still found being a part of a fashionable group exciting.

There were a few regulars who showed up every time and others who came and went with Bertie's whims. Although Lori was sensitive about Bertie paying all the rental fees, it was taken care of so smoothly that there was no chance for real embarrassment.

The first time the rich girl greeted her, Lori knew that her welcome was only perfunctory, an act of good breeding. It was obvious that Bertie was willing to buy an audience of those she wanted in attendance—even willing to pay the price of an unwanted girl friend when necessary. Maybe she hoped that eventually Kyle would show up alone. Unwittingly, her generosity provided some of the most intimate moments Lori and Kyle ever shared. One in particular was framed in her memory, and it was the one she relived most often.

The last week in March they had gone to Aspen for their spring break. Out of next quarter's book fund, Kyle bought bus tickets to the famous resort. The trip was a pleasant one, and Lori tried to enjoy every minute of it as she sat beside him in a swaying bus filled with holiday-bound young people.

Although the mountain passes were still snow packed, an early spring thaw had piled slush on the road and had caused water to flow again in ice-choked rivers. Everybody in the bus chuckled at the sight of some hardy fishermen who waded in hip boots out into the chilly currents of the Roaring Fork River. Lori couldn't believe they were trying to fly-fish for trout in a river that still floated chunks of ice. All through the bus there were loud guffaws at such ridiculous enthusiasm. Fortunately the ardent fishermen couldn't hear the jokes made at their expense or they might have retaliated with some scoffing of their own.

Just beyond Glenwood Springs, Lori caught sight of a herd of deer grazing in a snow-filled meadow. Tips of dried grass protruded just enough above the snow to tempt the white-tailed animals, which someone identified as mule deer because of the shape of their ears.

"Happy?" asked Kyle as she slipped her arm through his. "Your eyes are sparkling like the snow out there. This week's going to be worth the money. Just think! On the slopes all day. Music, dancing at night! There's no resort in the whole world like Aspen!"

No one, least of all Lori, was going to argue with that. Once the lure of silver had brought bright-eyed prospectors to the slopes of Aspen Mountain. Historical landmarks like the Red Onion Saloon and Jerome Hotel remained in the midst of converted old Victorian buildings and newly established shops and chalets. The booming mining camp of the 1880s had become Rocky Mountain Ski County, boasting that a third of all skiers coming to Colorado chose Aspen and nearby Snowmass. The young, and not-so-young, skiing enthusiasts pouring out of cars, buses, and trains were just as bright-eyed and eager in their quest of silver snow as the first prospectors had been. Kyle and Lori surged along pedestrian malls, breathing deeply the intoxicating, thin mountain air as anticipation brought new color to their cheeks.

There was wealth everywhere, but most of it had been brought in by land speculators and financial manipulators. The McPhees' condominium was in one of many complexes built along aspen-covered slopes. The condominium looked across Roaring Fork River, with a glimpse of the mountains of Independence Pass. Its clubhouse offered indoor racquetball and squash courts, a sixty-foot swimming pool and several saunas. As Bertie collected her group, Kyle whispered to Lori, "This is going to be great! I bet it's the best skiing we've ever had."

But Kyle was wrong. Fickle Colorado weather did not cooperate with their holiday plans. The same warming trend that had brought fishermen into the Roaring Fork River changed the snow surface on all slopes to crunchy slick ice. As a result, Bertie's invited guests decided to desert her hospitality for some better skiing conditions in Steamboat Springs, a resort farther north. The guests' departure left the condominium empty of its usual mounds of people huddled in sleeping bags. Gone was the continual blast of rock music and laughing, beer-drinking merrymakers. The unexpected peace and quiet was like a sudden shift from a subway station to a novice convent.

Kyle and Lori would have preferred to leave with the others, but financially it was out of the question. They were tied to Bertie's hospitality. When she asked them to do her a favor, there was only one answer they could give.

"My parents have decided to fly out for a few days' vacation," she explained. "I'll need to get this place back in order. I have the names of the couple who do the usual cleaning, but I'd feel better if someone were here to supervise. Will you stay?" In actuality, the request was a demand on their IOUs. "I'll go with the gang to Steamboat and then meet my folks at Stapleton when their plane gets in. We'll drive back up on Wednesday afternoon."

Lori understood perfectly. In exchange for her previous hospitality, Bertie wanted them to get the condominium presentable again. "And I assume you would like us to be gone by the time Senator and Mrs. McPhee arrive," offered Lori candidly.

"Not at all! I want him to meet Kyle—and you." She gave a flip of her long hair. "Dad's always asking me about my friends. I want him to see how respectable they are."

"Respectable?" Kyle gave her one of his side grins. "I've been called a good many things by pretty girls, but I'm not sure that I like respectable."

"That's because I haven't had the chance to know you very well," she quipped.

"Maybe that's just as well—"

"Oh, I don't know. I'm willing to take my chances." She lightly touched his arm. "Sorry to be leaving you here, but—" She gave a shrug. "Oh, well, maybe next time. Off to Steamboat! Come on, gang." She turned away and herded a half dozen chattering guests out the door.

Lori was used to this kind of teasing flirtation. Kyle's open devotion to her always made it light and innocent. At first she had needed Kyle's constant reassurance that he wasn't interested in the propositions that came his way. In answer, he stroked her soft blonde head tenderly. "I'm happy with my tawny kitten, all purring and declawed. You're not like the others. Especially not like my mother."

"What was she like?" He never talked about his family. She only knew that his mother was dead.

"A shrew!" And that was all she ever got out of him. If he had not treated her so lovingly, she would have been certain that he hated all women, despite the fact that he could twist any of them to do his bidding any time he chose. Although she wanted to know everything about her beloved, she respected his silence as he respected hers. She didn't tell him about her mother and father, who had always been strangers to her. From birth she had been raised by baby-sitters, day-care attendants, and hired companions. When she was in the fifth grade, her parents were killed in an automobile accident and Aunt Adele, her father's spinster sister, took in Lori. Belonging to someone had made those years the happiest in her life. But she didn't want to talk to Kyle about Aunt Adele.

Her aunt's idea of a proper escort had been the very meek and boring Sunday school leader who had called properly the summer Lori graduated from high school. She knew Kyle would laugh if she told him about Aunt Adele; so out of respect, she let the subject of family ties remain a neglected item of conversation.

As soon as they had the condominium to themselves, they wandered hand in hand through the plush surroundings as if they had suddenly come into an unexpected inheritance.

"Just imagine! Four whole days in this place—alone!" breathed Kyle. "Rosie Perkins and her Lotus Garden Apartments can't quite compete with these accommodations." Laughingly he picked her up in his arms, swung her around, and carried her into the master bedroom.

"We shouldn't be in here," she gasped as he tossed her onto an oversized waterbed.

"Of course we should. Squatter's rights!"

Then, as always, any protests were quickly forgotten. They could have been any couple on a honeymoon as they laughed, made love, giggled, and chased each other in foolish horseplay.

Jake and Sarah Norris arrived to do the housekeeping and were on the premises during the day but went home at night. Lori got along well with them, mainly because she scurried about doing half of the cleaning chores herself, feeling somehow that she was working her way out of debt. Kyle teasingly called her his "Lady of the Chalet."

Frequently he dragged her away from work to the complex's outdoor swimming pool, which was set in a snow-filled meadow under a huge, steaming plastic bubble. "Do you think I should go into politics," mused Kyle as they lounged in a warm Jacuzzi. "I could switch to a political science major. I'm not all that crazy about chemistry."

Science had not been easy for him, and a master's degree would be necessary for any good job. They were both sick of school! Getting a college degree seemed to be nothing more than an endurance contest, with little relevancy for any real future accomplishments. Kyle had been searching to find out what he really wanted to do with his life and getting more discouraged with every class.

"You'd be good at politics," she granted. "People like you . . . so they'd vote for you. And you can talk anyone into anything." She laughed as she blushed. "How well I know!"

"That's only fair, my love. Since you make me feel like I can do anything." He touched her hair in a familiar, caressing gesture. "How was I lucky enough to find you?"

"You looked under the right rock, I guess," she quipped.

"Would you like politics? Being in the limelight and all that? I want to choose a career that would make you happy. I don't think you really like being with a lot of people."

"Yes, I do. But I'm not good with them, the way you are. I could take the public—if that's what you wanted."

He gave her his crooked grin. "How would you feel about being the First Lady of the land?"

"I already am," she said simply, with a catch in her throat and filled with the wonder of being loved by someone like him. How had it ever happened? It was a mystery—one she didn't want to unravel.

The senator's entourage of several cars arrived shortly afterward. Immediately cameras began to flash as doors opened and reporters bounced out. Lori and Kyle went outside to greet the arrivals.

Bertie and Senator McPhee laughed and exchanged quips with six or seven reporters who followed them up to the house. Mrs. McPhee remained in the car, apparently refusing to be a part of the melee.

As Bertie reached Kyle, she slipped her arm around his waist and drew him forward.

"Who's that, Miss McPhee?"

"Someone special?"

"Hold it, please."

"This way!"

"One more, please."

"A friend, Miss McPhee?"

Bertie smiled and nodded as the cameras clicked. Kyle laughed in an embarrassed way and then stuck out his hand for a shake with the senator. Bertie made the introduction while pencils flew and a barrage of new questions drowned out the senator's words.

Lori had hung back, out of the crowd, and one young girl reporter, unable to get to the front of the gathering, spied her and asked rather dubiously, "Are you anybody?"

"No," answered Lori. "I'm afraid not." But as Kyle turned and caught her eye in an intimate wink, she knew with sudden warmth that she had lied to the girl.

*Six*

There was no word to describe the next few days except "hell." She and Bud moved around the house like two caged lions, giving each other as much berth as possible. Both of them tensed at every telephone call, which was always someone trying to sell storm doors or steam clean their carpet.

Lori refused to eat with him. She snacked early or waited until he had finished before taking a plate to her room, the deck, or the solarium. She hated to admit any credits in his favor, but enticing smells began to fill the house every afternoon. Apparently he was using a lot of his idle time to pursue his culinary interests. If the kitchen and family room became his domain, the deck and solarium became hers.

Trying to save what she could from the havoc Bud had wreaked upon the plants gave her some immediate purpose. She lowered the heavy planters hanging from the vaulted ceilings in the family and living rooms, threw out the plastic ferns, and potted the new greenery that, with some tender loving care might survive.

Bud watched her with a disdainful expression on his face as she carefully lowered the heavy planters to the floor for replanting and then laboriously pulled them back up and hooked the chain again on the wall hook.

"What are you going to all that trouble for?" he asked, sprawled out in his TV chair.

"I don't have any other containers to put them in," she responded, sweetly sarcastic.

"That's a hell of a lot of trouble if you ask me. You're going to have to lower them every time they need water."

"I haven't got anything better to do!" And she flounced back to the solarium.

At first she was so nervous; she paced up and down between the wrought-iron tables, wondering how long she could keep from fleeing down the steps away from endless swirling questions that brought no answers. She dragged one of the fancy pillow chairs from the living room into the solarium.

She sat in the deep chair with her legs drawn up under her chin and tried to find some pattern in the past that had brought her to this moment. It was true that she liked house-sitting because it gave her a built-in identity during the time that she shared another's house and possessions. Before her parents were killed in a car accident when she was ten, there had been no place they called home. Her mother had never been the homebody type. She had worked to put Frank Martin through law school and then had continued as one of the best legal secretaries in the huge New York law firm that took him in as a junior partner.

Lori had been an unexpected, and unwanted, intrusion on their careers from the very beginning. As they moved from one fashionable apartment to another, Lori had spent her growing-up years in day-care centers and pre-schools, and when she was ready for regular school, they found a private one that would keep her until six every night until someone picked her up—very often a baby-sitter because her parents were involved in evening conferences. It was on the way home from one of these late night affairs that her parents had been struck broadside by a diesel truck.

Her father's sister, Adele, came after her and took her to Kansas City. Despite her aunt's sincere efforts to adapt her life to include a painfully shy and colorless child, Lori had always felt she was as much an intrusion on her aunt's well-ordered life as she had been on her parents'.

When she and Kyle found each other, she felt that at last she had found a "home" for herself. But that hope had only survived the eight months they had lived together. Her small efficiency apartment in Kansas City was like the impersonal, sterile ones her parents had always rented. But when she was house-sitting, in a real home, she vicariously enjoyed the warmth and love that was revealed in the collected possessions and clutter of family living.

Bud and his conspirators couldn't have picked anyone better for their little game of make-believe. Her own identity was as blurred as the woman in the photograph, and there was only one person who had ever sharpened it.

Kyle . . . Kyle . . . She put her face in her hands and muffled the name that came out like a sob.

Bud had taken a bedroom off the hall, so their paths did not cross very frequently on the upper floor. Rather than go through the family room to get to the solarium or living room deck, she used the outside steps and balconies.

Sometimes as she leaned against the railing and stared at the mountains, he would come up behind her. Suddenly she would feel a coldness on her neck and turn around. There he would be, looking at her as if he had to make certain his captured specimen was still harmlessly fluttering about in its prison.

"How much longer?" she would ask.

"I don't know. We'll have to wait and see."

"Have you taken care of that recording? I'm not going to wait much longer," she threatened with white lips, knowing that the bluff wasn't going to work.

Without answering, he turned away and went back downstairs.

"I mean it!" she yelled, rather hysterically. "I won't wait much longer."

The nightmare went on. Empty days. Empty nights. Three weeks of agonizing waiting. It was an eternity of mental anguish and emotional drain. Every day Lori felt her self-control disintegrating in the charged atmosphere, until she wasn't sure when she would go screaming from the house like one who had exhausted all of her emotional reserves.

The telephone rang once more.

She heard it from the deck. Bud had insisted that she answer all the calls since it was Mrs. Brandon who would receive the important "something."

With the chronic trembling in the pit of her stomach, she crossed the living room to pick up the small princess phone.

"Hello. Mrs. Brandon speaking." Her voice was steadier than she felt inside.

"This is Pacific Airlines," said a sweet, mechanical-sounding voice. "We want to inform you that flight 276 from Bangkok, Seattle and Denver will be arriving two hours late. The new arrival time will be four twenty-three this afternoon."

"But—"

"Thank you for calling Pacific." There was a hum on the line that told her there was no one on the other end to answer any further questions.

"What is it?" Bud demanded in a tone that showed an impatient anxiety. "For God's sake, who was on the phone?"

"Pacific Airlines. A woman—she said that flight 276 from Bangkok was late—two hours. She said it would arrive at four twenty-three."

"That's all?"

She nodded, searching his face for some kind of understanding, but it was plain that he was as confused as she was.

He looked at his watch. "Well, we'll have to meet it. It's about an hour to the airport. Get ready to leave by three."

"Do you think . . . maybe, they let Kyle come home?" As soon as the name Bangkok registered, her thoughts were on Kyle, and even as the rational part of her brain was taunting her hope, she had put it into words.

"Don't be an idiot! Of course not. I don't know what to expect, but we won't find out anything with you standing around blabbering like a love-sick fool. Do something with your face and get out of those dirty jeans."

Apparently her casual clothes had irritated him as much as his immaculate attire had irritated her. He had expensive tastes in food and clothes. She had never seen him without coordinated outfits, including white summer shoes and a variety of Indian shell necklaces around his tan neck. He had continued to play golf early every morning, but the bronze Matador had remained in the driveway the rest of the day.

This would be the first time they had left the house

together. Neither had been willing to leave very often, fearful that the message might be missed or delayed.

Even now as she slipped into a crisp, yellow pantsuit and hung a gold medallion around her neck, her thoughts were on the telephone message. What did it mean? Maybe it was a mistake, a wrong number. Still, she had identified herself as Mrs. Brandon. She brushed her hair and tucked it back with two small combs. She patted a touch of blue color to her eyelids. That would have to do. If it were Kyle—her foolish brain still fumbled with the hope —he would find her changed. But then five years were enough to change them both. Suddenly she was frightened in a different way, as if she were surely going to see him again that very afternoon. Maybe he would just walk away from her, or worse, give her an indifferent smile and say, "Oh, yes, I remember you. We had fun, didn't we?"

Standing in front of the mirror, she tried to smile at the pale girl standing there. Her lips curved up but no smile reached her eyes. They were wide and frightened.

As they drove toward Stapleton Airport, Bud gave her the quick once-over. As usual he looked like a fashion plate in beige slacks and plaid shirt.

"Well, do I meet with your approval?" she goaded him, irritated that she was under some kind of inspection.

He only grunted and gave his full attention to the road. Obviously he was searching in his mind for some understanding of what might happen when they got to the airport.

"Maybe it's a wild goose chase," she taunted above the blare of the car radio.

He glared at her.

"Well, it might be. Maybe they got the wrong number —or something," she ended lamely.

"Didn't you tell them your name?"

"Yes, but maybe she didn't hear it—or misunderstood what I said. The person acted as if I knew what it was about and hung up before—"

"I know—I know! Well, there's only one way to find out, isn't there?" he said impatiently. "We'll meet the plane and find out if there's anything on it for us." He seemed in control of the situation, but Lori noticed his knuckles were white on the steering wheel.

When they got to the airport they missed the signs and arrows that directed them to a lower parking area. She knew he was going in the wrong direction when he drove up the ramp, but she only bit her lip and kept silent when he started swearing.

There was no place to park the car on the unloading strip, so they went past all the terminals and drove back down to the lower ramp, where they finally found an open stall about two blocks from the Pacific Airlines entrance.

"What if it isn't a person?" Lori questioned as she tried to match his long stride. "Won't we have to go to the baggage area for a package?"

He jerked to a stop and swung around to face her. "Did the call say it was from the Pacific freight office?"

For a minute her mind went blank and she couldn't recall anything specific about the call. "No. . . . do freight flights have a number like passenger ones?"

"When we get there—if we ever do"—he said as he grabbed her arm and pulled her along—"we'll find out."

Flight 276 from Bangkok was a passenger flight, unloading at gate 16. They walked through a long annex to the proper waiting room. Lori saw from one of the round clocks that they had fifteen minutes to wait. During those long minutes, she wished that she smoked. It would have given her something to do with her hands. Usually she was a people watcher, especially enjoying the bustle of people coming and going at an airport, but today the sight held no joy—in fact, she didn't even see those who mingled around her.

Bud seemed to go through a pack of half-smoked Winstons. He couldn't stay in his seat and kept going to large windows overlooking the landing strips.

He's as nervous as I am, thought Lori, and somehow his discomfort made her calmer. His confident doctor role irritated and disturbed her. Maybe he wasn't as much on top of the situation as he pretended. And then the next thought drove away any sense of ease that was beginning to build. Maybe he knew who was arriving on flight 276! If it was one of the "we" he had spoken about and he was worried about their arrival, then the situation might not be better for her—in fact, it might be worse. Although she hated Bud, he had been a lenient jailer and impostor, and some of the worst fears about living in the same house with him had been unfounded. As far as she knew he had never approached her bedroom. She might not be so fortunate with someone else. With millions of dollars at stake, the most ruthless kind of people could be involved.

When the jet taxied up to the loading tunnel, Lori was on her feet beside Bud; their eyes were fastened on the entrance where unloading passengers first came into view. Still halfway expecting to see Kyle walk through the opening, her glance quickly passed over every passenger as fast as they came through the door.

Evidently whomever Bud expected to see did not show up either, for both of them were staring at the the opening when the last passenger went by. As they looked at each other, they wore matched faces of bewilderment.

Then the stewardess appeared, leading out a little Oriental girl who was traveling alone. Lori and Bud started to turn away when the stewardess called, "Dr. Brandon?"

Bud froze, turned, and then nodded. Smiling, the stewardess stopped and motioned to someone still in the tunnel. Then she came forward toward them with a warm expression on her face.

"Your children had a good flight," she said. And as she gave the little girl's hand to him, a second stewardess appeared with a sleeping baby boy about six months old, whom she handed to Lori.

As both stewardesses beamed at the united family, Lori looked down at a dark-haired baby who had opened large brown eyes and was staring, unblinkingly, back at her.

Lori searched Bud's face for some kind of understanding, but he was looking down at the fragile little girl with the same kind of disbelief. When Lori heard someone suddenly laughing in an abandoned, uncontrolled manner, it was only from the expressions of the stewardesses that she realized it was herself!

## Seven

As Bud took the baby from Lori with an air of ownership, she protested in anxious tones, "We can't do this! We can't take them!"

He gave no sign of having heard her and beamed down at the baby as any proud father might do. A small identification card was pinned to its blue kimono. Kee Brandon: eight months old. Destination: Dr. and Mrs. Philip Brandon, Denver, Colorado, U.S.A.

The little girl continued to stand passively beside them, wearing the same kind of identification card. Lang Su Brandon: six years old. Destination: Dr. and Mrs. Philip Brandon, Denver, Colorado, U.S.A.

"Dr. Brandon, the baby just ate," said the stewardess with the same air of reporting that a professional nurse might use. "But there is another bottle ready." Then, because his hands were filled with the wriggling child, she handed a large cloth satchel and a claim ticket to Lori. "The baggage will be ready in just a few minutes."

Obviously glad that the flight was over, both women smiled their good-byes and went back on the plane. They saw strange reunions every day, so the bizarre little family, frozen like some tableau, only brought a shrug of the shoulders and was instantly forgotten.

"We can't take them," repeated Lori, this time loud enough for him and anyone else to hear.

He shot her a warning look that was as sharp and ominous as any he had ever given her. Then he shifted the baby in his arms. "Give me the claim check."

He took it without another word, or even a glance at her or the little girl. Then he spun on his heels and walked away, leaving her staring at his retreating back. He seemed to have dismissed both of them completely as his long stride took him down the corridor.

Fury overran Lori's sense of bewilderment. He must be out of his mind! What on earth was he planning to do with these children? Well, she would have no part of it. Angrily, she started after him, and then, remembering the little girl, she turned to wave her along. As her gaze fell upon the statuelike child, wearing baggy pants and a shapeless shirt, both so big that they made her small arms and legs look like toothpicks, her fury was submerged in a wave of compassion.

How terrified she must be, thought Lori. The baby might not know where he was, but this six-year-old did. And such strangeness would be enough to terrify an adult, let alone a sensitive child.

Lori knelt down beside her. "Lang?" She smiled, touching a tiny arm reassuringly. Huge, unblinking eyes, framed by jagged black bangs, moved only slightly in their mask as a solemn, steady gaze bore into Lori's face.

"Lang? Lang Su?" repeated Lori. There was a slight nod but no change of expression.

Then Lori stood up and pointed down the corridor and then to herself and Lang, trying to communicate without words that they were going to walk down the hall. She held out her hand and Lang put a listless one in hers.

Most children would have been looking at everyone and everything. Even if language were a barrier, strange surroundings would have captured their attention. But Lang moved along like a mechanical doll, no response of any kind in her petite, stiff frame, her gaze straight ahead.

As for Lori, every step they took seemed to bring new confusion. Lord, what are we going to do? But the words were more of exasperation than a prayer. Bud must think that the children were the key to something. But what? After the first shock, he had reacted quickly, taking the baby with an ease strange to most men.

But Lori was terrified of children! She knew nothing, absolutely nothing, about babies or kids. She had avoided elementary education because she felt ill at ease with young children. How a teacher had enough nerve to shut herself up all day with thirty of them was something Lori could not fathom. Her high school students were near enough to being adults that she could relate to them as people, and not strange little creatures of a different world.

Aunt Adele had not enjoyed children either, and except for a few relatives, none had come to inflict their noise and sticky fingers upon Aunt Adele's well-ordered house.

Lori hadn't decided against children of her own—someday. In daydreams she had imagined how beautiful any baby of Kyle's would be, and she knew when the time came she would be ready for it. But these little foreign children added more terror to a mounting wave inside her that threatened to sweep her away from the tenuous hold she had been maintaining on her self-control.

"Let's wait here." She motioned the little girl over to a small bench in a waiting area where there was a gift shop and magazine store. People were milling in and out of the stores, but Lori didn't look at any of them as she sat down. She had to have time to think, to marshal her thoughts before Bud swept them away in a masquerade that would sacrifice them all.

Lang Su sat stiffly on the edge of her seat. Her thin legs dangled out of her too-short pants. Lori fleetingly wondered what she was thinking and marvelled that she appeared so self-contained—or was the word withdrawn? She felt she ought to say something to the child, but the challenge of communicating without words was more than she was up to at the moment. What shall I do? What shall I do? The question made a thumping screech inside her brain, made her head ache with the rhythm of the words.

There were officials here at the airport that she could approach. "There has been some mistake," she could hear herself saying. "We cannot take these children because we are not who we seem to be. They must belong to someone else. You see—" And then her mental conversation broke down. The rest of her explanation would bring an end to the impersonation and, as Bud had promised, an end to Kyle's safety. But how could they involve two innocent children in the charade? If she told the truth, what would happen to them? How could she know when she didn't have a glimmer of an idea why they had been sent to Dr. and Mrs. Brandon in the first place?

Beads of perspiration formed on her forehead and she

hunted in her purse for a tissue. Lang watched her as if the sight of the American lady sweating when she wasn't working was of interest to her. There seemed to be a judgment in the child's eyes that made Lori even more ill at ease. Why couldn't she show an interest in something else, thought Lori defensively, uncomfortable under the little girl's unwavering stare.

"Hot," said Lori to her, trying to smile and pantomine the word by fanning herself with her hand. Then she felt foolish, realizing that air conditioning belied her words. Actually, it was probably chilly to the displaced Oriental child.

At least Lang seemed less like a mechanical doll now as she gazed from Lori to the nearby gift shop. Like most airport shops it was filled with toiletries, plants, toys, and thousands of other items that travelers might buy.

Lori was startled when Lang's tiny hand reached out and touched her arm. Then the child pointed to the window of the shop.

"What is it? What do you see?"

Lang's pointing finger leveled at a yellow Winnie-the-Pooh bear. Then she looked back at Lori to see if she understood.

"The bear? Is that what you'd like? Well, why not? Let's go spend some of the 'doctor's' money."

Lang's hand had lost its limpness this time as she took Lori's hand. In the shop Lori picked up one of the soft plush toys that was on a display table. "Like this one?" she asked as she handed it down to the child.

Lang Su grabbed the bear as if it were a life preserver. It seemed unlikely that even an adult could pry it loose from her again. Then she raised saucerlike brown eyes up to Lori and said in understandable English, "Thank you very much."

"You're welcome," Lori managed with her mouth hanging open in complete surprise. Then the memory of her pantomime antics made her feel like a fool. "Why didn't you tell me you spoke English?" she demanded churlishly. "I must have looked ridiculous waving and pointing like that."

"Lady didn't ask." This softly spoken reply, which seemed more reasonable than Lori's demand, made her feel that somehow she had managed to make an ass out of herself in front of this child.

It wasn't the best psychological moment for Bud to appear. "There you are," he said impatiently. "I got the suitcase. Here—take the baby and I'll bring the car up to the front."

In an instant he had deposited a wriggling mass into her arms. The baby was wide awake now and seemed more than sixteen pounds as he twisted and turned in order to sit upright in her arms. Kee was without any of Lang's passiveness as arms and legs shot out in every direction.

"We've got to talk *now!*" Lori tried to step in front of Bud to bar his way out of the shop. Then she gave a cry, "Ouch!" The baby's clutching hand had made contact with her swishing hair, and pain shot through her head from the jerk he gave it. Then as she struggled to disentangle his tiny fingers before he succeeded in scalping her, Bud managed to outmaneuver her.

"There's plenty of time for talking when we get—home."

Home! How dare he use that word for a prison . . . a horrible mass of stairs and crazy-shaped rooms! Its emptiness and coldness poured over her. She couldn't go back. She couldn't. She had to get out.

"Wait!" But he was already through a group of people entering the shop and nearly out of sight. As everyone looked at her peculiarly, she realized how shrill her voice had been.

A sales clerk shifted a pair of black-framed glasses uneasily on a narrow nose. Her expression clearly stated, "Boy, you sure meet all kinds when you deal with the public."

An overwhelming desire to run made Lori hold the baby away from her as if she were about to deposit him on the nearest counter or in the arms of the thin-lipped sales girl. Only a firm jerk on the edge of her jacket delayed the impulse and made her look down.

Clutching the Pooh Bear with one arm, Lang had picked up a brown and white plush monkey with the other hand. "Keewie likes monkeys," she said.

"Those are on sale today." The clerk was beaming now, scenting another sale. "I think it's just wonderful that these beautiful little children are coming to America to live," she cooed. "Their little slant eyes are adorable. I was working that night when they brought about five hundred to Denver—you know, the airlift from orphanages. My goodness, what a sight! All those tired, crying babies and scared new parents. They looked just about as bewildered as you do," she said frankly, then added reassuringly, "but they've all settled in good now. Don't know what would have happened to the poor things if they'd been left over there."

During this recital, Lang had been trying to hand the monkey up to Kee.

The sales girl continued her monologue. "It was a good night for business, too. A toy makes every one feel better. And all kids know what they want." She beamed at Lang.

Perhaps her irritation with Bud spilled over to Lang and the sales girl, but Lori felt that she was being neatly manipulated by both of them. Firmly she took the monkey from Lang and handed it back to the clerk. "He's too young for that kind of toy," she said in her first motherly action. "Maybe a—rattle—or something like that." She avoided looking down at Lang while the exchange was made.

"He already has one," Lang was mumbling, with a stubborn jut to her chin.

Kee was the only one happy with the transaction. He grabbed the handle of a combination rattle and teething ring with a deathlike grip and began to wave it around in the air with uncontrollable abandonment, promptly bopping Lori on the head with it.

Several giggles came from Lang while the salesgirl smiled broadly. The salesgirl had lost ten dollars on the exchange. The little girl's eyes had lost their dullness and there was a sparkle in them that had a hint of derision about it. A creature much older than six years seemed to peer out from that petite face as she watched Lori's irritation.

Propelled by growing frustration and anxiety, Lori swept them speedily out of the shop and through the front doors just as Bud pulled up. As he got out and came around the front of the car, she met him at the curb.

"I'm not going anywhere with these kids. I want to talk to you—"

"Right now—here?" His black eyebrows raised up in disgust, and a quick hand motion indicated arriving passengers, airline personnel, and zealous red caps handling piles of luggage.

"We can go back in—"

"Where to—a bar? A restaurant?"

The picture of what Kee would do to a nicely set table was not reassuring. Without answering, she shoved the wriggling baby into his arms. With the expression of someone fleeing from disaster, she spun around and started away.

Immediately Kee let out a piercing howl that stopped everybody for fifty feet right in their tracks—Lori included! Each yell increased in volume until surging traffic noises were drowned out in the outburst and countless staring eyes came to rest upon the couple with the screeching child.

Even Bud's composure disintegrated with the volley of rising screams coming from a pair of lungs that sounded big enough to fill an Olympic stadium.

Lori stood riveted, unable to continue her flight. Bud hastily handed the mass of noise and flailing arms and legs back to her. Almost instantly Kee's cries began to diminish, and as Lori gazed with bewilderment at the now tranquil infant, his round lips parted in a contented toothless smile.

"He likes you," said Bud, sighing in open relief. "Get in," he ordered.

She might have made it away from him even then, and away from the cooing baby, but when Lang voluntarily slipped her tiny hand into hers, holding it as tightly as she clutched Pooh Bear with the other, the moment for escape was lost.

As if resignation brought its own kind of release, she managed a reassuring squeeze and hid her trembling lips from view as she ducked into the car.

# *Eight*

Whoever said that the art of motherhood was an instinctive trait had never had to call upon such instincts in a situation like this, thought Lori, sitting with a strange wriggling baby on her lap and a wide-eyed, adult little girl beside her.

She kept glancing at Bud's profile as he drove, trying to gain some understanding from his concentrated look. It was obvious from the way his forehead furrowed that he was doing some heavy thinking.

Her own anxieties had lessened, and an enveloping numbness made her feel detached from the reality of the situation, as if she were apart from the events that were sweeping her along toward some catastrophic end.

Kee had found her gold medallion and had discarded his new rattle in favor of the necklace. He had been gurgling and tasting it with the air of a gourmet. As he bit down on it with his bare, slobbering gums, he looked up at her with an air of satisfaction. It seemed to her he was sitting up very erect for an eight-month-old baby, and she wondered how much his bright eyes were actually seeing as he gazed out the window at houses, cars, and trees flashing by.

Lang Su seemed as disinterested in the view out the window as she had been in the airport. Still hugging her bear, she cautiously reached out and turned a radio knob as if she knew what it was. As music came on, she looked up and gave Lori her first smile. It was fragile and fleeting, but it was a smile.

"Do you like music?" Lori asked.

Then before Lang could answer, Bud said something to her in a language that sounded like Chinese. Lang swung her gaze from Lori to him, responding in the same tongue.

Lori's numbness was swept away before a new rising bewilderment. "You know Chinese?" she demanded.

"Not Chinese. It's a Vietnamese dialect."

"You were in Vietnam?"

"No, I learned to speak it in Brooklyn." He shot her a look of disgust.

She didn't know why she should be surprised. Somehow she had assumed that the rest of the "we" was with Kyle overseas and the United States part of the operation was Bud's. Now she realized that even though her pretend husband didn't seem to be in control of things, he must have personally known Kyle and he must have been overseas quite awhile to learn the language. A flood of new questions surged up in her mind, and with them a new determination that he would no longer evade her questions.

Now he was chattering with Lang who responded with one-syllable words, which Lori assumed might be "yes" or "no."

Irritated that they were conversing behind her back, she broke in rudely. "She speaks perfect English, you know."

But apparently he didn't, for one dark eyebrow of his went up. Lori felt an unreasonable sense of smugness. He thought he was so all-knowing. Then, to prove her point, she pointed to the stuffed animal. "There are some good stories about Pooh Bear. Would you like to hear them?"

As Lang nodded solemnly, Lori flashed a triumphant look at Bud. Lang relaxed her rigid little spine and leaned back in the seat so that her head was resting against Lori. Instantly Lori's momentary victory seemed shallow . . . and cruel. Her promise to read stories indicated her willingness to continue with this family charade, but there was no way that she was going to adopt instant motherhood. When they got the children out of earshot, she and Bud were going to have it out. The quick look that Bud sent her made her wonder if she had made the declaration out loud.

When they reached the house, it was obvious that if

there were any parental instincts at all, they rested with Bud. Plunging into the role of fatherhood as if it were the only possible behavior, he directed "Operation Settling-In." He was the one who took charge of making the adjoining balcony bedroom into a kind of impromptu nursery.

Every time Lori tried to corner him he would cut her off briskly, "For God's sake, Marty. Let's get the kids settled before you go into one of your marathon talking acts."

When they had first come into the house, Lori had put the baby down on a couch in the family room; her arms ached from carrying her lively bundle up those steps.

"Don't leave him there!" yelled Bud as she walked away. "He'll fall off." He dropped the suitcase and Lang's hand and darted. But his reactions were not fast enough, and Kee had tumbled off even before Bud's last words were out.

Kee's Olympic screams vaulted to the high ceilings, filling all the open spaces of the house with rebounding yells. He refused to be placated despite Bud's "It's all right, fellow. You're okay." He patted the baby's bottom as he glared accusingly at Lori. "Don't you know anything about taking care of kids?"

"No, I don't. You fouled up there. Why didn't you pick someone else for this fiasco?"

"Because I didn't know— There, there, don't cry." The baby's eyes were scrunched up and his tiny nose hidden behind a wide open mouth that emitted shrieks like someone under dire torture. "Here, you try."

Lang's solemn eyes had gone from one to the other during this exchange, like one following a tennis match.

So back into Lori's arms again came the shrieking bundle. She held him tightly, fearing that his next thrust would jerk him from her arms. This strange hold seemed acceptable to Kee, however, and his cries began to soften into gurgling whimpers.

"Well, you've got him fooled, anyway," Bud said in obvious relief. Then glancing at his watch, he added, "I'll have to get to the stores before they all close."

"You're not going to leave me here—alone?" she gasped, horrified.

His look was scathing. "I have to get some things for the nursery. Come on, I'll get you and the kids settled up there. You all ought to be safe enough until I get back." He spoke as if he were reassuring three children instead of two. Then he picked up the battered suitcase and cloth bag and motioned for them to follow as he led the way up the circular stairs.

"The floor will be the best place to put the baby until we get a playpen and crib. Don't leave him on the bed unless you're sitting there," he instructed bluntly, as if she might repeat her stupidity again. "I doubt if there is much in the suitcase except a few clothes. Here's the diaper bag. He probably needs to be changed."

"You do it," she sputtered, suddenly as horrified as if she were facing some kind of graduate exam.

But Bud was already in the doorway. He paused, a flicker of amusement in one corner of his mouth. "Oh, you'll do fine—Mother!" Then he scooted out of sight before she could throw something at him. She was positive she heard him laughing all the way downstairs.

Lang brought the diaper bag as Lori laid Kee on the massive Italian-style bed. Lori was hoping that the bag would contain the kind of disposable diapers that were always being advertised on television—already shaped with handy sticky tape on each side. But the square piece of gray muslin she drew from the bag had no shape, and not a hint of the right way to fold it to fit Kee's wriggling bottom.

As Kee tried to turn over in every direction, she gingerly took off a pair of plastic panties and began to undo a wet diaper. Two safety pins were rusty as she withdrew them, carefully watching to see what else Kee might have left in the diaper for her. She realized later that a potent smell would have left no doubts in her mind about a full diaper. But this time Kee was just sopping wet. She studied the way the diaper was folded as she withdrew it.

But before she could pick up the dry diaper, Kee let go again with an arched stream of water that would have drenched them both if Lang hadn't quickly flung the dry diaper down on him.

"He always does that," she said, as if apologizing for his lack of manners.

Finally, with a lot of coaching from Lang and encouraging chortles from Kee, the diaper was put into place, very loosely. In fact, it threatened to wriggle down his legs when she put him on the floor to play while she unpacked the suitcase.

Bud was right. There was little in it except more clothing, in the same style as what they were wearing. There was another rattle, which Lang drew out with a kind of I-told-you-so look. But it was a large, heavy gourd and Lori was satisfied to see that Kee preferred the lighter plastic one she had bought for him. It was easy to see why Lang clung to her Pooh Bear. There were no toys in the suitcase for her.

At the bottom of the suitcase was a large brown envelope. Lori drew it out and started to open it. At that moment Kee let out one of his murderous shrieks. He had turned over and banged his head against the claw foot of a chaise longue. A large egg-size bump rose immediately on his forehead. Even the floor isn't safe, thought Lori, trying not to think about what Bud would have to say about her baby-sitting capabilities now.

Kee refused to be consoled by her reassuring pats. Walking up and down with him, she said, "Maybe a bottle will stop his crying," and she looked at Lang for agreement.

Down to the kitchen they went. Kee's cries lost some of their volume but he continued his fretful whimpering. While she heated a bottle in a pan of water, Lori stared at it impatiently, patting Kee on the rump, and wondering why it took forever to heat up.

When she thought the milk was warm enough she shook out a few drops on her arm. It seemed all right, but she was only guessing. How hot was too hot? As Kee grabbed the bottle and began to suck it greedily without any expression but pleasure, she let out an audible sigh.

She carried him back to the family room couch and laid him down again. This time she sat on the cushion beside him. His large dark eyes stared at her unblinkingly over the top of his bottle, a sucking motion milking the rubber nipple. Slowy, heavy eyelids flickered down, finally closing in sleep. His cheeks were tearstained and the bump on his forehead had an ugly yellow cast to it. He

71

was a darling baby, but he sure didn't know a mother when he saw one, she thought wryly. When there were only a few drops left in the bottle, he let it slip from his mouth. He was fast asleep. She felt a deep sense of satisfaction.

"He's asleep," she whispered to Lang who was sitting at her feet, bouncing her bear on the floor as if they were out for a walk.

"Are you hungry?" A flash of guilt that all her time and energies had been spent on the baby dissipated her sense of accomplishment. She slipped off the couch onto the floor beside the child. "Shall we see what's in the fridge?"

Lang stopped her play and looked blankly at Lori. "Fridge?"

"Refrigerator—ice box."

A smile of understanding turned up her lips slightly. Without responding she got to her feet and held out her hand to Lori.

"Just a minute." Lori put a chair beside the sleeping Kee. "See, I'm learning," she said to the little girl, hoping that the bump on Kee's head would go down before it revealed her inadequacies to Bud.

Where in the hell was he, anyway, she thought as she studied the choices in the refrigerator. Gone were all the delicatessen items. Now fresh shrimp, cuts of beef, mushrooms, bean sprouts, and other peculiar-looking fresh vegetables filled up all the bins. There was nothing so mundane as peanut butter and jelly. She shut the door with an exasperated bang and was about to search the cupboards for some canned food when Bud came in.

He was laden down like Santa Claus and smiling just as merrily. "I think I got everything we need right away —playpen, bottles, baby food, disposable diapers, and something special for you." He winked at Lang and drew out a book—*Winnie-the-Pooh and the Tight Squeeze.*

For the first time Lang lost her little-adult composure. She let out a squeal and her little arms trembled with excitement. She pointed to the yellow bear on the cover. Pooh was stuck in a hole while Rabbit, Christopher Robin, and his friends were trying to pull him out. "Pooh Bear," she said and precious laughter like rare tinkling chapel bells drew the three of them together in a moment of intimacy.

As Bud shifted his gaze from Lang to Lori, his expression did not change to the open derision she had come to expect when he looked at her. She was included in the warmth of his smile, and a thrust of response swept through her body. Startled, she realized his open disdain and mockery had hurt. She did not want him to look upon her with abhorrence even if she couldn't stand the sight of him. His short gray hair was growing out and curling against his head. That's why he keeps it short, she decided with a sense of smugness. He hates curly hair. And as her eyes locked with his, she felt as if she were seeing him for the first time. For a brief instant she forgot how he had misused her to gain his own greedy ends.

Then valid feelings of hurt and anger rose to keep their hatred flaming. "We're starved. If you're through playing the good guy, please change some of these weeds into food."

The coldness that came into his eyes reassured her. She knew what ground she was on now, made firm by the antagonism between them. He was not going to manipulate her through these children. She didn't know how they fitted into the situation and she didn't care. The rules of the game had not changed. She had one purpose only for involving herself in this masquerade: Kyle! "And after dinner we can decide whom to call about the children," she added firmly.

"I'm not sure you'll want to do that, Mrs. Brandon—"

"I'm not Mrs. Brandon!" And you're not Dr. Brandon, she thought angrily.

"I know," he admitted crisply. "And since you took the children from the airport under that pretense, the authorities would consider such an action kidnapping." And as her knees threatened to buckle, he asked with that schizophrenic twist of his, "How about shrimp with bamboo shoots tonight?"

# Nine

He was an excellent cook and showman. Just as if he were one of those Oriental chefs who make an elaborate production of preparing meals before their customers, Bud flipped shrimp from his cutting board into a sizzling wok with the flourish of a juggler. He handled sharp cutting tools with ease and waved them around with such exaggerated swagger that Lang's solemnity disappeared. Peals of childish laughter followed his every gesture, urging him to further dramatics with the persuasion of a continuous encore.

Lori remained outside the circle of their levity. Although a few moments' consideration had dismissed the kidnapping threat as another of Bud's maneuvers to keep her in line, she felt anything but jovial at this weird dinner party. As Bud chopped onions and mushrooms, she imagined how just as easily he might wield a knife in softer flesh.

Bud handed her a glass of white wine, and she tried to put such macabre thoughts out of her mind and concentrate on enjoying the perfection of the meal. Neither of the other two dinner guests seemed aware of her aloofness. As soon as the meal was finished she mumbled a habitual, "Excuse me," and rose to leave. But Bud refused to let her make such an easy exit.

"We've got to take all these things upstairs. You take up the playpen and I'll carry Kee. We'll put him in it for the night."

Although her instinct was to spit "Do it yourself or call in someone else," the words never got to her vocal cords. She rationalized that they ought to get the children settled as soon as possible so she and Bud could have this thing out.

Fortunately Kee didn't wake up in the transfer, and as Bud laid a new blanket over the sleeping baby, he whispered, "I'll get a crib later." There was no doubt from the way this strange man gazed down upon Kee that his Achilles' heel had been found.

Lori made a mental note of this discovery. A weak flank in the enemy was a valuable piece of knowledge —one she might desperately need before this nightmare was over.

Lang had been bathed in the large tub by Lori, who felt extremely clumsy and nervous as she passed a washcloth over the tiny brown body. Lang had reverted to her mechanical responses, and Lori's nervous chatter brought scarcely more than a slight shifting of her large dark eyes.

After her bath, the child sat in the center of the huge bed like a lost puppy in the middle of a field. All laughter was gone from her face, and her eyes held a solemn, watchful gaze that resembled a protective wall. Her little brown hands were like claws as she clutched Pooh Bear.

Lori's intention to flee the room as soon as possible disappeared. "Would you like me to read some of your new book?"

A slight nod, but no smile.

If this barnlike house seemed cold to an adult, how much more frightening would these ultra-modern surroundings be for a child from halfway around the world?

Lori pulled the little girl back to the pillows and settled down beside her as she opened the book. She refused to meet Bud's eyes as he moved about the room putting baby paraphernalia on an elaborately carved dresser.

" 'Edward Bear, known to his friends as Winnie-the-Pooh, or Pooh for short, was walking through the forest one day . . .' " As Lori read, Lang stared at each page of colorful pictures. Slowly the little girl's rigidness eased away. Her body began to curve against Lori's as Pooh pranced his way to Rabbit's house and the calamity of too many honey pots.

Bud left the bedroom at just about the place in the story where Pooh was blaming his predicament on the fact that front doors were not made big enough.

As Lori read, an automatic consciousness pronounced the words, while another part of her mind dealt with much different thoughts. Lang had spoken so little. How much English vocabulary did she have? She seemed to keep up with the story, but was she only picture-reading? Where had she learned English? The plane had come from Bangkok, yet Bud had said they were speaking a Vietnamese dialect. There had been nothing on the identification tags about their nationality. Then she remembered the brown envelope. Probably there were official papers of some kind that would answer some of her questions about the children.

She speeded up her reading. Lang's eyes were as wide open on the last page as they had been when Lori began the story. There was no sleepiness in them. " 'So, with a nod of thanks, he went on with his walk through the forest, humming proudly to himself. But Christopher Robin looked after him lovingly, and said to himself, "Silly Old Bear!" ' "

Lori smiled down at Lang as she closed the book. Instantly the little girl's contented look faded and she did not return Lori's smile. Instead, she held the book up. "Again," she said solemnly.

Lori laughed and eased herself off the bed. "Not tonight. Maybe tomorrow."

Quickly she tucked the covers around the child, avoiding looking into those depthless eyes. "You need a good night's sleep. It's been a busy day." And then she touched a kiss to the tiny forehead and turned away. Some wise part of her demanded that she keep herself detached and free from entanglements that could grow from intimate moments like this one.

Purposefully she went to the double closet and quickly opened the sliding doors wide enough to pull out the weathered suitcase she had placed on the floor. She knelt down beside it and fumbled with an old latch until the lip flipped open. Only emptiness met her eyes. Nothing! The envelope she had hastily flung back in the suitcase when Kee banged his head was gone. Lori stared at the bottom for a few seconds, reassuring herself that she had really held such an envelope and had replaced it in the bag. She was positive.

Lang had been watching her, wide-eyed, from the bed.

"I'm looking for that brown envelope. Do you know where it went to?"

No response—not even a blink from those all-seeing eyes.

"Do you know what I'm talking about?" demanded Lori impatiently, irritated that Lang consented to talk only when it suited her fancy.

As only silence greeted her from the child, Lori shoved the suitcase back in the closet, intent on getting downstairs and confronting Bud as quickly as possible. The sight of that lonely little hump in the middle of the huge bed caused her to pause in the doorway. "I'll leave the bathroom door open. If you want anything, just call. I'll be in the other bedroom. Good night, Lang Su." She waited but there was no response.

As Lori stepped outside the door, she glanced over the balcony railing. Bud was stretched out in front of the TV. Her exasperation over the missing envelope exploded. She charged down into the family room with all war banners flying.

"What did you do with that envelope?" she demanded without any preamble.

Bud raised one eyebrow. "Envelope?"

"Don't play innocent with me! There was a brown envelope in the bottom of the suitcase. Now it's gone."

"I don't know anything about it."

"Liar!" Her voice had a hysterical edge to it. She breathed deeply to settle a surge of helplessness that swept up in her at his denial.

"What's so important about an envelope?"

"Tell me what's in it and I'll know."

"Sorry, I can't help."

"Who do those children belong to?"

"Dr. and Mrs. Brandon."

"The real Brandons—*not us!* Maybe you can sacrifice two little children to your treacherous game, but I can't. Kyle wouldn't want me to. Playing house with you is one thing but—"

"They're better off here for a while than they would be in Vietnam," he interrupted in a smooth tone that contrasted highly with her jagged rising voice. "There's no place for two orphans who have been rejected by the

American parents. We'll keep them here and then later—"

"You're insane! I'm through. Do you hear? You haven't given me any proof that Kyle is alive. I warned you that if I didn't hear his voice, I would know you're lying about him. I'm calling your bluff, Mr. Whoever-You-Are."

That seemed to sober him. Triumphant, she leaned back in a cushion chair and crossed her legs in a gesture of relaxation. She had changed to a cotton peasant dress on their return from the airport. One sandaled foot swung slightly in the air as she forced her hands to lay quietly on the arms of her chair. Her voice had a firmness in it she didn't feel. "I care about those children, even if you don't. The longer they are unsettled the harder it's going to be for them. When your game is over, they're going to be uprooted again. Lang doesn't act as if she can take much more, and the baby—" she paused, trying to gauge his reaction without really looking at him. "He's a darling. How can you take a chance on what might happen to him if you keep him in the middle of this thing?"

When he didn't reply right away, hope sprang up. Maybe she was going to pull it off. If she could use his feelings for Kee to give this whole thing up, she would be out of this nightmare and they would let Kyle go. The baby might be the lever—if she only knew how to use it. But if she applied pressure in the wrong way, it might collapse any chance of saving Kyle. Could any baby mean as much as three million dollars to a man like Bud? It didn't seem likely. Still, he was sitting there, slumped down in his chair with his hands pressed together near his chin, as if he were deep in contemplation.

The urge to say something more, to push him toward the thing she wanted, was too much for her. "Kee deserves a real home, real parents who care about him. And so does Lang. If it's true that the Brandons arranged for their adoption, then the sooner another family is found for them, the better. We can just tell the authorities they arrived while I was house-sitting. Someone will take—"

He moved fast, jerking her out of the chair with such force that she was flung halfway across the room. She stumbled, righted herself, and started to dart away from his explosive fury. But he had her by the shoulders, shoving her backward until she fell onto the couch. "You lying bitch! You don't give a goddamn about the kids. It's your precious Kyle's skin you're trying to save." His wrath gave an orange cast to his tanned skin, and as he bent over her, his expression was one of a diabolical creature. "Isn't it? Isn't it? It's always Kyle. Every time you say his name, your face shines—like he's something holy." As he pressed her back into the cushions, he brought his face close to hers and glared at her with such ferocity that she closed her eyes against it.

Suddenly his voice softened and his words were coldly measured. She could tell from the warmness of his breath that he had not moved his face away from hers. She tried to turn away from him. "Why the kids don't see through you, I don't know. You're not much good at being a mother, or a wife—and I bet there's ice in your veins instead of passion." As if to prove his last accusation, he jerked her head about and she felt his lips on hers. He kissed her harshly, pressing her backward until his body lay full length upon hers.

She struggled against him but he was immovable and gradually her will to resist dissolved and the hands that pushed against him were no longer defensive. An involuntary response in her own body sent warmth shooting into her loins, and her body arched to meet his. Then as her moist lips opened to receive his, Bud roughly shoved her away from him.

"I don't take Kyle's leavings," he said contemptuously as he rose and glared down at her. Then he turned and left; the back door banged loudly behind him.

With her face burning and her lips still smarting from the pressure of his kisses, she fled upstairs. It was as if he had stripped her naked and then turned contemptuously away from what he saw. She was consumed with shame and a mixture of feelings that defied classification. Cold fury dissipated the warm flush of her body and she knew she would never forgive him—or herself.

Inside her bedroom she shut the door, leaning up against it, her choked breath sounding like a roaring in her ears.

A faint stirring drew her eyes to her bed. A tiny curled-up mass lay sleeping in the middle of rumpled covers.

Lang Su had found her way through the adjoining bathroom, and she and Pooh Bear were sharing her bed and pillows.

With hot tears blurring her vision and sobbing constricting her throat, she struggled into a nightgown and then eased herself in beside the sleeping child.

She muffled her sobbing into the pillow. "I hate him! I hate him!" And her hard voice sounded like someone else as she whispered, "If he touches me again—I'll kill him!"

# *Ten*

K ee woke her up at three thirty, screaming at the top of his lungs. She was in the middle of a dream, running down a subway tunnel with the screeching brakes of a train sounding just behind her. Bud was standing between two roof pillars lashing her with a whip to keep her on the tracks.

Baby cries mingled with the train's shrill brakes. Without full consciousness she bounded from her bed. Standing befuddled in the middle of the floor, she tried to orient herself as the dream faded away. Piercing screams continued. The present swirled into focus and she hurried to the nursery bedroom.

Bud had reached it before her. He was staring at Lang Su's bed. "Where is she?"

"In my room."

As they glared at each other, the screaming baby faded into the background. Bud did not look like the satanical creature who had attacked her last night. His other personality was in command this morning. His gaze fell before hers did. He made a gesture with his hands that could be construed as an apology. "About last night— I'm sorry, Marty."

"Take your apology and stuff it!" she spat, surprised that her high school students' vernacular fitted the occasion so perfectly.

Instead of flaming his anger, her reply made one eyebrow go up, and then his lips twisted into an amused smile. "Touché. No apology—no forgiveness. But a compromise? Unless you've decided Kyle isn't worth it?"

He knew where her Achilles' heel lay and he had no scruples about using it.

"I want that message from Kyle. No delays! No promises! And don't you ever touch me again!"

He nodded. "Agreed. You go along with the kids for a while and we'll both get what we want."

At that moment Kee decided that the present level of screams wasn't doing the job. His arms and legs went rigid, and he looked as if he were about to hold his breath until he lost consciousness.

As Bud grabbed him up from the playpen, the baby bellowed loudly, satisfied that someone was paying attention at long last.

"What's the matter with him?" asked Lori, frightened that he was in the throes of some kind of a fit.

"He's hungry and dirty. That bottle of milk didn't see him through the night. He should have been fed some baby food." There was censure in his tone as he handled the irate bundle of noise.

"As I recall, you hadn't brought any back when he fell asleep." Her disposition had never been the best in the morning, and she wasn't about to take any criticism in the middle of the night.

"We'll feed him now. He's disoriented anyway, so maybe he won't get into the habit of eating at this time."

"He damn well better not," swore Lori. "I'll get the food," she said quickly as Bud started toward her with a very fragrant Kee. And before he could protest, she was out of the room. I outmaneuvered him that time, she muttered in satisfaction.

By the time Bud came down to the kitchen, lugging an exasperated Kee, she had milk heating and a jar of pears open. Maybe Kee's stomach was ready for pureed spinach at three in the morning, but hers wasn't.

This time Bud was quicker. He handed her the baby before she could hand him the food. As awkward as anyone has ever been, she held the baby on her lap while she tried to maneuver a spoonful of food past his waving fists. When she was successful in reaching his mouth, more food seemed to bubble out than went in. By the time she had emptied the small jar, she had pear juice in his hair, down her neck, and spattered over her nightdress, which, she realized, should have been covered with the matching robe that she had left forgotten on a bedroom chair.

Fortunately Bud hadn't seemed to notice her state of undress and her disheveled look. He had been fussing about the kitchen while she wrestled with Kee, probably smiling secretly at her ineptness. Except for squeezing some icky liquid vitamins into the baby's mouth, he had left the two of them alone.

"What's that?"

"Something he needs every day."

"How do you know?"

He looked pained. "Maybe the druggist told me so."

As she took Kee to the family room couch, laying him down with his bottle as she had done before, she felt that she had victoriously come through some demanding initiation. She let her head fall back against the couch. Good God! How do mothers survive? she thought.

Bud brought in a tray of juice and some crisp pastry rings. "Coffee will be ready in a minute. Do you want to join Kee for breakfast?"

"At three in the morning!"

"Time is relative. Besides," he consulted his watch, "it's four o'clock now. Early dawn. The best part of the morning."

He was insufferable—overbearing, ruthless and definitely psychotic. The fact that he had put on a striped terry bathrobe even though he had reached the bedroom first infuriated her. Now he was acting like some social director, as if last night's assault had not happened or had been forgotten.

"No, thank you," she said crisply. With the children around it would be difficult to go their separate ways, but she would manage it. "I'm going back to bed." And with a protesting growl in her empty stomach, she flounced out of the room and took the carpeted stairs at a near run.

As she came into view on the balcony above, light outlined her figure under the filmy lace nightgown. Bud put down a glass of freshly squeezed orange juice and called up to her. "Tell me, why do you bother to wear anything at all?"

Flushing hotly, she shut the bedroom door with a loud enough slam to have awakened Lang. Fortunately, the little girl seemed to be able to sleep through anything, even Kee's tirade.

She stripped off the soiled gown and showered—which made her more awake, and hungrier, than ever. Stubbornly she crawled back into bed with Lang, and lay wide-eyed, cursing Bud as she pictured him below, enjoying his breakfast while he watched an early morning television broadcast.

It was nearly six o'clock when she dozed off, just about the time that Lang woke up. A not-too-gentle hand began to shake her shoulder.

"I'm hungry."

Lori groaned and managed to let one heavy eyelid flicker up. She saw Lang's solemn face three inches from her own. She closed her one eye, muttering, "Tired. Too tired."

"Kee's awake."

That statement jolted her into consciousness. She listened but couldn't hear any demanding screams.

"I gave him his new rattle."

"Good girl. Good girl." Lori started to snuggle down again. Bud must have put the baby back in his playpen. "Go ask Bud for breakfast."

"He's gone . . . with his bag of sticks."

Now anger had her wide awake. Where did he get off, thinking she was on twenty-four-hour call while he paraded around a golf course? They were going to get a lot of things straightened out before this fiasco went on any longer.

Her firm intentions came to naught. The impersonal routine they had established for so many waiting days disappeared. Although both of them were still keyed up for the arrival of "something" that would put an end to the abhorrent deception, the daily routine became physically exhausting and she longed for the days when she had been bored.

At first she tried to tend the children on the deck, which had a solid railing for Kee's protection, or in the solarium. But there were too many demands that took her into the kitchen or family room—Bud's domain.

And since she shoved as much responsibility for the kids as she could onto his shoulders, her demands put him in and out of the balcony bedroom.

Many things took a cooperative effort, and they found themselves working side by side in a situation that would have been unbearable if it hadn't been for the presence of the baby or Lang. But even in the closest quarters, there was a wall between them.

Bud never made any kind of overtures to her, but continued to treat her with the same kind of disdainful tolerance he had maintained from the beginning. She, in turn, realized how much she detested everything about him.

"Where is Kyle's message?"

"Coming."

"It better be!"

The house no longer resembled an immaculate showplace. Toys, clothes, and general clutter were spread in every room. Furniture had to be moved so Kee couldn't wriggle near any steps. He had a tummy crawl that Lori swore could cover distances faster than a walking child. And the first time he pulled himself up on something, standing on wobbly legs, Lori let out a shriek that brought Bud running.

"What the—?"

"Look! Look! Kee's standing!"

Putting down her Pooh Bear, Lang laughed and pointed. "Keewie walk!"

"Oh, no!" shuddered Lori, and even Bud laughed at her look of consternation. Kee spread his mouth in a wide grin and chortled, obviously pleased that everyone was giving him the recognition due him.

Bud continued his shopping sprees. No wonder he had such an avarice for money, thought Lori. He sure knew how to spend it. She wondered how long his share of three million would last. Nothing seemed too good or too expensive for the baby, and Lang Su came in only slightly second in his generosity. What's he trying to prove, Lori wondered suspiciously. It was as if he feared that somehow his little game would blow up if the children became dissatisfied.

He even bought Lori a watering can, as if he were tired of seeing her and Lang water the hanging baskets with a pop bottle full of water. The plants were doing well, a fact Lori pointed out to him with open smugness. Something made her want to keep baiting him—maybe it was his casual pose of superiority.

Although occasionally he took Lang with him, it was Lori who was surrounded night and day by the children. She had finally given up tucking Lang in her own bed, only to wake up during the night to find the little girl snuggled in close to her.

Despite this kind of intimacy, Lang's reticence was not softened enough so that Lori could ask her questions about her background. Lang continued to talk only when there was immediate relevancy, and only when she wanted to. She gave Lori that flat, detached look when she tried to pump information out of her. Since Lang was not a spontaneous talker, no accidental bits of information were forthcoming in childish chatter. Lori was as much in the dark about the children after two weeks as she was on the day of their arrival.

Lang became her shadow, following her into the bathroom, into the shower, and into bed. Since Lori continued her habit of talking aloud, Lang often came to her rescue when she was exasperated with some baby-tending duty. Kee seemed delighted with her bumbling efforts and gleefully shared his bath water with her, managing to leave her kneeling in a puddle of bath water, her hair and face almost as damp as his as she lifted him out of the big tub. He even joined in the conversation with expressive, nonsensical sounds that seemed quite appropriate at times. Except when he was hungry or wet, his disposition was quite sunny, and as he played with Lori's nose, lips, and hair, she found herself doing all kinds of dumb things to make him laugh and squeal.

She read to Lang and took her for a walk down to the mailbox each day. Her heart was always in her throat as she reached into the box, silently praying that some strange package or letter would be there. But nothing came, not even a package the size of a cassette tape. One day her summer check came, and a letter from Mrs. Wallace, the director of the House-Sitters Association.

Lori gave a hysterical giggle as she read it.

"What's the matter with you?" demanded Bud gruffly. He was obviously disappointed that the mail hadn't been more lucrative.

"It's a letter from my boss. She wants to know if everything is going normally."

Bud didn't laugh. "How did you ever get hired as a house-sitter? You're a hell of a housekeeper."

The mess and clutter were getting to him. He had been making more and more remarks about a "pigpen." He had continued with his early morning golf and most evenings prepared a meal for the three of them. Some of the Oriental dishes seemed familiar to Lang, and she cleaned her plate appreciatively while Lori played with a spoonful of strange grasses and bleached nuts. It seemed that Bud's responsibility for cleaning up began and ended with the kitchen. He kept his cutting tools and stainless steel cookery shining and grumbled about the rest of the house.

It wasn't that Lori didn't see the need for any of the housekeeping chores. Aunt Adele had instilled a sense of cleanliness and orderliness in her, but the dear lady had never lugged around a heavy sixteen-pound baby from morning till night until her arms ached with fatigue. Now Lori made a mental plea for forgiveness for misjudging the demands of motherhood and for being critical of those homes that were less than immaculate.

Keeping a small apartment tidy with only one adult living in it was nothing like the carnival of duties arising from tending children. And this monster of a house would have taken three hours to vacuum. Kee's crumbs disappeared into deep pile carpets, to be felt when bare feet pattered over them and ignored otherwise.

"You have so much money—hire a cleaning lady." Bud's criticism was like salt on raw, taut nerves.

"I don't think it's wise to have strangers about. Too many things can go wrong."

"Then you'll have to suffer the house. I'm too busy playing mother."

Although Bud was a great shopper, this didn't include the grocery buying. He would scribble a list of things he wanted and place it and some bills under a salt shaker on the kitchen counter. This was the signal that Lori was expected to make a trip to the shopping center. Although she grumbled about it as she brushed Lang's hair and tied a scarf around her own, the time away from the house was welcome, and if she had been forced to honesty, she would have admitted that she thoroughly enjoyed the errand.

Lang enjoyed it too. She sat on her knees in the front seat beside Lori and glanced about with an expectant expression on her face. Lori could not help but compare the difference between her now and the first ride home from the airport. It was becoming easier to bring a quick flash of a smile to her lips, and more than once the little girl had surprised Lori by chuckling deep at some situation she found amusing along the street. Lang Su still did not chatter like most children her age, but gradually she was becoming responsive to Lori's remarks. Of course, Lori had expertise in the monologue, and so the two of them went in and out of shops with intimate companionship that found Lori babbling about prices and merchandise while Lang kept by her side and looked up with understanding and contentment.

Lang was never more than a couple of feet from her side. Although the child grew weary with the long lines at checkout counters, she never wandered off and Lori had made a habit of rewarding them both with ice cream cones at a fabulous 58 Flavors Shoppe just around the corner from the supermarket. Often Lori became so engrossed in hassling with a clerk or searching for some imported condiment Bud wanted that she forgot the quiet little girl trailing at her side.

"Thank you," she smiled at a freckle-faced carry-out boy standing by the car loaded with groceries. She wondered if she was expected to tip him. She had never been sure about it, and by the way he took off, she guessed he wasn't sure about it either. It was then that she discovered Lang Su was nowhere around.

"Lang! Lang Su!" Lori called, spinning about and running all the way around the car. She looked up and down rows of parked cars and walked a little distance this way and that. Her heart began to make frantic thumping noises in her neck and chest.

She was certain Lang had followed her out of the store. But had she? All of Lori's attention had been on her grocery carts and the teenage boy who was helping her push them. Now she couldn't remember Lang at the checkout counter at all. But she must have been, Lori reassured herself as she hurried back to the front of the store. Her eyes searched frantically up and down the crowded sidewalk, and then she shoved her way back into the store, oblivious to scowls sent her direction as she plunged through.

"Did you see a little dark-haired girl?" she gasped, grabbing an arm of the freckle-faced lad who had carried the groceries. "The one I had with me?"

Obviously puzzled by this distraught woman who had been so calm a moment ago, he shook his head slowly.

Lori appealed to the check-out clerk and all the people lined up at her counter. "I've lost my little girl! Please! Someone help me find her. She's so tiny—and she doesn't talk—"

"Just a minute, I'll call the manager." The clerk gave Lori a smile of reassurance. "It'll be all right. Kids get lost all the time."

But Lang Su was nowhere in the store. Lori went up and down every aisle at least twice, praying at every turn that she would see that fragile little frame walking in front of her.

"Oh, my God! Someone's taken her," sobbed Lori, putting an agitated hand against her lips.

"Do you want to call the police?" asked a rather officious manager, irritated by this demand upon his valuable time.

The word "police" brought back a surge of instant control. She took her hand down and moistened her lips. "No—no! I'll look some more. Maybe she went somewhere else. I'll look—Thank you!" And she fled out the front door. How could she go to the authorities? They would ask her all kinds of questions. They wouldn't settle for any flimsy story and then . . .

She went back to the car again, hoping she would find Lang Su standing there waiting for her. But the little girl was not there. "Dear God, let her be all right . . . Don't let anything happen to her." Like a whirlwind the prayers went swirling through her head. What could have happened? Was she lost? Had someone taken her? Who? When? Where? Like a magnet drawn back to the last place she had seen Lang, Lori started back to the store. If Lang had wandered off—but she never did—but if she had—she would come back to the store, reasoned Lori. Where else would she go? The ice cream shop?

As this possibility hit her, Lori went at a half run down the crowded sidewalk. She shoved aside any slow-paced walkers who got in front of her. What did she care if they thought her a madwoman? At that moment of anxiety Lori would have gladly disrobed, screamed, or pulled her hair out if that would have brought Lang back into her arms. Lori turned the corner and thankfully she saw Lang Su standing at the curb about four store fronts down the street. She was licking an ice cream cone. A man was with her, but Lori didn't even glance at him as she spurted forward, then stooped down and gathered Lang, ice cream cone and all, to her breast.

"Lang—Lang," she said in a voice that was so void of strength it was a mere whisper. "I was so worried—so afraid—"

"I thought someone might be worried about her," said a voice so familiar that Lori jerked her head up and stared in disbelief. Rex grinned. "I didn't know she belonged to you, Pretty Lady. How are the plants doing?"

But Lori stood up stiffly, not returning his smile. Somehow she knew that Rex was not the innocent deliveryman he had seemed to be. Perhaps her anxiety had to find a release, but the coincidence was too great.

"Why did you take her?" she demanded, her eyes afire and her hands clenched in a hard fist. Unconsciously she moved so that her body was between him and Lang's. If she hadn't gotten there in time, no telling where he was going to take Lang.

Rex's smile faded as if he had just been reminded what a kooky lady she was. "I didn't take your little girl. I met her in the ice cream place a moment ago. She had ordered a cone but didn't have the money to pay for it, so, being the gentleman that I am, I came to the aid of the damsel in distress."

It could be true. But it could be a lie. It wouldn't have been the first time that a stranger coaxed away a child with something sweet. Lang would never go off like that and try to buy an ice cream cone. Or would she? Lang had shown herself to be determined when she wanted something—like Pooh Bear. While these mental gymnastics kept her staring at Rex, searching his face for the answers, he shifted to one foot and started licking his chocolate cone. Then when it seemed that Lori wasn't going to lash out with those clenched fists, he asked sociably, "Would you like a cone? I'd be honored to buy another double with pistachio nuts." He offered politely, taking another lick of his cone and then grinning at Lang, who was peeping around Lori's leg, licking her ice cream.

Lori felt like a fool . . . as if both of them were laughing at her dramatics. But, damn it, she had been scared to death. "No thank you," she responded coldly and took Lang's hand. "We have to be getting home. I'll talk to Lang about going off by herself and taking gifts from strangers."

"A good idea! But now that we're not strangers, maybe I'll see you again sometime, Lang." And he turned and sauntered off as if he were God's gift to the female sex.

By the time they got back home, Lori had put the incident in perspective. There was no reason to make something sinister out of the incident. As the store clerk said, children got lost every day. It was this macabre charade that gave a sinister overtone to everything. And yet, her mind would not let loose of the facts. Denver had millions of people in its city limits. There must be hundreds of ice cream shops and thousands of delivery-men. It took a real stretch of fate to put Lang Su and Rex together in the same one at the same time.

If she hadn't glanced in the rearview mirror as she turned into the driveway, she might have accepted the coincidence. But for a brief second she saw an unmarked delivery truck slowing and stopping at the side of the road, in a curve out of view of the house. Lori's fingers suddenly trembled as if they had palsy. She dropped the keys. Without looking for them, she pulled Lang into her arms and carried her up the steep staircase to the house. She closed and locked the door behind them. She would not play into his hands next time.

Bud came into the kitchen just after she had set Lang down. She was leaning back against the door, trying to catch her breath.

"What's the matter with you?" he demanded with a gruffness that might have been concern or irritation. Lori chose to think the latter. Since she had probably made a fool of herself once already today, she wasn't eager to make it two in a row.

"Nothing," she snapped, deciding not to share her anxieties with her arrogant jailer. "The groceries are in the car—and so are your keys."

"Oh, were the keys too heavy for you to carry up all those stairs?" he asked sarcastically.

"Stuff it!" she spat and brushed by him before he could see the tears of frustration that were welling up behind her eyes. Both Bud and Lang stared after her as if she were displaying a childish temper tantrum. And her behavior *was* childish. How much simpler things might have been if she had talked about her anxieties.

The next afternoon, Lori was in the bedroom nursery, putting Kee and Lang down for their afternoon nap. She assumed Bud was alone in the family room, watching TV. But suddenly the loud voices floating up through the open bedroom door were much too distinct to be coming from the set. Someone was in the room below with Bud.

Curious and apprehensive, she quickly gave Kee his bottle and stepped out of the room; then she looked down over the balcony into the family room below. Mrs. Holmes stood there, exchanging more than idle conversation with Bud.

The exchange between Bud and the pretty Oriental woman was heated. Their voices were raised and hands were slicing the air in quick gestures.

They were not speaking English, but anger in any language can be easily read in body movements and facial expressions. Bud's eyes had that frightening metal look, making his gaze as cold as a cutting knife. He took a step toward the woman as if he were going to bash her about as he had done to Lori and the pots of flowers.

Lori's breath caught in her throat and her hands gripped the railing so tightly her knuckles were white. She must have gasped audibly, for Bud stopped his movement and both of them swung about and raised their eyes up to the balcony. They both seemed to wait in a suspended silence for her to speak.

"I—I thought I heard voices," Lori stammered.

And then the most terrifying scream went up behind her. Lori swung around and saw Lang Su standing in the doorway. She had left the big bed and had followed Lori out. As the little girl caught sight of the impostor cleaning lady, she began to back up, screaming, as if a bear trap had snapped about her slender body. Eyes that were habitually flat and expressionless now darted in terror.

Below Mrs. Holmes had bounded forward, shaking a fist at the child and expelling a series of quick expletives that matched the hatred flashing from her eyes.

Lori could feel herself rising on tiptoe, like a mother bear.

"Get that woman out of here, *NOW!*" Then she turned and encircled the terrified child in her arms.

## Eleven

It took nearly an hour to get Lang settled down. Lori held her tightly, rocking slightly on the bed as the child sobbed and trembled in her arms.

"It's all right, darling. Please don't cry. You're safe. Lori won't let anyone hurt you."

There was nothing passive and withdrawn about the little girl now. She accepted kisses and caresses as she pressed her tear-wet face tightly against Lori's neck. Her tiny hands clutched Lori as if the devil himself were reaching out to snatch her away.

As Lori consoled the child, a consuming anger rose inside her. What had happened to the child to bring about this kind of response? What was Mrs. Holmes to Lang? How could any adult show such open hatred for a child? Lori had really forgotten about the woman. "One of us," Bud had said. Another impostor after three million dollars!

As the child quieted down, Lori was tempted to question her, but resisted it, fearful that it might cause Lang to renew her trembling and sobbing. Exhausted from the emotional unheaval, the little girl at last slipped into sleep and Lori eased herself away from the bed.

She went downstairs with mounting fury. Her anger had already passed combustion level. But the spark needed to ignite the explosion was absent. There was no one in the house! Both Bud and Mrs. Holmes were nowhere around.

The energy generated by her wrath demanded release. Back upstairs, for the first time she marched down the upper center hall to the last bedroom, the one Bud had taken. Without knocking, she flung the door open and walked in. She stopped in the middle of the floor. The presence of the unseen man enveloped her. The whole room was dominated by his personality. She was irritated to see his bed neatly made, clothes out of sight in the drawers and closet, and only a few expensive toiletries on the dresser.

There was a photograph in a gold frame on a bureau. Curious, Lori picked it up and studied it carefully. Bud was in the center, flanked by two women. It was difficult to tell whether or not they were all the same age. The dark-haired girl looked a little older than the smaller one, who had reddish highlights in her hair. Sisters, maybe, thought Lori. It must have been taken some time ago, for Bud's hair was long, in a stylish cut that put gray wavy puffs and sideburns around his grinning face. He had his arms around their waists in an affectionate squeeze. Lori had never seen that happy, carefree expression on his face. She set the picture down with a bang. For some reason she was irritated by the happy group which seemed to be mocking her.

As Lori went through the closet, searching pockets of Bud's beautifully coordinated outfits, it seemed to her that he had been expecting her, or someone else. Surely no one automatically kept everything in this perfect order. As if he were there laughing at her futile efforts, she started searching a dozen pairs of shoes with resentful frustration. Damn him anyway! There had to be something—like that brown envelope—that would help her understand all these mysterious relationships.

It was by accident that she found what she was looking for. When the last shoe came up empty, she was so uptight that she gave in to the impulse to throw something. And she let the shoe fly! She aimed at the harmless wall, not daring to break anything like a window or mirror. Bud's shoe bounced off the white wall just above his bed, leaving a black mark where it hit. The jar of the shoe hitting the wall shook loose a modernistic painting that hung just above the headboard, and as it came crashing down, a corner of the frame hit the carved bedpost. Before her startled eyes, the molding broke apart at one end, leaving the edge of a brown envelope showing between the picture and the cardboard backing.

She allowed herself a loud laugh as she gleefully drew out the brown envelope and sat down on the smooth bed to investigate its contents. Inside were two sheets of paper. One was a Catholic christening certificate and the other an adoption form. Both were for Kee. The certificate listed his name as Kee Phamn. The only signatures on it were those of the godparents: Philip Allen Brandon and Lois Marie Brandon. The adoption form was also from a Catholic institution, and a Sister Marie Elena had signed it as well as the Brandons.

She felt like someone reaching into a Christmas stocking only to find one piece of stale candy in the toe. What had she discovered really? The Brandons had adopted the baby. She had already deduced that much from the identification slips when they arrived. Lang's papers must be someplace else but they probably read the same way.

Now she was furious with Bud for having made such a secret about the envelope. He could have told her what was in it instead of lying about having taken it. Of course, there might have been something else in it when he took it. Still, why would he be so careful about hiding the envelope if he had taken out anything? Maybe to give you something to hunt for, an inner voice pricked her. As long as you were hunting for a harmless envelope, you might overlook finding something more important. As she tossed this possibility about, it seemed to match the kind of thing Bud would do. She sat on the bed and carefully surveyed the room again. She saw nothing more that might help her with this speculation.

She got to her feet, debating whether to smooth out the bed and put everything back in order. With a stubborn jut of her chin, she marched out, leaving the shoe in the middle of the floor, the broken picture on the pillow, and the rounded shape of her fanny on the bed. He might as well know she was not about to take any more of his lies without active investigation. It wasn't until she was back in the family room that she realized such a warning might just make him lock her out of his room the next time.

All afternoon she waited for him to return so that she could demand some answers about Mrs. Holmes. No matter how he reacted, she was going to insist that the woman never come into the house again. Lang was still disturbed when she brought her and Kee out onto the deck after their naps. Usually Lang played with her Pooh Bear, caring for him just as Lori tended Kee, but today she just sat listlessly in a deck chair and refused to answer Lori even in monosyllables.

Lori brought them in early when gray banks of clouds began to build against the mountains. Soon the blue sky was gone from view as afternoon rain showers spread across the city. Dark strips from clouds to earth showed where heavy rains were streaming downward, and flashes of thin, jagged light brought accompanying thunder.

Perhaps it was the storm, or the shadowy house, or that he was fussy, but nothing she did seemed to satisfy Kee. He was disinterested in his rattles, and he protested loudly when she tried to put him down in his playpen. He even spit out the nipple from his half-finished bottle. He felt a little warm to her touch, but she had no idea if it was a fever or just her own flushed body. She had heard people talk about teething, but she didn't know whether that was just an old wives' tale. Maybe he was really sick.

By dinnertime, she was not only nervous and exhausted, but her anger toward Bud had taken a new direction. How dare he go off and leave her like this? She hadn't realized how much she unconsciously relied upon him for support. Even though she felt that she was doing everything for the kids now that he was gone, she knew better. Her back ached from carrying Kee around on her hip, and she felt the faintest prick of conscience that perhaps she hadn't been quite fair. He had carried the baby up and down the stairs and had prepared most of the meals.

It wasn't until she had put a boiled potato and a slightly charred piece of ham in front of Lang that the little girl spoke. She looked at the plate and then asked, "Where's Bud, Lowie?"

"Lowie doesn't know," she said honestly and with some irritation. Then she saw that flat, dull look come into Lang's eyes and she added with false brightness. "But I'm sure he'll be along soon."

All evening, the storm increased in ferocity, and the TV weathermen kept interrupting programs to announce a tornado watch for eastern Colorado. Pounding raindrops and peppering small hailstones created such a din against the large expanses of window glass that the whole house seemed to shake from the battering. Lori expected some of the windows to cave in upon them with every new wave of the downpour. She could amost feel the house slipping down the hillside.

It was the longest evening she had ever spent in her life. Claps of thunder vibrated through the house as streaks of lightning struck on every side. Lang cowered at her side, quietly whimpering, while Kee shrieked and flailed the air with his arms and legs. She took the children into her bedroom. With heavy drapes drawn, it seemed to offer the most protection from the holocaust outside.

She tried to follow through on a nightly routine, but Kee just would not settle down. She tucked Lang into her side of the bed, where she lay stiffly with rounded eyes watching as Lori walked the floor with Kee. Finally the storm diminished and the exhausted baby fell into a fitful sleep. Lori took him into the other bedroom and settled him down—she hoped until morning.

She went back into her own room and undressed for bed. Lang was still wide awake. Lori read *Tight Squeeze* all the way through again, her voice weary and unsteady. She told Lang a couple of impromptu stories. Finally she firmly kissed the little girl good night and promised not to leave the room.

She was too tired and too apprehensive to go to sleep herself. She picked up a paperback book she had packed in her suitcase in that other life when she had expected an uneventful house-sitting job. Pulling one of the chairs into a dim light, she sat down to read. Lang watched her every movement, obviously suspecting that Lori was going to slip out at the first chance.

Lori smiled reassuringly and then fastened her unseeing eyes on the page of print. What am I going to do if he doesn't come back? Instead of being jubilant because her jailer had gone, a new kind of terror met her head-on. If Bud didn't return, the play was over! She should feel relieved, but she was sick to her stomach. She could visualize herself going to the authorities and explaining this mess. Bud had been right. Taking the children from the airport and keeping them all this time could be interpreted as kidnapping. She had no right to keep the children five minutes without notifying the proper authorities. Even though the Brandons were dead, Kee and Lang could not be brought home like a couple of stray kittens and a claim made for them. Even a normal family—which this certainly wasn't—would be acting against the law to make off with two children the way she and Bud had.

The whole impersonation was a fraud. She could be legally prosecuted for her part in it. She had played a role that might well be an accessory to a crime as serious as murder. She had known it from the beginning. The Brandons had been killed. Her silence could only be interpreted as that of an accomplice.

She knew that Kyle might well be dead, probably had been all along. Her story about cooperating to bring him to safety would be met with raised eyebrows and disbelief. No one could be that stupid! Hot tears formed at the corners of her eyes, and she lowered her head so that her face would not be visible to the pair of watchful eyes on the bed. Even without Bud, there were others who could link her to the impersonation. Her old landlady Rose Perkins, the deliveryman Rex, and even Mrs. Holmes, not to mention the stewardess and the thin-lipped salesgirl at the airport.

And the mysterious "Something." Her head jerked up. Maybe Mrs. Holmes had brought it. Maybe that's what they had been arguing about. This new thought jabbed her like a corkscrew. Bud's disappearance made sense if you looked at it in that light. He had stuck around long enough to get what he wanted. Maybe she would never really know what it was. This new speculation made her angry instead of frightened. She could still see the two of them looking up at her with menacing gestures. Whatever happened to her, she was going to do everything she could to hang the noose around their necks, as well as her own.

When she finally gave up and went to bed, the long night was spent in very little sleep and a lot of restless turning. She was aware of the soft stillness that followed the storm's fury. Toward morning she fell asleep for a few hours, still trying to decide on some definite action she would take if Bud had not returned during the night.

She knew he hadn't when she awoke to Kee's cries. There was no enticing smell of perked coffee to greet her. She knew without investigating his bedroom that he had not come back to the house.

Tired and with nerves stretched taut to the breaking point, she took care of the morning chores. All the time her mind swirled with ways to handle the impending crisis. She moved around the house leadenly, mentally lashing herself for not having confronted Bud and Mrs. Holmes yesterday. If she had talked to them, she would have had a little warning that they were about to leave her holding not only the bag—but two misplaced children! They were probably on their way to Mexico or some such place.

She discovered how wrong she had been when she flipped open the morning paper. On the front page was a picture of a small car being pulled out of Cherry Creek. UNIDENTIFIED WOMAN DROWNED IN CREEK. It might be a coincidence, for surely there were dozens of dark-colored Triumphs in the Denver area, but the thing that took moisture from her mouth and brought the conviction that Mrs. Holmes lay under the canvas was the bent bicycle rack on the back of the car.

As her gaze moved to the words of the news story, her eyes stopped again, this time on the person directing the proceedings in one corner of the photograph. Although Rex was dressed differently than when he had delivered her plants, there was no mistaking the well-built blond-haired skier. Only the caption under the picture didn't mention his name. It simply read, "Denver detective discovers body of drowned woman during height of last night's storm."

# Twelve

The eight o'clock morning news on channel four reported the story, showing flashing lights and a wrecker pulling a green Triumph out of the swirling waters of Cherry Creek.

Once more she saw Rex conversing with two uniformed policemen. The same sketchy story was repeated. A Denver detective had seen the rear end of the car sticking out of the water. Identification and notification of next of kin was underway.

No one seemed certain about the time of the accident. Maybe just after she left here, thought Lori. She snapped off the TV. The truth seemed obvious. Bud had somehow been responsible for the accident. They had been arguing when Lori saw them from the balcony. She remembered what menacing looks they had given her before Mrs. Holmes lashed out at Lang. Maybe Bud had taken what he wanted from her before shoving her car into the water. As Lori thought about it, she became convinced that Rex would discover foul play. The heavy rainstorm had helped Bud get away and delayed discovery of the car until he was a long way from the scene. Just where, she would give a lot to know.

It all adds up, she said aloud over the roar of a vacuum cleaner. She threw her energies into housecleaning since her pent-up energies demanded some kind of release.

Lang sensed her agitation and insisted on being at her side every minute. As the little girl followed her like sticky glue, Lori smothered the impulse to order her away. Instead, she faked some reassurances that Lang seemed to see through with her too-wise eyes.

"Let's see if you can write your name for me," sug-

105

gested Lori, putting Lang at the round table with pencil and paper. If she could just keep her busy, maybe she would quit searching Lori's face for answers that she didn't have.

Luckily Kee was displaying a better disposition today and banged happily with a spoon and pan in his playpen. Every time she walked by him, he gave her his radiant toothless smile.

What am I going to do? Would they trace Mrs. Holmes back to this house? An electrifying thought went through her. What had Mrs. Holmes done with the purse she had stolen? Would they find the shoulder bag in her car? If they did, she would be tied into this murder as tightly as she was into kidnapping charges.

There was no way she could deny pretending to be Mrs. Brandon—not with Rex being a detective. He had impersonated a deliveryman to get inside the house. She didn't know why. He must have known she was faking it. She was chagrined when she remembered her fumbling efforts to find the solarium. As she recalled the conversation, she realized he had given her plenty of opportunities to say she wasn't Lois Brandon. Maybe he had been hoping she wouldn't incriminate herself by this false representation, but she had stubbornly insisted she was Mrs. Brandon. He would even have had a forged signature if Bud hadn't come in at that moment. Maybe he didn't arrest her because he needed more evidence, something concrete—like accepting two children as her own!

She sat down on the couch and put her hands over her face. Both Bud and Rex had done their part to embroil her in the deception, and even if she could cut free now, there was still Kyle's safety hanging over her. She couldn't be sure he was still alive, but she was certain that before she finished telling her story to the police he would be dead . . . like the Brandons and Mrs. Holmes.

"Lowie hurt?"

"No, darling. I'm fine." Lori quickly brushed her hands past her eyes, spreading wetness across her cheeks. "Let's see what you did. Oh, that's good, Lang. You have a pretty name." She tried to put all her thoughts into playing school and hoped Lang wouldn't notice her trembling hands as she printed a few more letters for Lang to copy. "That's Pooh Bear's name. Can you write it?"

At last it was time for their nap. Lori put the children down and then went out on the deck to marshal some kind of plan. All right, so Bud isn't coming back. For one reason or another, he pulled out. If he killed Mrs. Holmes to get something he wanted, he would most likely leave the country. That means he's out of this situation for good. But even as she reconstructed events along this line, she couldn't accept it. Why not? an inner voice pricked. You've seen his anger—even felt it. Suddenly her lips were burning again from the pressure of his kiss. You fool! She whirled and sat down on a deck chair, twisting her hands. "I don't believe it. I don't believe it," she said aloud. "He didn't kill her. I know he didn't." And a memory of him dressing Kee in new sailor rompers came back. She remembered the look of love on his face. No murderer acts like that! Really? taunted the voice. And how many murderers have you known?

She got to her feet then and paced up and down the deck. He's been gone nearly twenty-four hours. Quit stalling. It's over. If Bud got what he wanted, Kyle is probably safe. You did what you promised. Don't you understand? Kyle will be freed! Why didn't she feel elated and satisfied? "Kyle. Kyle." She repeated his name as if it were some kind of magic incantation that would weave a spell around her as it had always done. But the magic was gone. For the first time, she felt no surge of longing at the sound of his name. As she stared into the distance, she couldn't even bring into her mind's eye a clear picture of what he looked like.

What is the matter with me? She fled into the house and picked up the white princess phone. She listened to the dial tone, but her fingers refused to dial the operator. Slamming down the receiver, she went into the nursery bedroom.

Kee was sleeping on his tummy, with his head turned to one side and his little rump stuck up in the air. Long, dark eyelashes lay on his honey skin, and his little arms were stretched out above his head in a contented position. She replaced a light blanket over his chubby bare legs and feet.

Lang Su was asleep until Lori approached the bed. Her eyes flew open and instantly widened as she saw Lori's intense expression. Without speaking, the little girl scooted across the bed and put her arms around Lori's neck.

Holding Lang tightly against her, Lori knew that the pretense was not over. She was still trapped. Maybe this time by something stronger than an old love affair.

She had become used to Lang's little body snuggled closely against hers every night. She had felt that trusting hand in her own for too many hours of the day to fling it suddenly aside as if now her trust were unimportant. Lang did not even look like the strange child standing so mechanically at the airport. Lori had trimmed her bangs and evened the straggling hair, and brushed it morning and night until it shone like a raven's glossy wings. When her all-seeing large eyes looked at Lori now, they weren't flat and expressionless, but glowed with an emotion easy to read—love.

Kee had woven his own net around her, securing her as tightly in his affections as his sister. How could anyone not be captured by the cooing, happy baby who changed every day, demonstrating some new development that brought laughter and happiness to them all?

Of course, the lock on her new entrapment was dependence. She had never really been important to anyone else in her whole life. Not her parents—their lives were full and complete without her. Her Aunt Adele had taken her into her home, but Lori had neither added to nor detracted much from the fullness of the life that her Aunt had known before her arrival. Not even Kyle! Bud had been more dependent on her than Kyle had ever been.

The truth was difficult to deny. She knew that Bud's love of the children had reached her as an overflow. Because they had become so important to her, she could not completely reject someone who had the same kind of feelings. Even though he was gone there was no way she could really escape from him or the children.

The authorities would come. She knew that. It was just a matter of time—a few days, a few weeks. Then the children would be taken away. Kee and Lang would be uprooted again. There was an ache in her chest as she thought of it. She knew the longer she kept them the more precarious became her position, but as she snuggled them to her, she knew she lacked the strength to call the authorities. She would wait until . . .

# *Thirteen*

Once the decision was made, practical problems arose. When her present supply of food and baby necessities ran out, she would have to go into town. Her small check wasn't going to stretch over many twelve-dollar taxi trips.

They could make it a few days on what they had. Fortunately, Bud had ordered a dairy delivery, so she marked an order for eggs, cottage cheese, ice cream, and orange juice, plus the usual order of milk. She might have to write Mrs. Wallace for an advance on her house-sitting job, which might not be a bad idea, anyway, since she wouldn't receive one cent when the impersonation story came out.

As she stared into the refrigerator, filled with the makings for gourmet dishes, she swore, "Bud, where in the hell are you?" This time, her voice contained more apprehension than anger. She didn't know when the first worry about him had flickered into a growing concern. Since she had completely rejected the idea that Bud had been responsible for Mrs. Holmes's death, the next possibility jolted her like a painful stab. Bud might be as dead as Mrs. Holmes! Even as she closed her eyes against the thought, she pictured him floating face down in the water.

"Oh, no!" Surely there would have been something in the news about it. It had been two days since he disappeared. But maybe they hadn't found his body—or maybe they had and were waiting to see what she was going to do. But why?

"I don't know. I don't know." She put a hand to her forehead.

"Lowie sick?" Lang slipped her hand into Lori's.

Lee Karr

"No, I'm fine." She gave a reassuring squeeze. "I think I saw a pile of sand behind the house. Let's go make a sandbox."

The telephone's commanding ring interrupted their plans. Lori set Kee back down in his playpen. He instantly screamed his displeasure, but she scarcely heard his cries as her trembling fingers hovered over the receiver.

The phone's ring still had the power to send moisture from her mouth and a tightness to her chest. Only now there wasn't any Bud breathing over her shoulder. She was alone! Whatever events this call put into motion, she would have to carry out by herself. On the fourth ring she grabbed the receiver and said a tense "Hello?"

"Is Dr. Brandon there?" The man's voice was indistinct, slightly muffled, with the hint of an undefinable accent.

"No, he isn't."

"Do you know when he'll be back?"

"No, I don't," she answered quickly and rushed on. "Would—do you want to leave a message?"

"No, I'll call back." A definite click and then a dead hum.

Slowly she replaced the receiver, frustrated by the abrupt end to the conversation. She felt anxiety building into new heights of uneasiness.

Who was it? Someone who wanted Bud—or someone who wanted to know if she were alone? And if the latter were the case, for what reason?

Suddenly every moment became precious as she realized her hours with the children were numbered. Imperceptibly the children had become "hers." Aunt Adele would have scoffed at such ridiculous feelings, but Lori wondered if the dear lady had ever seen a toothless smile as beautiful as Kee's or seen love shining from eyes as intense as Lang's. Lori knew that her aunt had loved her but there had been no physical demonstration of it. Such a display of open affection was not a part of Aunt Adele's makeup. As Lori grew up, there had been no one to hug and snuggle, not even a kitten. Now Lori bestowed all this pent-up affection on Kee and Lang, who, for the moment, had only one person in their lives. As she fed, bathed, and played with them, she found a happiness that

112

was made all the more intense because of its tenuousness.

Lori was too keyed up to sleep after the children were in bed that night, even though she was physically exhausted. She decided to go down to the kitchen and make a cup of hot chocolate. She had just poured the milk into a pan when the telephone rang again.

It was the same voice asking for Bud.

"He's not here. Please—who is calling?" Anxiety tinged her high-pitched words.

"Just a friend. I'll call back."

"Wait—" But the phone went dead again.

This time Lori slammed the receiver down angrily. "You just do that—but see if I answer!" As if her little display of childish behavior had solved something, she turned on the TV and tried to become interested in an old movie. When it was over, she was more awake than ever.

As she turned off the television set, she became aware of the echoing vastness of the house. There were parts of it, like the dining room, where she had scarcely been, and others, like the living room, that she only used as a path to another room or to the outside.

"No need to get the jitters," she told herself as she rinsed out her cup in the kitchen.

But the house, for all its spaciousness, suddenly seemed confining, as if the high ceilings with their mammoth hanging planters, walls of large triangular windows, and bulky, thick furniture, all were pressing in on her. She had felt uncomfortable in the sprawling impersonal surroundings from the very first moment, but tonight she felt vulnerable and somehow more of a captive within these walls.

An overwhelming urge to get outside caused her to go quickly up the circular steps and through the living room, its numerous furniture groups like black blotches of living things. Almost frantically, she flung open a glass door and sped out onto the deck.

It was idiotic to let a mass of wood and cement affect her as if it were some monster about to devour her. Still, she had experienced the same kind of feeling the first time she had viewed the house. If she had acted on it, she never would have stepped out of the taxi. But she had denied the sensation then, even as she was trying to do now. "It's just a building," she said aloud to a gentle night breeze. Throwing back her head in a defiant gesture, she drew in some deep breaths of air.

Then she heard a sound like the crunch of gravel in the darkness below her. She froze. Every sense reached out to confirm the noise. She held her breath, waiting to hear it again. It was fainter the second time, but still distinct over the whine of chirping crickets and distant sounds from the highway.

Someone was at the base of the house, in the rocky ledge below!

"Who's there?" Her voice was sharp and the summer night, which had seemed so protective a moment ago, now surrounded her ominously. "Who's there?" she cried again.

A sudden quietness answered her as crickets ceased their chirping, validating an alien presence in the rocks where they held their nightly serenades.

Turning, she fled back into the house. As she slid the glass door shut and pushed in a steel lock, she realized that even as she locked the intruder out, she was locking herself in. Her fears of the house were psychic and the presence outside was real and tangible. There was no question about which one she was going to honor first.

For nearly an hour she remained in the dark living room, staring at the glass door where the intruder's form would be silhouetted against the sky when he came up the outside steps to the deck.

What she planned to do when that moment came, she had not firmly resolved. But no one appeared. Tired and emotionally exhausted, she finally went back to the nursery and crawled into bed with Lang.

She lay there stiffly, staring unseeingly at the ceiling, trying to comprehend the sinister maze that kept her frantically running, seemingly without purpose and without end.

When Kee woke her up at six, she had only slept for three hours. But the terror of the night had faded away and it was a new day—one that was to change the pattern of her days in a way she did not expect.

Later in the afternoon when she heard footsteps on the back stairs, she tensed, waiting for a commanding knock on the door. But none came. There was just a banging of the back screen. Then Bud walked in!

She had been cutting up an apple for Lang, and as Lori saw him, she froze with her knife held up in the air like a weapon.

"I hope that knife isn't going to be a part of your greeting," he grinned wryly, looking more tired and unkempt than Lori had ever seen him.

Once she found her voice, she lashed out. "How dare you run off like that?" And she blinked quickly against tears that were filling her eyes.

"Miss me?"

The conceited, arrogant fool! Because she couldn't think of anything caustic enough to say, she fled the room, stumbled up the stairs and through the living room, out onto the deck.

Tears blurred her vision as she leaned against the railing. "He's back. Oh, thank God, he's back." She knew she was blubbering, but for once she didn't care. "He's not dead. He's alive. He's back."

As he came up behind her, she felt his hands. He turned her around gently. Foolishly she went into his arms, burying her head against his shoulder. "I—I thought —you were dead."

"Now if you had said 'wished you were dead,' I could understand that," he teased. "Come on, now. You're going to make me think you were worried about me." He stroked her head the way she did Lang's. "I'm sorry. I thought you'd be elated to have me out from underfoot for a few days."

She drew away, facing him with tearstained cheeks. "Where were you? What happened? Why were you so angry with Mrs. Holmes?" The questions came tumbling out.

Bud chose to answer the last one. "Because she accused us of lying. She claims that 'It' is here. That we're

115

holding out on her. Has something arrived that I don't know about?"

Lori shook her head. "Nothing. Absolutely nothing. When I first heard about Mrs. Holmes, I thought you had done it." She felt his whole body stiffen.

"Done what?"

"Killed her—pushed her car into the water."

"Pushed her car? She's dead?"

Again Lori nodded. "And then I thought—you might be dead, too. I didn't know what to do—" she pressed against his chest, pouring out all her anxieties about the children, Rex, Mrs. Holmes. "I decided to keep the kids until someone made me give them up."

He began to laugh.

She pulled away. "What's so funny?" His reaction dried up her tears.

"Do you realize you've been talking nonstop for five minutes, Marty, and you haven't once mentioned Kyle with that sick-dog look of yours?"

What she would have replied would not be known because at that moment they heard Lang's voice raised in a shrieking cry. Both of them ran into the house and down the steps as if they themselves were on fire.

Lang was pointing at Kee. The baby was lying on the floor of his playpen with his eyes bulging and soundless heaves coming from his chest.

"Apple," said Lang, pointing to his throat.

"He's choking," screamed Lori.

Bud jerked him up, expertly laid him over one arm, and gave a quick squeeze just below the rib cage. Nothing happened. Bud tried again but the piece of apple did not come up.

"Damn," swore Bud. Then he brushed by Lori and ran into the kitchen with Kee still hanging over one arm.

He jerked open the dishwasher, which was still steaming from a two-day load Lori had just washed. He took one of his cutting tools and in a quick motion had Kee on a work counter. As Lori watched horrified, he thrust the small point into Kee's throat. Immediately blood spurted and there was a swish of air into Kee's chest. "Give me one of those plastic straws. I'll insert it until we can get him to the hospital."

Her lips were stiff and the words came out in a hoarse whisper. "You *are* Dr. Brandon!"

"Yes. My bag is upstairs under my bed. Get it!"

Ironically she found it right under the place where she had sat the day she searched his room. On the satchel in gold-leaf letters was a name. Philip Allen Brandon. M.D.

# *Fourteen*

There had been only minutes between Kee and death. If Bud had not been there to perform the tracheotomy, making a new air hole into his throat, the alert little baby would surely have died.

Fortunately, a private ambulance service answered Lori's frantic call in an unbelievably short time. When the ambulance arrived, Lori argued about going with Kee. "He needs me," she protested as Bud carried the baby down the steps. "I want to go!"

"There's no reason. He's out of danger now. You'll just be in the way. Stay here with Lang."

And with that he climbed into the ambulance and gave a nod to the attendants to shut the back door. With a shriek of sirens, it rolled quickly out of sight.

She knew that he was probably right but that didn't make the waiting any easier. Lang had watched the drama with a guarded look in her eyes. Her little body seemed stiff enough to break as the ambulance screeched away.

Back in the house, Lori tried to reassure the child that it wasn't her fault Kee had choked. "You didn't know that Kee couldn't have apples. He's all right now. Everything's fine."

But even as she said the words, the most unexpected thing happened. Lang began to cry, "I sorry, I sorry." She sobbed against Lori as if her little heart would break. Lori found herself unexpectedly crying with her. Reaction to the near tragedy caught up with them both. They felt better after they had consumed a pile of tissues and ended up with a feeble smile on Lang's face and relieved laughter from Lori.

"Now it's up to bed for you and nap time. Where's Pooh Bear hiding?"

119

With Lang sleeping quietly, Lori eased off the bed and went into the solarium to think. Numbness had worn off and the time had come to adjust her thinking to include the revelation that Bud was not the pretender he had seemed to be. She felt stupid for not having suspected the truth before. Bud had never really acted like an impostor. He had been too smooth, too much at ease with the role. She had thought more than once that he looked like a professional man with his immaculate wardrobe and his expensive tastes. His handling of the baby had always been sure and efficient. From the beginning he had known what to buy, and he had spent money easily, as if he were used to having some wealth.

When she accepted the fact that Bud was truly Dr. Philip Brandon, then the rest of the charade seemed more bizarre. Forcing her into the impersonation of his wife only made sense if he were the thieving murderer she had once thought he was. It was his feelings for the children that had changed her view of him, and yet she still had no evidence that basically he was any different from the man she had met the first night. "It's only my feelings about him that have changed," she muttered in a kind of horror.

She got to her feet and busily started watering her plants, scarcely noticing what she was doing. He was still after the "something" that Mrs. Holmes said had already arrived. That was a lie. Nothing had been delivered except these plants, and Bud had made sure their containers were free of anything mysterious.

As she waited for Bud to return, her brain seethed with a multitude of ifs and whys. She wondered if Bud was a renegade of his profession, and if so, how he was making out at the hospital. She was tempted to telephone but managed to wait until he returned that evening. A taxi brought them both back.

Everything had gone well, he said, carrying in a pale, sleeping Kee, who wore a simple bandage over two stitches in the tiny slit in his throat.

"It's a simple operation," Bud explained after they had put both Kee and Lang down for the night. "His throat is going to be sore for a couple of days, not from the incision but from the scraping his trachea took when we dislodged the piece of apple."

"Lang was crushed about giving it to him, but she didn't know. After all, she's seen me give him a cookie or cracker to suck on. I tried to reassure her that it wasn't her fault. She's such a sensitive little thing." She paused and then shot a quick dart. "Is she yours?"

Bud only smiled wearily. He had looked disheveled and tired when he first arrived, and his appearance hadn't improved any during his sojourn at the hospital. "No, but Kee is." Then he slipped his arm around her waist. "Thanks for being such a good mother to him. Now let's fix a pitcher full of martinis. I owe you some explanations."

Lori didn't intend to argue that point. "Where did the 'Bud' come from, Dr. Brandon?"

"It's a nickname. My sister gave it to me."

She had expected him to be his usual evasive self—leaving her with more questions than answers. But as he settled himself beside her on the couch, he talked, almost continuously, without raising his eyes from his glass, swirling the clear liquid and now and then bringing it to his lips.

"I married Lois four years ago when I was practicing medicine in San Francisco. She had been living in the Far East for about twelve years and had come to the States on a brief business trip. Her father was one of the early advisers President Kennedy sent to Vietnam before the war really exploded. His family followed him there, and somehow Lois got into the export-import business." He paused and sipped his drink. "I found her fascinating. She had contacts in all parts of the world. She was shrewd and, I found out later, unscrupulous, but on the outside she was fragile and lovely, with wide innocent eyes like yours. So . . ." He shrugged. "We were married without my family even meeting her. I volunteered for a government health corps and went to Vietnam with her." His lips twisted into a bitter smile. "But our paradise honeymoon was brief. Almost immediately we lost contact with each other in all the ways there are. Lois was up to her pretty neck in the black market, smuggling, and dope traffic. I think she knew how the war was going to turn out, and she was busy stripping that part of the world of all the wealth she could lay her hands on—illegally, of course."

He got up and poured himself another martini. Lori had some feminine curiosity about the woman he had married, but she was afraid to ask anything, fearful that he might take it in the wrong way and clam up on her. So she sat quietly and waited for him to sit down beside her again.

"I didn't know what was going on at first. The field hospitals were hell! Wave after wave of casualties came in on us day and night. The army units were overrun and our little volunteer program couldn't begin to handle the civilian population. Young kids with blown-out eyes and dangling limbs screamed and died on our tables. Whole families came in charred and burned, or cut up like they had been on a butcher's block. While I was up to my elbows in injuries, Lois was expanding her operation into Cambodia and Thailand. She had no trouble finding disgruntled GIs to do her work and stimulate drug traffic." He paused, as if he weren't certain how to go on.

She made it easy for him. "Was Kyle one of them?"

He nodded. "There wasn't any way for the army to keep an accurate account of those missing in action or captured. All kinds of soldiers were wandering around and will probably be surfacing for years. Somehow Kyle got into an intelligence unit, which allowed him to move around secretly and incognito. Perfect for Lois's needs."

She stiffened. Bud could be lying to her, putting his own interpretation on the situation. She couldn't give up believing in someone who had meant so much to her. "Maybe you're wrong. Maybe it just seemed like he was working with her. Maybe Kyle—"

Angrily he swung around to face her. "Why do you say his name like it's something sacred. That sonofabitch isn't worth one breath. You should have seen the way Lois had him in tow. No, I'm not mistaken! Christ, the two of them were a matched pair. What they couldn't sell at exorbitant prices, they smuggled out."

"But how do you know?" she stubbornly protested. "I mean, how did you find out?" He wasn't going to rush her into abandoning Kyle without more substantiation than just his feelings. But even as she protested, she remembered how Kyle had always resented the wealthy students at the University of Denver. He had railed bitterly against the poverty that had forced him to quit school. He probably would have been ripe for trading this war for a get-rich scheme. Working as an intelligence agent suited him, too.

"But what happened? How is my impersonation going to help him? What happened to Lois—and who is Mrs. Holmes?"

"Whoa!" He laughed, obviously relieved that she seemed to have accepted Kyle's implication without a scene. He didn't realize that recent events had put her in a kind of limbo, where her feelings were fuzzy and inconsistent.

He chose to answer her last question. "Mrs. Holmes worked for Lois. Her maiden name was Hang Phamn and her sister, Mela, was a volunteer in one of the field hospitals—as good a nurse as I've ever seen. Mela had a disposition like Kee's, all sunny and laughing. She was the only bright thing in a miserable, dirty existence. As Lois and I split up, I turned more and more to Mela and—" He drained his drink. "How about another martini? You're two behind."

"Did you love her, this Mela?"

He snorted. "My dear little romantic, when hell is bursting on your doorstep, you don't worry about defining your feelings—you just react. My personal world was in a catastrophic state, and so was everything else around me. Mela put some moments of sanity into it. I wasn't surprised when she told me she was pregnant. We were both happy about it, and I knew Lois was as fed up with our so-called marriage as I was. But there wasn't any time to work things out. Mela was due to deliver any day when all hell broke loose. The United States started moving troops out, and there was a frantic rush for the border. The four of us made it into Thailand—"

"You and Mela—?"

"Lois and Kyle. We tried to arrange quick passage out of Bangkok. Lord, we spread money around like it was water, greasing every official's palm that we could find. Everyone smiled at us, nodded, and took the money, but permission to leave was always denied. I realize now that we were fools to think we could slip out unnoticed. Kyle's connection with the U.S. Army was unverified. Lois's operations were well-known, and the authorities were more than casually interested in her dealings . . . and in what she might be trying to take out of their country. Since I was her husband, I was thrown in the smelly sack with her, and, of course, no one was particularly concerned about a pregnant Vietnamese girl." He stared into his drink and swirled the clear liquid around in the glass. "But those days of waiting were the best we had. Mela and I found a little place of our own, not much to look at, but it was high on a hill and away from the city's turmoil. There was peace there . . . a honeymoon retreat, you might call it." But he gave a laugh that had more pain than gladness in it. "Anyway, " he continued after he had drunk deeply, "I delivered Kee there about five o'clock one morning as the first rays of sunlight came through bamboo shades to fall upon his little round face. He was a happy baby from the first. Maybe because—"

As his voice cracked, Lori felt tears moisten her gaze. It was all she could do to keep her hands folded in her lap instead of touching him. He was quiet for such a long time that she was afraid he would not continue. For once in her life, she kept her mouth shut and waited.

"After Kee was born, I began to help in a nearby hospital, while Mela spent her days at a Catholic orphanage. A deep friendship developed between her and Sister Elena, the nun trying to care for the countless refugees and orphans. We were hopeful that our permission to leave would come any day. And then—and then—it was all over! Just like that!" He tried to snap his fingers but the gin was having its effect. "Some goddamn terrorists planted four or five bombs around the city, and one of them exploded in a place where Mela had gone to buy food. She and a dozen other innocent people were blown to hell!"

His hand was unsteady as he poured another drink. His eyes were beginning to glaze and his speech became more labored. As he sat down beside her again, she wondered if he had ever talked to anyone about this before. She doubted it very much.

"I went to Lois. She had been busy organizing her import business so that she could continue when she got back to the States. It was at that time that she contracted to buy this house. I forced Lois to adopt Kee, swearing I would see her spend the rest of her life in some stinking jail if she refused. She laughed at me but she did as I wanted. While we waited to leave, she made numerous helicopter trips around Thailand, no doubt arranging to buy, smuggle, or steal priceless items. Kyle told me about the jade she had laid her greedy hands upon. I warned her that she would land us all behind bars, but she just scoffed and called me some choice names." He laid his head back and closed his eyes. "I didn't know her helicopter had gone down until the Thai authorities descended upon me. Both Kyle and I were immediately arrested and interrogated. They found enough illegal stuff in Lois's possession to hang her a dozen times. Kyle maintained that he had been working with Lois as a part of his job to uncover black market activities—"

"Maybe he was!" said Lori expectantly. Hope spurted like a geyser in her thoughts. It could be that Bud was only putting *his* interpretation on the relationship between Lois and Kyle. It might not have been a business partnership or anything romantic.

"Like hell! The authorities didn't buy it either. But he's smooth—real smooth. He convinced them that Lois had already arranged for all the info, like names of contacts, addresses, and dates of shipment, to be delivered to her here in Denver. He swore that his name would not be on the list. He claimed that he was as interested in finding out her contacts as anyone. By this time our own government had been alerted, and they got into the act too."

He sat up. "It was Kyle's idea that someone impersonate Lois and recover the information. You had written to him about house-sitting, so it was an easy matter to request you for this job. Of course, the resemblance between you and Lois is undeniable. He suggested that you would be more than willing to enter into any scheme that would save his beloved neck. I guess he wasn't wrong."

Lori couldn't tell whether it was disappointment or

disgust that coated his words. "But, I don't understand. Why did you get involved?" she prodded.

"Because they wouldn't let me take Kee out of the country unless I did. The Thai authorities didn't like the plan one bit. But our boys threatened to stall a three-million-dollar aid program if they didn't cooperate."

"So that's the three million dollars."

"Of course, the Thai officials were anxious to recover everything Lois had arranged to smuggle out, but all of it probably didn't have a three-million-dollar value. As I said, Kyle's smooth, and he convinced everyone that Lois had arranged for all her business details to be delivered to her when she moved into her new place in Denver. In the end I had no choice but to play the game. They would hold Kyle and the baby until the package had been received and handed over to U.S. officials."

"But—"

"I know. Kee's arrival really had me floored, but since I had to leave the baby with Sister Elena, I figured she had outsmarted everyone by sending my son home with some other orphans who had American adoptive parents."

"Lang?"

"I'm afraid Sister Elena is going to be on her knees a long time to do penance for forgery. I was as surprised as anyone that the Brandons had adopted a six-year-old girl. At first I thought that Lang Su was just one of the sister's orphans that she had decided to send into a good home, but—"

"But Mrs. Holmes knew her," interrupted Lori. "What is Mrs. Holmes to Lang?"

"Her aunt . . . Lang is Mela's child. I still can't believe it. When Mrs. Holmes was telling me about it the other day, I threatened to break her neck if she was lying to me. Mela was afraid to tell me that she had an older illegitimate child. When we left for Bangkok, Mela arranged for Mrs. Holmes, who had married an American lieutenant, to bring Lang to the States with her. But Lieutenant Holmes didn't like the idea. In fact, he didn't believe his wife's story about Lang being Mela's child and accused Mrs. Holmes of being her mother. When Mela wrote her sister and told her we had been detained in Bangkok, Mrs. Holmes brought the child—but it was too late. Mela was dead and I was under arrest, so Mrs. Holmes just dumped Lang at the orphanage."

"How terrified the child must have been to be abandoned like that. And when she saw Mrs. Holmes the other day she must have thought the woman had come to take her away."

"I'm glad the sister sent her to me with Kee. But I don't know why Mela was afraid to tell me . . ."

Maybe he didn't, but Lori did. Too many women and children had been deserted by American soldiers for a lot less reason than that. "But I don't understand why Mrs. Holmes was so angry with Lang."

"Because she cost her a husband, so to speak. The American lieutenant chose to desert her the minute they got here. He probably would have anyway, but Mrs. Holmes blamed Lang. He never did let go of the idea that Mrs. Holmes was trying to pull a fast one on him. She settled her hatred on the child."

"But how did Mrs. Holmes find you—how does she fit into all this?" She knew that Bud was exhausted and all those martinis were slowing him down to a snail's pace, but there was so much she had to know.

"She came to Denver to put the bite on me. For Mela's sake I have tried to help her out. And for a little cash she was willing to help get the house in order and go along with our impersonation scheme. But she was blackmailing me for more."

"And now she's dead."

Bud ran a hand through his thick hair. She could tell that he was trying to get his thinking under control. His head must be rolling like a television out of focus. "Tell me again—what did the news say—exactly."

"That detective, Rex. You know, the guy who delivered the plants and the one that took Lang to the—" Then she stopped, realizing that she hadn't told Bud about that incident. At his puzzled expression, she said, "Never mind." And then very quickly she related the few facts surrounding Mrs. Holmes's death. "It might have been an accident—but if it wasn't—*who killed her, Bud?*" Her voice was higher pitched than she realized.

"I don't know any more about it than you do. Quit looking at me like that."

"Then where were you?" More than one blackmailer had met a violent death.

"Right after she left, I caught the next flight to San Francisco. I had to check with some government officials to see if the whole charade was off, now that I had Kee, which was the only reason I cooperated with their little scheme in the first place."

"Is it—off?" She leaned forward. Maybe Kyle had been freed too.

But Bud closed his eyes and leaned his head back on the cushion. "I'm afraid not. They're half convinced that we're holding out on them. Even accused me of having the jade and data so I could carry on my dear dead wife's illegal activities. They say they have enough on Kyle and me to keep us behind bars for years. And— Kee would go to someone else."

It was the tenderness in the last words that caused her to reach out and smooth back the hair from his forehead. "It won't happen. We'll find what they want!" Now that she had the whole picture, she felt a surge of confidence. "If Lois sent those things to herself, at this address, they'll show up."

"But why is it taking so long? Kyle maintains that she told him everything had been arranged and she was ready to leave anytime."

"Maybe she didn't send them directly. There might have been some question in her mind about how soon she would be here to receive them. Don't you think so?"

He didn't answer. Four martinis were having a soothing effect on Bud—so soothing that Lori wondered if he were about to pass out on the couch.

"Let's get you to bed." She pulled on his arms. "You're exhausted."

He seemed to agree and let her navigate him to his feet, up the stairs, and down the hall to his room. Inside the door she gave him a gentle shove toward the bathroom. "A shower wouldn't hurt," she said brightly.

But he wavered unsteadily and then collapsed in a nearby chair. "You'll have to tuck me beddie-bye," he said with a sheepish grin.

"Why is it drunk people look so ridiculous?" she countered. "I'll take off your shoes and you can dress for bed —or sleep in your clothes!"

"Cruel lady," he slurred. "Cruel Marty."

As she knelt before him, he swung his hands around, probably intending to pull her into his arms, but he accidentally knocked over the gold-framed picture that Lori had replaced on the dresser instead of the bureau.

She picked it up and handed it to him, watching as he carefully put it back and then continued to stare at it.

"Who are they?" asked Lori. "Your sisters?"

Bud poked a wobbly finger at the tall dark-haired woman. "This one—Audrey—two years older than me."

"And the other?"

He didn't answer as he brought the picture closer to him. "Beautiful Brandy. Beautiful little Brandy. Her hair looks like that in the sun—all coppery and soft." He touched the picture as if he could feel texture there. "She was going to be Brandy Brandon." He gave a drunken laugh. "We laughed about that. Brandy Brandon. Brandy—" And his smile wavered as if its upward turn were about to collapse. "Gave her up for that bitch I married."

Lori stood up, wanting to look away from the expression of pain and longing that covered his face, but she was mesmerized by the intensity of feelings that came pouring out with such strong vibrations. Embarrassed, she felt it was an invasion of his privacy to take advantage of his drunkenness, which bared his soul in this fashion and exposed his deepest emotions. She turned away.

He made no protest as she left the room and continued to stare down at the picture as if he were trying to draw solace from it.

"He's still in love with her," Lori said aloud as she went down the dark hall, and a truthful voice within her answered, "Yes, you fool!"

# *Fifteen*

If she had been able to forget the picture of a pensive, love-sot Bud staring at a photograph, the next few days might have been the happiest she had ever known. But her own feelings were in a tangle. In some deep region of her being, where reason had no place, she knew that she wanted Bud to look upon her with some degree of affection instead of the mocking, scornful manner he had adopted from the beginning. Even though she reassured herself that it was her resemblance to Lois that caused it, the same logic did not keep her from reacting personally to his open contempt.

When Bud came down to the kitchen early, full of plans for the day, Lori was strangely irritated with him, as if he had deliberately strung her emotions on a yo-yo. Even as he gave her a breezy "Good morning," she wanted to confront him with some questions about Brandy and to delve into the personality of this Philip Allen Brandon who was dominating too much of her thoughts and emotions.

But with a gurgling Kee throwing Pablum in every direction and Lang upsetting her milk, the time wasn't appropriate for discussing the more serious aspects of life.

As Bud sopped up the spilled milk with a sponge, he said, "I feel like a picnic. Let's go to Elitch's amusement park and let the kids have fun on all the rides."

"But—"

"No buts! We all need a day out."

"Doctor's orders?"

He shot her a quick glance to see if she was being sarcastic, but faint smile lines around her eyes seemed to reassure him. "You might say so. You look like a steam kettle about ready to blow, and since we don't know how much longer it will be before Lois's package arrives, I think we'd better try to relieve a little of the pressure here. A day away from this monstrosity of a house would do you good."

His real intent is to keep me masquerading, thought Lori, until he can secure the thing he wants—Kee. His concern over my welfare is superficial—and selfish. A few days ago she would have told him what he could do with his solicitation, but even as she silently railed against the shallowness of his concern, she nodded agreement. Maybe such a day's outing would help her get her head on straight.

Both children loved the amusement park. Although Lang held Lori's hand for dear life when they first walked by a beautiful merry-go-round, she made no protest when they all climbed aboard. By the time they had had three rides on horses going up and down to gay music, Lang was laughing openly on a black and white pony beside Lori, while Kee chortled and issued baby squeals in Bud's arms on a pink mount just behind them.

From then on Lang climbed aboard every ride eagerly, looking small and fragile, waving to them as she went by. Every time Lori caught sight of her glowing face, she felt herself swallowing hard against an emotion that threatened to bring tears to her eyes. There was nothing mechanical about Lang today, and instead of a solemn, adult little girl, a spontaneous, giggling six-year-old was in her place. Even though Lori might have verbally denied it, a feeling of "mine" had descended upon the child, and she looked around to see if anyone else was appreciating the beautiful little girl who was laughing with such abandonment.

Bud carried Kee around on his shoulders, and more than one person pointed out the happy, squealing baby showing his open-mouth smile to everyone.

"We'll have to get a stroller before our next outing," he said as they sat down on a garden bench to rest.

His reference to the future brought a foolish thrust of

pleasure to her, and she found herself laughing openly with Kee.

"I told you the good doctor knows best. You look ten years younger than you did this morning. In fact, you're the prettiest gal around."

It was more foolishness to believe him when she knew his motives, but it took more strength than she had not to respond to such flattery.

As people strolled by them, they smiled at the happy family. The two beautiful Oriental children raised some eyebrows, and some bold ones murmured, "Lovely children," pausing as if they hoped for some further conversation. With that professional air of his Bud simply nodded, while Lori had a hard time containing herself as she imagined what their expressions would be if they knew the truth of the situation.

More than one young girl's eyes paused as she appreciated Bud's wavy gray hair and tanned skin. Even Lori was stimulated to say, "You look a lot like Burt what's-his-name, the songwriter, with your hair like that."

"Now that you mention it, I do play a mean chopsticks. But you're going to have to wear your sweaters tighter, Angie."

It was delightful to waste the day in such levity, and when they went back to the house, its oppressive atmosphere went unnoticed in Lori's happy exhaustion.

During the next few days they took short trips—mostly shopping and to the city parks. And if the daytime hours were family affairs, then the evenings became at-home dates.

Even though Lori knew exactly why Bud was trying to make her as contented as possible with all the flowery attention, she only rarely confronted him with the truth, baiting him with some sarcastic remark that showed him she really wasn't all that dumb. Most of the time she dressed up for the fantastic dinners he prepared and thoroughly enjoyed the kind of companionship that had not been part of her life for such a long time.

Surprisingly enough, that's all they did—talk. Bud never came any closer to her than across the table, and when she remembered the way he had looked at Brandy's picture, she knew she did not have to fear any romantic advances from him. His attack on her before had only been out of anger because she had threatened to send Kee away. Now that he had her cooperation, he didn't have to release his anger in such a fashion. And she was glad! If he didn't want Kyle's leavings—neither did she want Brandy's.

This was the message she continued to reiterate to herself as more of her time and thoughts became interwoven with his. Now that they had begun to get away from the house, any prolonged confinement within it became unbearable. Just a few days in the old routine made everyone so short-tempered and disagreeable that Bud would suggest some new excursion.

"But shouldn't we stay close to the house in case 'it' comes?"

"Maybe the information isn't coming to the house," he said. "I've been thinking . . . Lois might have arranged for 'it' to be picked up."

"But where? You know how big Denver is!" She spread her hands in a helpless gesture. "How will we ever know?"

"Perhaps someone will contact you if we make ourselves visible. Let's visit one of the shopping malls, like Cinderella City. If they've been waiting to hand you a package, a busy place like that would give them a chance. Besides"—and there was a glint that might have been a twinkle in his eye—"it's time I bought 'Mom' a present to show my appreciation. And I'll bet Lang Su is ready for another Winnie-the-Pooh book. Aren't you, doll?" There was no doubt what her beautiful little smile meant.

So off they went to Cinderella City with its huge fountain and colored malls stretching so far in every direction that it took only five minutes for Lori to become completely lost.

Bud was a shopper! He rented a stroller for Kee and down the crowded corridors they went—Bud and Kee in the lead and Lori holding Lang's hand as they trailed behind. Lori had never seen such a mammoth shopping center. On one level they covered Rose Mall, the Blue Mall, and on another the Shamrock Mall, all of them blocks long!

At first Lori couldn't think of anything else but the possibility that someone might be watching her every move, waiting to shove the mysterious "it" into her hands. Every person who approached her or brushed by her side was suspect. She tried to be casual as she searched every face and glanced around every store they entered.

Bud was displaying his usual casual aplomb. Once he growled at her, "Will you relax! This is supposed to be fun."

Lang and Kee were convinced it was some kind of a holiday. While they were shopping in the Blue Mall, Bud spent at least a hundred dollars in a children's shop. They had so many packages that he had to take two trips out to the car with them.

Lori and the children waited for him in a huge center rotunda. She watched a diamond-studded fountain as water rose in white feathery spumes and then fell with rhythmic roars into a giant pond. Some of her pent-up tension began to ease. If anyone had wanted to contact her, he would have done so by now, she reasoned. Bud's speculation had only been a bad stab in the dark.

Of course, there were lots of people about—families, couples, teenagers, and singles—all milling about in the huge place. On the second floor, where the vaulting fountain reached a crescendo and then fell back to the floor below, there was a balcony. Lori's eyes searched the railing for anyone looking at her suspiciously.

Kee was slobbering happily on a new rubber turtle that squeaked as he squeezed it. Lang sat beside Lori and flipped through the pages of her new book, *Winnie-the-Pooh and the Honey Tree*. She had already begged Lori to read it right then and there but had to be content with a promise of "Later."

No, there was nothing out of the ordinary in the scene. The only attention she got was from smiling passersby who couldn't resist the sight of a happy, chortling baby waving his toy enthusiastically, with a wide tooth-less smile on his face.

The proud sense of "mine" enveloped her again, and

a new feeling of completeness caused her to relax back against the bench. It was just about that time that she realized that Bud had been gone a terribly long time—much longer than it took to carry packages out to their car. Almost at the same instant she felt a prickling sensation that someone was staring at her. Very slowly and very woodenly she turned her head and raised her eyes to a man standing a few feet to the left of the bench.

He acknowledged her stare with a slight bow and then approached. He was of slight build, obviously of Mediterranean extraction, and wore a foreign-cut dark suit. In almost every way he fitted the sinister messenger Lori had been expecting.

Her hands came together in a nervous clench and all moisture went out of her mouth. This is it! Dear God, let me do the right thing.

"Madame." He gave that slight bow again. "Pardon, please." He waited for her stiff nod. "Forgive intrusion . . . Lady understand . . . other cultures?" He indicated the two Oriental children at her side.

She nodded again, wondering if this might be some kind of a password ritual. What was she supposed to respond? Maybe Lois had set up the dialogue to prevent anyone but herself from receiving the vital data. Better not say anything—just stall. She nodded again.

"If Lady . . . be so kind . . . direct, please, to elevator. Unable to climb stairs." The man lightly touched his chest. "Need elevator . . . please." He turned and pointed to the second floor railing above the fountain.

As Lori's eyes automatically followed his gesture, she saw a small dark woman at the top of the stairs who waved back at them.

"My wife," the man said simply. "Lady . . . direct, please . . . to elevator."

Lori closed her eyes and took a deep breath; a feeling of dizziness was making her head swim. Then she moistened her lips and pointed to a Penny's store behind her. "At the back. I saw an elevator there. By the shoe department."

He bowed and thanked her profusely. Then he went off with a crisp, erect walk through the doors of the bustling store.

"Who was that? What did he say?" Bud was at her side instantly. "I saw him talking to you as I came in."

"He—he—" And then she started giggling. She put one hand up to her lips to try and stifle her laughter. "I thought—" she gasped, her chest suddenly heaving with mirth. "It's so funny! He looked . . . so right!" she roared.

"He wanted the elevator," piped up Lang, coming to Lori's rescue.

"The elevator?" echoed Bud and then started laughing too. Lang Su gazed at them both as if they had lost their senses. She had been on an elevator once and hadn't seen anything terribly funny about the ride. Grown-ups! She let Bud have her place next to Lori.

"What took you so long? I thought you had gotten lost." Finally Lori blew her nose and stopped laughing.

"I did. But accidentally on purpose," he confessed, looking sheepish and self-conscious. More and more she had been seeing a little-boy look that was definitely too darn appealing. "You've . . . you've been such a good sport about everything . . . I . . . wanted to say 'thank you.' "

Then Lori noticed the small sack he was fingering. He held it out to her. "A present."

"You don't have to—"

"I know I don't have to! But I wanted to buy you something. Now be a good sport, Marty, and take it."

She knew she shouldn't even open it. If she didn't see what it was, it would be much easier to refuse. But even as she hesitated, Lang began to dance up and down at her side. "Open it, Lowie! Open it!"

Her hands were trembling as she pulled out a small black box from the sack. Receiving any kind of a present was a rare experience for her. Aunt Adele had thought gifts foolish and Kyle had never had money to spend on her. The gift that lay inside a box from Silversmiths, Inc. made up for quite a few presents. It was a lovely turquoise ring and bracelet set, fashioned in a needlepoint pattern with tiny round blue stones set in the middle of silver droplets. Lacy, intricate, lovely! She couldn't say anything.

"Don't you like them?" asked Bud anxiously. "I know

you don't wear much jewelry, but Indian silver can be worn casually. And these pieces aren't heavy-looking like some. The stones are a nice color. The blue is . . . a lot like your eyes sometimes."

But as she raised up her head and looked at him, he couldn't verify the color. Her eyes were too full.

*Sixteen*

She realized too late that she had lost control of her emotions. If angry antagonism had remained between them, her feelings could have been leashed and heeled. She would have recognized his overtures for what they were. But she had been lonely for such a long time! Imperceptibly she forgot how the very sight of his bronze face and silver-gray hair had made the hackles of anger rise up on the back of her neck. Now she looked at his waving cap of hair and resisted the impulse to touch a curl dangling over his ear. Doubtless his bedside manner had been responsible for part of his successful practice. Even as she tried to steel herself against this charm, her own needs made her as vulnerable and pliable as any patient he had ever had. He was an entertaining conversationalist and knew the art of being an active listener.

A few days after their shopping spree at Cinderella City, they sat in the family room having a mid-morning cup of coffee. Lang and Kee were at their feet happily playing with a new pile of toys. In response to a general statement Bud made about parents and children, Lori said honestly, "My existence was an accident. An unwanted complication in the lives of two people who were completely happy and satisfied."

"Most babies are surprises, Marty. Very few are really planned," he reassured her. "You know the old saying, 'I wouldn't take a million for the kids I have but I wouldn't give you a nickel for another one.' Your situation isn't unique."

"Yes, it is! Once a baby gets here, it is usually welcome. My folks wouldn't have given a nickel for me even after I was born. They probably would have sent me to Aunt Adele in the beginning if they hadn't wanted to keep up appearances. I wish they had! In her own fashion she loved me more than they ever did." Then she blushed and stammered an apology, wondering why her tongue had been loosened like that. "I'm sorry to bore you with a soap opera."

"I'm not bored. I've always found people interesting. I could tell you some stories that sound like science fiction." Then he shared some experiences from his days in medical school, its pressures and frustrations, and the satisfactions of his San Francisco practice.

"Don't you have to get back to practicing medicine pretty soon—I mean, the way you spend money!" Finances had always been such an important part of her life, she couldn't imagine living even one day without that concern.

He laughed. "The big spender, that's me! However, I'm quite solvent at the moment. I made a nice profit when I sold my practice in California and my old man left a trust for Audrey and me that won't run out tomorrow. Besides, I enjoy buying things for people. Brandy used to get furious at me for arriving at her house with my arms full of stuff that I happened to see and like."

Lori stiffened. Her gift hadn't been special in any way. He must have thought her a fool for reacting so emotionally. It was obvious that he bought presents for his own pleasure. How many other women were wearing jewelry he had bought because he liked to spend money? "Where did you meet her?"

"Brandy? We were at University High School together. She was interested in science too. At one time she planned on being a doctor. Our classes fell together when we went to college. And her folks belonged to the same club as mine . . . so we saw a lot of each other."

Good Lord! No wonder Bud mooned over her picture. Beauty, brains, and money! For some reason Lori didn't want to hear any more about her. A leaden feeling in the pit of her stomach startled her. Why should she care about this Brandy Whatever-Her-Name-Was? A warning bell went off even as she denied her feelings.

She tried to remember that this Philip Brandon, with

his solicitous manner, was the same, hard, unfeeling person who had forced her into this pretense for his own benefit. It was dangerous to endow him with benign characteristics or to put credence in anything he said. He was intent upon insuring continued possession of his son. That was the true motivation for everything he did. He really didn't give a damn about her or Kyle. He had done everything he could to ruin what had been between them. Those vicious innuendos he had made about his wife and Kyle were sickening!

She knew about Kyle's ability to attract other women. Some girl, like Bertie McPhee, had always been throwing herself at him. But he had always kept them at a distance. She didn't trust Bud's evaluation about what had happened between Lois and Kyle in that distant corner of the world. And yet, deep down, she questioned whether or not, after five years' absence, she could completely trust her own feelings. How desperately she needed to believe that nothing had changed between her and Kyle. Maybe everything that Bud had told her was a lie. Maybe the children were not really his at all —but somehow involved with Kyle! Maybe that's why Kyle's note had said, "Do as they say." Was it wishful thinking to believe that he was depending upon her to keep Lang Su and Kee safe?

Nightly she read Lang a story and soon the little girl's eyes closed contentedly in sleep. Lori turned off the light and then tossed restlessly with insomnia. She couldn't stop analyzing and speculating what might be the truth in the things Bud had told her and what might be lies. Away from his confident manner, his remarks lost some of their overtone of credibility. He could be lying his head off! If only she could talk to Kyle, or just see him. One look would tell her whether or not Bud was maligning him for his own purposes.

One night her mental anxiety brought on a nightmare. Kyle stood before her, his handsome features so clear she could have reached out and lightly caressed them as she had done so many times before. But his expression was not loving—but accusing! Abruptly he took the children from her. She could hear Kee's cry and see Lang reaching out for her. His voice was cold. "You promised not to change! You promised to stay the same!" His accusations rolled over and over in her dream, like a scratched, broken record, getting fainter and fainter as the familiar figure faded away from her. "No! Come back! Come back!" Her voice was shrill and she awoke in a sitting position with sweat pouring down her face.

Although Lang could sleep through almost anything, Lori's cries had awakened her and she sat up sleepily in the bed beside Lori. "Is it morning?" she asked, befuddled.

"No, darling. I'm sorry I woke you. I had a dream. A bad dream. Now go back to sleep." She gently laid the child down on a pillow and cradled her with one arm. Soon the little girl was asleep again, but Lori stared unseeing up at the ceiling, adrenaline still pouring through her system.

Her dream seemed to be a premonition that somehow Kyle was already lost to her and the children would be next. *What shall I do? What shall I do?* There were no sounds but the quiet breathing of a sleeping child to answer her agitated questioning.

The next morning at breakfast Bud asked, "How about a drive up into the mountains?"

Lori paled and set her coffee mug down with a startled bang. "I don't think so," she answered, her breath suddenly coming in short jerks. The word "mountain" was a cue, and instantly those halcyon days she had spent with Kyle at the McPhee condominium swung her away from the present into a poignant past. She couldn't bear to go back to Aspen—and remember.

Bud peered through a fallen shock of curly hair. "I can tell from that sick-dog look that some beloved memory is enshrined in your bleeding heart. My God, Marty, haven't you mildewed long enough? Your Victorian, self-sacrificing loyalty to Kyle is sickening!"

"And so is a grown man blubbering over a picture of a copper-headed girl!" she retaliated, instantly pleased with the flush that made his tan ruddy. "You seem to be willing to pay a lot of homage to the past yourself." An emotion she refused to label jealousy brought forth a volley of caustic references to his behavior the night he had allowed his feelings to surface during his drunken state. She knew she was hitting below the belt but she couldn't stop herself. After all, she rationalized, he had asked for it, making scoffing, degrading remarks about her own memories.

It was the first barrage of angry words they had exchanged since Bud's return. Lang Su stiffened in her chair and looked from one to the other. Her deep eyes flattened, and she set down her spoon as if her food had suddenly turned rancid.

Bud angrily put down his coffee and brown liquid spilled on the table. "That's not true!" he lashed back at her. "You're such a damn romantic—"

"Better than an unfeeling realist!"

"Is that what I am? You say 'realist' like it's a dirty word! Well, that dream world you live in is pathetic! In fact, your whole life has become a shrine—"

She shoved back her chair and jerked to her feet. "You wouldn't understand," she screeched, cutting off his next word. "You misinterpret everything!"

"Oh, do I? Tell me it isn't Kyle! Tell me there's some other reason you don't want to go to the mountains—"

Without answering, she turned away from the table and started out of the room. Lang Su gave a cry and lurched out of her chair after Lori.

"Marty!" Bud's controlled voice stopped her in the doorway as Lang grabbed her leg in a scissor hold. In order to move Lori would have to drag the child along.

"Lowie stay." Lang raised dark, soulful eyes.

"Come back, Marty." There was more of a request than an order in his tone. "I'm sorry."

As Lori patted the little girl's head she was ashamed that she had brought such a look of unhappiness into that precious face. "It's all right, honey. Don't get \
Bud and Lowie enjoy fighting."

She came back to the table, sat down, and pu\
Lang up on her lap. She looked at Bud. "I'm sorry too. All right, we'll go—but not to Aspen." Her eyes challenged him, daring him to continue the battle.

"Good enough. There are quite a few resorts to choose from. How about a day in Estes Park? Thompson Canyon is a nice drive and not very far. You get the kids ready and I'll pack a picnic lunch that's out of this world." Then he swung Kee out of his high chair and gave him a toss that brought delighted giggles from the happy baby. "Okay, Tiger?"

Lori dressed Lang in a pretty yellow summer top and denim pants. She combed her hair into two ponytails and tied them with ribbons over her ears. Then she sent Lang to get Winnie-the-Pooh ready while she slipped into her beige jump suit. Impulsively she tied a chiffon scarf the color of her turquoise jewelry in a soft loop at her throat. There was a luminous glint in her eyes that almost made her look like a stranger to herself as she stole a glance in the mirror. A rising sense of excitement caught her by surprise.

It took another ten times longer to get Kee and his paraphernalia ready, but at last the car was packed. Bud stuck a Colorado map in the glove compartment. He had bought a car seat for Kee that he placed in the back with Lang and Pooh Bear. Both children had become used to car travel by now and enjoyed peering out the window or playing with toys piled up on the seat.

They took Interstate 25 out of the city, heading north. Layers of mountains lined the western horizon where a front range of rounded verdant hills was speckled with houses at the base and up piñon pine slopes. The highest mountains of the continental divide were smoky blue as they receded into the distance. Raised pointed peaks tipped with snow glittered against a periwinkle sky.

The highway was straight and flat, cutting through farmland stretching eastward in squares of variegated greens all the way to the Kansas state line. For the first time in many weeks, Lori thought about her small duplex apartment, closed up and stuffy in a moist steambath ___ner. As early as May she had lain in bed, clammy ___ky during sultry Kansas nights. Now as a breeze ___mountain slopes slightly lifted her hair and bathed ___ neck in coolness, she realized how much she dreaded going back to her sterile existence as a lonely schoolteacher. This year would be worse than ever!

She turned to Bud. "Do you think we ought to be away from the house like this?"

"One afternoon won't make any difference," he reassured her but she saw the knuckles on his hands whiten as he gripped the steering wheel. "I've decided we'll only wait a few more days and then try something different."

"What?" Her eyes jerked up to meet his.

"Don't worry about it." But he was smiling at her wanly, in the same fashion he might have given encouragement to a patient scheduled for risky surgery.

They skirted several towns like Longmont and Berthoud, small farming communities clustered along the highway as it plunged northward toward the Wyoming border. Knee-high corn promised a good yield from irrigated fields where water shone in silver strips between rows of deep green plants. Cut alfalfa and bales of fresh hay brought sweet, poignant smells into the car, but their noses quivered several times at the odor of a feeding lot. They laughed as Lang Su uninhibitedy said "Phew!" and grabbed her tiny nose in a protective gesture.

By the time they turned onto Highway 34, which took them west into Thompson Canyon, Lori had begun to relax from the bustle of getting ready and was enjoying seeing a part of Colorado that was completely new to her. At the mouth of the canyon was a pretty town, poetically named Loveland, that flaunted its own lake. Lang Su squealed delightedly over a huge Indian totem pole that had been erected on its bank. Several water-skiers were making silver ribbons in the water, and Bud pulled the car over to watch them for a few minutes.

He confessed that he was no slight hand at ocean surfing and waterskiing. Anything that took money seemed to be a part of his life style, thought Lori. From what he had said there had always been enough wealth in the family for him to pursue his interests. Could it also be that he would not hesitate to supplement any lack of funds by less-than-legitimate means? She shoved the prickling thought away.

"Loveland. Nice name for such a pretty place. Don't you agree? Maybe we should come back sometime and see if the town can deliver what it promises?" he teased and laughed at her sudden rise in color.

She was happy. The feeling surprised her so much she almost rejected it as being false. There was a warm sensation inside her that filled her and surrounded her like an aura. Bud seemed to sense it because his expression softened as he looked at her. "I knew that color matched your eyes," he said appreciatively, glancing at her chiffon scarf.

She didn't answer but turned and looked out of the window. The mountain road was climbing sharply. Rock cliffs rose on both sides and narrowed the canyon to a two-lane highway and the width of the Thompson River. A large sign advised, IN CASE OF FLOOD, CLIMB TO HIGHER GROUND. As Lori let her eyes slide upward over lichen-coated rocks in greens and reds, she couldn't help but observe, "Climb where?" If a wall of water came sweeping down the narrow ravine, it would be impossible to get a foothold on mountain cliffs whose steepness challenged the ablest of mountain climbers.

"Don't worry. It doesn't look like rain today. Although mountain weather can be fickle," he admitted. "I hope you brought some wraps for the kids."

Lori didn't answer, realizing that she hadn't. She peered upward, arching her head to see the sky. No sign of rain clouds. Besides, if it should turn cold, they could stay in the car. But even as she rationalized her forgetfulness, she felt like a typical flatlander, ill prepared for the mountains. But this was only a picnic, not a camp-out!

They chose a wooded dell, Glen Haven, for their picnic. A tiny stream flowed through a gentle ravine with inviting grassy areas. Bud ignored some larger camping grounds and stopped instead under some trees where there was room for only one car. A blackened rock fireplace showed that it had been the choice of other picnicking campers. There was a silence and solitude about the spot that gave the illusion that they were miles from anyone else.

When they unloaded the lunch, Lori discovered that Bud had carried out his promise. Somehow he had managed barbecued chicken, butter rolls, fruit salad, brownies, coffee, and lemonade. Kee sampled the offerings on everyone's plate before he settled back on a blanket with his bottle and prepared to take his afternoon nap. Everyone's appetite was so healthy they were all stuffed before they realized it.

"How about a hike up that hill?" proposed Bud. "Exercise is the best way to work off a meal like that."

"Maybe," granted Lori, "but I think Kee has the right idea. You and Lang go ahead and be mountain climbers. I'll clean up the lunch things and then stretch out beside Kee."

"Fair enough." Bud held out a hand to Lang.

"Can Pooh come?"

"Sure, why not? We may meet a member of his family on the way."

"Christopher Robin, too?"

"We might," granted Bud solemnly.

Then Lang started laughing. "You're silly, Bud. This isn't the Hundred Acre Wood."

Lori snickered and Bud gave a shrug of his shoulders. "What do I know!"

She watched them walk away. Immaculate as always, Bud wore light blue western pants with a darker shirt. As he knelt down beside Lang and pointed out a furry little chipmunk, Lori felt a catch rising in her throat. *Love begins with love*, she thought, watching them. A child learns about love with his small hand in a big one. Then if the experiences are right, the love is there to draw upon later, in a loving that brings about another child who . . . *A beautiful circle*. She sighed as she lay back on the blanket beside Kee.

Clouds like puffs of popped corn floating overhead were almost hynotic as she watched them. Mountain smells of pine needles, moss, and decaying wood wrinkled up her nose as she drew in the heavenly scent. Somewhere in the top of a ponderosa pine a blue jay was telling the world about his presence. The same warm, happy feeling she had experienced in the car came back. Her apprehension about painful memories had been groundless. There were no parallels between this summer picnic with a sleeping baby at her side and lovers' trysts so long ago. Last night's dream with its presentiment of tragedy had faded away, and in her present, fuzzy mood of contentment she wondered why she had been so upset by it.

She closed her eyes and recalled the picture of Bud kneeling beside Lang, his hair catching yellow tones from the sun and his arms bronzed with a deep tan. Up the hill she could hear Lang's high-pitched, lyrical laughter and Bud's resonant deep voice as they moved away through the trees. Lori knew that Lang Su would be safe. She could trust Bud—trust! Her eyes flew open. The word suddenly brought her face to face with a new truth. Trust? A voice mimicked the word inside her head. Yes, you trust him. Your feelings aren't the same anymore. *You're falling in love with Dr. Philip Brandon.* She closed her eyes tightly as if to shut out this line of ridiculous thinking. Her feelings of contentment had nothing to do with him! It was the children and the beautiful day. And then his laughter floated down the hillside, echoing slightly in crevices of rocks and dirt. The pleasure of hearing it mocked her. It's not true! It's not true! Her lips moved in a denial.

## Seventeen

She must have dozed because a crunch of footsteps and the sound of Lang's bubbling giggles awakened her.

"See what we found!" squealed the little girl as she dumped an armful of pine cones in Lori's lap.

"They're lovely," beamed Lori, wondering what she was supposed to do with them. In the commotion Kee woke up. He picked up a pine cone and immediately tested its taste. He spit and looked at them accusingly.

"It's early," said Bud. "Let's go into Estes Park and play tourist. I bet we can find some interesting shops there." He winked at Lang.

The youngster understood perfectly and clapped her hands excitedly.

"You're spoiling her," warned Lori sternly, but with a flicker of a smile tugging at the corner of her lips. She loved to see Lang bubbling and excited, expressing herself freely as a happy six-year-old ought to.

"I know. But spoiled women are the happiest. You ought to try it sometime."

"If I ever have the chance—"

"You do! I don't mind having two spoiled females on my hands."

"Sounds great, but—"

"But what?"

She shrugged. Her feelings were too complicated. A deep suspicion that she should be wary of good doctors bearing gifts made her cautious about any "spoiling" that came her way. And yet the temptation was there. She wanted to relax and accept his friendly overtures at face value. "I don't know," she said aloud and stood up. "Stop talking foolishness and help put all this stuff back in the car." As she picked up Kee, she impulsively planted a kiss on the top of his head. He felt so warm and soft! Her arms tightened affectionately around him.

Bud hadn't moved. He was watching her as if bemused by the scene. Then he shook himself out of the reverie. "How come I always end up on kitchen detail no matter where we are?"

"Just lucky, I guess," she quipped and chuckled as she went back to the car.

The road through Devils Gulch climbed to an elevation of over seven thousand feet before dropping into Estes Park Village, about seven miles southwest of Glen Haven. Lori's ears popped in the high elevation. Bud gave her a stick of gum to chew. "Thanks," she smiled contentedly, enjoying the mountain scenery. Log cabins and summer homes could be seen through flickering silver-leafed aspen and feathery ponderosa pines. In the distance, Longs Peak rose in proud domination over the lesser mountains in the Rocky Mountain National Park.

"Look at the size of those rocks!" Bud pointed to some huge white boulders that were double and triple the size of a car. They were strewed for nearly a mile along the North Fork of the Thompson River. "Just think of the water force it would take to move one of them!"

Lori shivered as she visualized flood waters that must have left them there. Another warning sign came into view, reminding them again about climbing to higher ground in case of a flood. She was glad when a series of sharp curves took them out of Devils Gulch and through more open mountain meadows.

By the time they reached Estes Park Village both children were ready to get out of the car, but they were delayed another fifteen minutes. The traffic was terrible. The narrow, two-lane streets were packed with cars. Bud combed Moraine Avenue, Big Horn Drive, and Elkhorn Avenue for a parking place and finally settled for a spot on MacGregor Avenue, nearly five blocks from the Park Center mall. "This will have to do," he said as he set the car's emergency brake.

Bud carried Kee piggyback as they window shopped. Most of the stores carried the usual amount of tourist junk but some nice specialty shops were scattered along the winding streets. Bud was especially taken by some original pottery deeply glazed in shades of indigo. Indian jewelery was offered everywhere, but Lori didn't see any she liked as well as the pieces Bud had given her.

She refused to go in an expensive import shop even though she was mesmerized by some exquisite Oriental gowns in a window. She shook her head when Bud tried to coax her in. "Can't you just see what Lang's and Kee's sticky cotton-candy fingers could do in a place like that?" She shuddered. "I'll settle for an ice cream cone."

By the time they emerged from the Old Fashion Shoppe, the weather had changed dramatically. Black clouds from a mountain thunderstorm had rolled over Longs Peak and were sending jagged flashes and booming peals across the threatening sky. Splashes of large raindrops began to pelt the street.

"Damn," swore Bud. "We'll have to run for the car. Maybe you should stay here with the kids and I'll pick you up."

"No, we can make it! A little rain won't hurt us!" She grabbed Lang's hand and hurried toward MacGregor Avenue, which she soon realized was farther away than she remembered.

By the time they had covered three blocks, it wasn't a "little rain." It was a downpour! Instead of large, gentle drops, slashing streams of water were coming down in sheets. Lightning cracked on wooded slopes just beyond the town. Instantly thunder rolled in deafening booms. Lang Su screamed and tried to hold her ears.

Where in the hell was the car? Belatedly Lori realized they should have waited out the rain, as the people who were familiar with mountain storms were doing. It was too late to turn back now. They were already out of the town center, struggling up a steep hill where they had left the car. Riverlets were flowing down both sides of the road and collecting in pools wherever there was a small depression.

Lori nearly went down on her knees as she slipped on the slick incline. With her head bent down against a blinding rain, she tried to keep Lang protected at her side as they tumbled after Bud and Kee. Wind, rain, and yellow snapping electricity bombarded them on all sides. Bud was hunched over Kee, endeavoring to shield him as much as possible. The baby screamed and jerked, his arms and legs sticking out in every direction, and threw Bud off balance.

It seemed more like hours than minutes had passed when they finally reached the Matador. All of them were drenched to the skin, shivering from the chill of wind and water, and breathless from the physical demands of fighting their way through the storm. Lang sobbed and Kee protested his misery at the top of his lungs.

They piled together in the front seat. Bud turned around and began searching the back for coats and sweaters. All he came up with was a jacket that matched his western pants.

"Where're the kids'—?"

"I—I—didn't—br—bring—any!" Her teeth were chattering so hard she could barely talk.

He swung on her. His eyes, flashing, angry, and demanding, bore into hers. "What? No coats? Sweaters? Anything?"

She shook her head.

"You idiot! You blasted idiot!" A furious look slashed her and she recoiled from his fury. No sign of her pleasant companion remained in this sudden schizophrenic change. With his hair plastered to his head and moisture beaded on his skin and eyelashes, he looked like a complete stranger, not the immaculate, jovial Dr. Brandon.

His anger terrified her. She edged back away from him, trying to soothe Kee. She swallowed an impulse to plead her case. She didn't need him swearing at her to know how stupid she had been to forget their wraps.

He flung his jacket at her. "Try to keep the kids warm with that." Then he turned the ignition as if the key were somebody's neck.

Even if Lori had not had her head down, trying to squeeze water out of Lang's dripping ponytails, she would not have seen anything out of the windows. Murky gray curtains of water blotted everything from view. Roaring thunder, pounding rain, and stabs of yellow light brought sobs of terror up into her throat. Her body shivered and a premonition of disaster settled upon her. It was as if the warnings had been there all day, but she had ignored them as she clutched at her own selfish happiness. Now the memory of steep canyon roads and rock-studded rivers screamed danger on every side of the blindly moving car.

Then it happened! Out of nowhere a four-wheel-drive vehicle loomed up in front of them, coming out of the pouring streams of rain like a vessel from the depths of the ocean. It was coming at them straight on! Bud gave a vicious turn of the steering wheel. Miraculously the Jeep roared by, missing them by a fraction of an inch. Bud immediately tried to recover from the quick jerk, but he overcompensated when he turned the wheel. In an instant the car was out of control—sliding, lurching, and pitching! The car vaulted over the side of the road and down a sloping hill, careening into a ravine where swirling water waited to receive the plunging automobile and its screaming occupants.

# Eighteen

The heavy car crashed down the hillside, tearing away brush, dirt, and trees until finally its rear axle was submerged in a roaring flash flood that filled the bottom of the ravine. Mud and debris began to collect around the sinking back wheels as the rear end of the car slowly lowered itself into rampaging waters.

It was fortunate that they were all in the front seat; otherwise they never would have gotten the children out of the car. The instant the car lurched to a stop, Bud flung open his door. "Out! Get out!"

Lori shoved the children at him, automatically obeying his authoritative commands. Stupidly she wasted a few seconds grabbing her purse and Pooh Bear. Before she could move toward the open door, the car began to sink under her! Bud jerked viciously at her arm, half dragging her through the door. Icy water swirled around her legs.

"Hurry!" shouted Bud, clutching both children in his arms as he turned away from her.

Higher ground, higher ground, higher ground, the words made a bizarre chant in Lori's head. But her legs could not gain any footing in the slimy mud. On hands and knees she labored after him up the rocky hillside. Trying to hold on to a drenched stuffed animal was an act of idiocy. Her shoulder purse dragged in the dirt, impeding her progress. She floundered, unable to think rationally enough to drop the purse and the toy.

A crack of lightning somewhere nearby jerked a scream from her constricted throat. Over the storm's roar, she could hear Lang's fearful cries a short distance above her. Undisguised terror in the precious little voice drove Lori upward. Strangely Kee was silent. None of the baby's usual shrill protests had been heard since the impact. The absence of his voice plunged cold fear into Lori's nearly numb body. No! No! He couldn't have been hurt! Was he dead? It couldn't be! She sobbed aloud. How could such an idyllic picnic have turned into this terrifying nightmare?

Higher ground, higher ground. Streams of water poured down her saturated hair and mingled with the tears of panic that filled her eyes. Loosened rocks spun out from under her feet and threatened to twist her ankle or bring her to her knees again. With every precarious movement upward, thick scrub oak branches reached out, maliciously tearing her clothes, leaving bleeding scratches on her arms and legs. She didn't know how Bud could possibly make it up the hillside weighted down with the two children. It was all she could do to make an agonizing scramble after him.

At last she heard him gasp, "The road!" He set Lang down, shifted Kee in his arms, then took one of the little girl's hands. Lori stumbled forward and grabbed her other hand. "This way . . . hotel." Blindly, in chain fashion, they floundered forward, down the road. Lori vaguely remembered Bud pointing out the Stanley Hotel as they came into town, but in her befuddled state she had no idea in which direction it might lay. Without protest, she followed Bud's lead.

Somehow they reached an unpaved road. Lori caught sight of a blurry sign, Service-Employees Entrance. Rain beat against them with unabated fury. The deep ruts and potholes in the rough road were filled to overflowing. Surging water nearly swept their feet out from under as they hunched against gales of wind and rain. *We'll never make it!* If flood waters could sweep mammoth boulders down a riverbed, four fragile humans could easily be tumbled into a watery oblivion. *We'll never make it!* She faltered.

"Marty!" Bud's shout whipped her. "Come on! Hurry, Marty!"

She raised a heavy head and a gust of wind jerked it backward. Her weary legs didn't want to work anymore. She let go of Lang's hand. Bud would take her on to safety. "Marty! The hotel! The hotel!" Through heavy, gray slates of rain, she made out the blotchy shape of a white clapboard building.

Bud gave out a weird noise that must have been a cry of joy. New strength came to all of them and they stumbled up a dozen stone steps leading to a wide veranda at the front of the resort hotel.

Bud butted a large front door open, and like drowning refugees from a capsized ocean vessel, they stumbled into the lobby and dripped mud, water, and grime all over the plush carpet. A group of sightseers on a commercial tour had been delayed because of the storm and were scattered about, seated in clusters on green and gold furniture. They gasped or stared with bulging eyes at the bedraggled family.

As if to announce their presence, Kee raised his head from Bud's chest and let out a beautiful ear-splitting screech. Lori laughed hysterically and swung Lang up in her arms. With as much professionalism as he could muster, Dr. Philip Brandon took charge. He demanded two adjoining rooms from a gaping desk clerk who swallowed an inquiry about reservations. Bud slapped down a credit card from his dripping wallet and grabbed two keys. Later Lori was to laugh, remembering how he had looked with mud running like wet putty down his face. There wasn't a clean inch of him anywhere and yet, somehow, he managed to project a professional, immaculate air.

Quickly he herded them past gawking onlookers into a tiny elevator that creaked and groaned upward, and then on to rooms 316 and 318.

"Strip!" he ordered once inside the first room, his own teeth chattering like castanets. "Get in the shower! Then into bed!" He opened a door into an adjoining room. "I'll handle Kee. Hurry now. Get yourselves warm!"

Lori's numb fingers fumbled with the tiny buttons on Lang's blouse. Trying to undo these small fastenings was like attempting to thread a needle with gloves on. The little girl was shaking uncontrollably and whimpering sounds came from her ice-blue mouth.

"It's all right, honey. It's all right now," Lori stammered. But the more she hurried, the longer it seemed to take. Finally they were both stripped of their clammy, drenched garments. They kicked off mud-caked, soaked canvas shoes and left everything in a dripping pile in the middle of the large bathroom. They quickly climbed into the ceramic tub-shower.

Blessed warm water sprayed upon their goose-pimply bodies. As soon as the worst chill was gone, Lori filled the tub with hot bath water. She and Lang soaked until a rosy pink hue replaced the blue tones of their skin a few moments before. Every bone in Lori's body ached and dozens of scratches upon her arms and legs smarted. She leaned back in the tub, exhausted from their ordeal. Lang Su, with the resiliency of youth, had dragged Pooh into the water and was diligently washing his face. Obviously she was more concerned about Pooh's condition than with their nearly fatal brush with death.

When Lori felt as if they would never be cold again, she set the dripping Pooh on a bath mat and dried off Lang, giving her hair a quick rubbing. Then swatting her affectionately on the behind, she ordered, "Scoot! To bed!" And without even a towel around their waists, they scurried across the room like two naked nymphs and bounded into a double bed. Burrowing under covers, they jostled each other, giggling, finally coming up with hardly more than their noses out of the blankets.

The bed was a large four-poster that blended in nicely with the decor of antiques. An early American wallpaper print was reflected in matching curtains, which were drawn against the storm. A pair of small bedside lamps gave muted light through milk glass shades. Thick doors and walls insured a hushed, protective feeling and did not even allow noise to drift in from Bud's room. Lori couldn't tell whether he and Kee were still in the shower or not.

Lang snuggled in close as she often did during the night. Lori put her head against the child's moist hair and sighed deeply. Fright had been replaced by blessed relief. How lucky they were! How very, very lucky! She closed her eyes tightly as grateful tears eased down her cheeks.

She was almost asleep when Bud came in with a wriggling Kee. The baby was ingeniously dressed in a diaper made out of a pillowcase. Bud wore only a towel hooked at his waist. The bath towel was decorated with a green strip bearing the name STANLEY, which happened to be draped down the middle of his front.

*I knew the hair on his chest was curly,* thought Lori irrationally, *but it's not gray!* He must have been a blond! The revelation seemed terribly important in the bizarre situation. Then she laughed openly at herself. Bud grinned back and deposited a gurgling Kee in her arms.

There was no way to keep the covers up around her neck as she scooted the baby in beside her. Kee promptly shoved the blankets down indecently low. She gasped as a cool draft of air hit her naked body.

"Nice work, Tiger," complimented Bud approvingly. "The view from here is quite . . . captivating."

"I might say the same," parried Lori quickly. "And educational too! To think that part of the male anatomy is named Stanley when all I've ever heard is John Thomas."

"So you've read *Lady Chatterly's Lover.* The truth comes out. Take off a woman's clothes and her true self emerges. Just for that, I think I'll undress too." He reached for an end of his towel.

"No," shrieked Lori in protest. "The—the children!"

"Oh, yes, the children." He raised one eyebrow in mock contemplation. "Do you think they're too young . . . or too old? Isn't there a trend toward early sex education? Can you think of a better time for show and tell?" Teasingly he reached for a corner of the covers. "Shall we show all?"

"Don't you dare!" Laughingly, she clutched the blankets. "You know we're supposed to stay covered up—doctor's orders!"

"Smart advice. And I think I'll follow it." With that he quickly scooted under the covers on Lang's side of the bed.

Their foolish banter was a welcome release from the recent physical shock and traumatic event. The adjustment from helplessness in a careening, tumbling car to safety in a heavenly warm bed made them all slightly giddy.

Lang squealed happily as Bud pulled her over against him. "Now isn't this cozy?"

"I like it," answered Lang simply. "Nice . . . family take bath together . . . now sleep together."

"Smart girl. Wish I could stay for a nap." Then he sobered, as if reflection on what had happened could not be held at a distance any longer. "My God, what an experience!" He shuddered. "I can't believe it! It—it happened so fast! We were on the road one minute and the next over the brink of a flooding ravine. No wonder people lose their lives in flash floods like that one."

Lori didn't want to think about it. It was too close. The near tragedy pressed down upon her and sent involuntary trembling through her body.

"Are we going to have a two-day picnic?" asked Lang Su innocently.

"I wouldn't be surprised," answered Bud. "I doubt that we'll be able to get our car pulled out very soon. What do you think, Marty?" He raised up on one elbow and looked at her. "Do you have any suggestions?" Then he grinned. "Any that are decent, under the circumstances?"

"No . . . I . . ."

"Shall we just forget the world out there and stay here as long as we like? No cumbersome clothes! No deadly charades!"

He was being facetious, of course, but there was an appeal in his teasing. If only they could enjoy a reprieve from all the insidious deception and its terrifying demands! She looked down at Kee who had fallen asleep in the crook of her arm. Thank God he was all right! The moment of contentment put everything that had gone before into a shadow. "I wish we could," she said honestly, looking up at him, forgetting how his anger always terrified her. The only thing she could remember now was that he had saved her life. She did not even consider that such a deed might have been done for his own purposes. If she had, she probably would have dismissed it as unimportant. She and the children were safe and well because of his relentless drive. "It would be nice, very nice, but I'm afraid Kee will wake up shortly and need food, clothes—"

"Ah, yes. The sensible Marty raises her beautiful but very practical head." He sat up against the headboard. She couldn't tell whether he still had the Stanley towel around his loins or not. "I guess I'd better see if the heater has dried out my clothes enough to put them on. Then I'll go out and see what necessities I can lay my hands on. The storm seems to have let up some. The police may be wondering about our abandoned car. Did you get a look at the sonofabitch who ran us off the road?"

Marty shook her head and for an instant the horror of that moment was back. "It happened—too fast. Some kind of four-wheel drive, I think. He didn't even stop—"

"Probably didn't see us go over. I shouldn't have been driving blindly like that. Well, let's put it behind us." But Lori knew he was seething inwardly about the other driver's lack of concern. And she knew that it was his anger because of her forgetfulness that had made him try to drive in the storm. Always ready to take guilt upon herself, she knew the whole thing had been her fault. If only she hadn't forgotten the coats—if only there had been no rain—if only— This ridiculous soliloquy was cut short as Bud climbed out of bed.

"You stay here and keep warm." He hooked the towel loosely around him. "What did you do with your clothes?"

"They're . . . in the bathroom," she answered, remembering the soggy heap in the middle of the floor. She hadn't even thought about hanging them up to dry.

She heard him rinsing something out, and then he came back into the room with some clothes over his arm. Quickly he spread them on a heater under the window. He held up a scrap of wet cloth that was a pair of Lori's bikini panties. "Are these yours? They look two sizes too small. And this?" He held up a bra. "Thirty-four B, C, D? I need to be sure of sizes, you know. I've always been a sucker for black lingerie."

She knew she should make some light, bantering retort but she couldn't. Somehow the conversation had become intimate. And as she looked at him standing nearly naked, moving with masculine beauty, his muscles arching under smooth, tanned skin, an emotion akin to desire swept through her. She looked away quickly and closed her eyes. Then as he moved past the bed, her heart gave a jerk. Even with her eyes shut, she could see the tufts of fair hair that curled on his chest and firm abdomen. She stiffened lest he should reach out and touch her, somehow creating a visible spark of electricity at the contact. But he only flipped off the light by her bed and went into the other room.

Both Lang and Kee were asleep before he softly closed his hall door a few minutes later. But Lori's heart was still racing. She had to get her emotions under control! His moods were as changeable as the weather—and just as dangerous. Instead of responding to his light, affectionate banter, she should be remembering his diabolical temper and be wary of the barbs hidden in his charm. Only the children were secure in his care. *He'll misuse you, if you give him the chance.* She told herself all this and more, but rational thought seemed to have little effect on her racing pulse and an aching need she thought sublimated long ago.

# Nineteen

At first Lori couldn't remember where she was. When she awakened she was grabbing Kee just as he was about to wriggle off the bed. Cool air hit her bare breasts as she sat up and then she remembered. Since the hotel room was still dark, she knew Bud had not returned. She was wondering what she was going to do with a hungry baby when she heard a key clatter in the hall door. Trying to imprison Kee with one hand, she clutched the covers over her breasts in a melodramatic fashion.

Bud's figure was silhouetted by the hall light as he opened the door. She recognized his shape even though it was distorted by sacks and boxes. He dumped everything in a chair before he went back and closed the door. Kee gave a squeal of delight and nearly lurched out of Lori's arm.

"Oh, you're awake." He turned on the light.

"Take him! He's going to be on the floor in a minute."

"What's the matter, Tiger?" He swung the baby up and gave him a light toss in the air. "Miss your old man?" In response, Kee's homemade diaper slipped off his fat little fanny and dangled uselessly around his knees.

"His old man better fix that diaper or he'll be in for a surprise very shortly. I hope there are some diapers in all that stuff," she commented dryly.

"Are you casting aspersions on my shopping abilities? For shame." A new beige leisure suit and maroon sport shirt had replaced his tattered clothes, and it was obvious that his spirits had improved as well. The rain must have stopped, for although his hair still hung in moist waves around his head, there were no water spots on his new outfit. Quickly he brought out a large box of disposable diapers and deftly changed Kee at the foot of the bed.

163

Then he laid the baby on his tummy in the middle of the carpeted floor.

"If you'll hand me my things," Lori motioned toward the heater, "I'll get dressed." She was still clutching the bedcovers around her.

"These?" Bud went over and gathered up the clothes he had carefully spread on the heater. "They're still damp, muddy, and—Look at this jumpsuit! Torn."

"It's all right," answered Lori. "Toss them here."

"Nope!" Bud shook his head. Then he came over to the bed, just out of her reach. "You don't want to put this stuff back on."

"Bud! Hand me my clothes!"

"Do you want to fight me for them?" He smirked and took a step backward. "Come on. Let go of those covers and come after them. No? Well, then I guess all of these go back in the shower."

"Bud!"

But even as she cursed, he went in the bathroom and dumped everything in the tub, turned on the water, and soaked them as much as they had been before.

"Why did you do that? You fool!" she swore at him.

"Because I've brought you something else to put on. Knowing your puritanical soul, you would refuse it—if you had a choice. Now you don't! Unless you're prepared to hide in those covers forever." He searched through his packages and brought a large dress box over to the bed.

All of the commotion had finally awakened Lang Su. "A present, Lowie! A present!" Clapping her hands, she ignored her nakedness and wriggled forward. But Lori couldn't.

"You open it for me, Lang," she said, still hunched down in bed.

When the lid came off, Lori blinked from the elegance of the contents. Beautiful rose-red satin was folded in white tissue. A pattern of tiny floral sprays, embroidered in silver and red miniature flowers, shone with unbelievable richness. As Lang Su drew out the resplendent material, Lori could see that the fabric had been fashioned into an exquisite Oriental caftan. She had seen the gown before! It was the one displayed in the window of the expensive import shop. Now it was here! Gingerly she reached out and fingered its soft, luxurious folds. "It's . . . it's beautiful!" she murmured. "Beautiful." Her words were hushed, almost reverent.

"Put it on."

Her startled eyes came up as if Bud had said something sacrilegious. "I—I couldn't! It's too—nice!"

"It's either that or bedcovers. You'd better hurry and make up your mind. Room service should be here any minute with a bottle for Kee and food and drink for the rest of us. Here, doll"—he tossed some sacks at Lang— "Bud didn't forget you." He laughed as she made paper fly in every direction. "You're my kind of female, Lang. Now I'll take your brother and get him dressed. Come on, Tiger." With the baby under one arm he started through the adjoining doorway.

"Bud! Wait!"

He looked back at the bed where Lori still cowered with only bare shoulders out of the covers. "Yes?"

"What—what about—underthings?"

"*Underthings?* Marty, you don't wear underthings with satin! It feels too nice against the skin." Then he shut the door quickly in case she was tempted to throw something at him.

With excited squeaks, Lang Su stuck her arms and legs into a flowered kimono top and matching blue pants. Then she hopped down from the bed and turned around in every direction while Lori made complimentary remarks. "Now you, Lowie. Put yours on!"

"In—in a minute." Lori slipped out of bed, taking the box and caftan with her as she went into the bathroom. After she shut the door, she stared down at the mass of muddy, soaked clothes in the tub. She lay her package on the counter and started wringing out her clothes and hanging each item on a crowded shower rod.

Bud hadn't missed anything! Unless she wanted to hide out in the bathroom or cower in bed, she had a choice of either a towel, sheet, or a gorgeous rose satin garment that would have made Aunt Adele purse her lips and pronounce it suitable for a harlot. Delaying her decision, she wiped off her muddy purse and took out a small cosmetic bag containing a brush, lipstick, and a compact. After giving her hair a vigorous brushing, she twisted it into a smooth French roll, searching in the bottom of her purse for bobby pins. Then, viewing her hairdo, she felt justified in touching her lips with a little color and slipping the caftan over her head. With a whisper it slid down her bare skin, clinging to every plane and curve of her naked body. Even her rounded nipples showed slightly under the smooth satin. It was indecent! A flush rose in her cheeks and was deepened by the fabric's rose-red color. There were yards of rich material flowing from full sleeves cut in floor-length drapes. The edge of a long circular skirt touched the floor as she turned.

She gasped as she looked into the oval bathroom mirror. A plunging neckline from a high collar exposed a wide swath of cleavage and bare skin to the waist! Then she remembered that a silver lamé scarf had been used as a cover-up on the window mannequin, but of course Bud wouldn't have bought that, too. "I might as well be naked," she said aloud in her usual habit of talking to herself.

She struggled with ambivalent feelings about the way she looked. A loud knocking on the hall door put an end to her vacillation.

"Lowie!" Lang Su yelled. "The door, Lowie." As Lori came out of the bathroom, the child squealed in a sing-song chant, "Lowie beautiful! Lowie beautiful!"

As she opened the door, an adolescent waiter's reaction verified that her appearance was something out of the ordinary. He managed to stammer "Room service" as his eyes bulged and an expression of awe covered his pimply face. He stumbled in with a heavily loaded tea cart, trying not to stare at the radiant creature who was dressed for a tête-à-tête with the Prince of Wales.

He swallowed hard as he held a pad out to her. "Would you . . . sign here?" he croaked.

Lori didn't look at the individual charges but the total bill was astronomical. Bud must have ordered something like pheasant under glass or a ten-course dinner. She hesitated, wondering if she should add in a tip or just pay the boy. Smiling nervously at him, she turned and glanced at Bud's closed door, wondering if he were going to ignore the situation. Then she went back into the bathroom for her purse and ended up giving the boy a five-dollar tip.

By the time the waiter left, she had begun to relax, liking soft folds moving with her body and enjoying for the first time the unbelievable comfort of no biting bra straps or pinching elastic bands. A well-developed conscience cautioned her that there might be dangers in the freedom she felt. As she knocked on Bud's door, she felt unnaturally free, as if the donning of such Babylonian apparel had allowed her to break away from habitual patterns of conditioning. "Dinner's here!"

"Good," he called. "Come in. Tiger's ready." He was just lifting the baby off the bed as she opened the door. "He's got his jamies on and—" Then he stopped. "My God!" he swore, gaping at her in a manner only a little more sophisticated than the bellhop's. "You're . . . you're beautiful!"

"Lowie beautiful," echoed Lang, slipping through the doorway.

"She is indeed! Beautiful!" His enthusiastic agreement brought a new flush of color to her cheeks.

"Lang Su beautiful too?" Wanting some of the limelight for herself, the little girl began to twirl in front of him, showing off her new outfit.

Laughing, Bud assured her that she was lovely, too, and the prettiest little girl in the whole wide world. "And now that my ladies are properly attired," he said pompously, "let's eat!"

By nine o'clock they had put the children to bed in Bud's room. The bed had been shoved against the wall so Kee wouldn't fall out, and Lori had wrapped a towel around a soggy Pooh Bear so Lang would be content. They went into the other room, leaving the door slightly ajar.

Bud turned the television set on low and sat down in a small armchair to watch. Lori poured them each another cup of coffee and then relaxed in an early American rocker. Lori finished her piece of fresh apple pie as they watched a musical special on a Denver channel and then began to doze when the news came on.

"Look at that!" Bud's remark jarred her awake. "The storm made the news."

Lori stiffened in her chair. For three minutes an announcer's narrative, accompanied by pictures of angry, flooding waters, brought the terror back. Bridges washed out! Cars swept off roads! And there had been fatalities! In ghoulish descriptions, all of the drownings were reported in detail. As the announcer dispassionately began listing the dead, Lori shuddered and quickly turned her eyes away. It could have been them! But for fate . . .

Abruptly Bud turned off the set. He came over to her chair and drew her up into his arms. "Don't think about it. It's over. We're alive, safe." There wasn't any suggestion of passion or desire in his touch. He could have been comforting anyone during a tense moment or painful memory. But Lori, suddenly reacting to their near tragedy, clung to him with rising emotion. A horrible sensation of plunging over the side of the road came back so strong that it brought a gasp of terror from her lips. "It's all right," he soothed. "Everything is just fine." Gently he raised up her chin. "Come on now. A beautiful lady shouldn't put tear stains on a rose satin gown." He let his hands slide down to the curve in her back and rested them at her waist. "There's nothing to worry about. We'll have the car pulled out. Go back to Denver. All of us fine and dandy from our two-day picnic. That's better. No more tears. Just pleasant thoughts."

The situation lent itself beautifully to his smooth, professional manipulations. Since his identity had been revealed, Lori's defenses against Philip Brandon had been steadily decreasing. His attentiveness, gifts, and displays of tenderness toward the children overshadowed his past deceptions and all his sporadic temper outbursts, which under analysis always seemed justified. Now his arms felt firm and protective as they wrapped around her back and waist. And in the circle of his warmth, her body responded. Stiff muscles became supple. Her breasts pressed against him as, almost involuntarily, her arms slipped up around his neck, her fingers laced through the tempting curls that hugged his neck. Her fright dissipated.

For a long time they stood together, silent and immobile. If Lori had pulled away then, he might have tightened his embrace to secure her. But she didn't. Her consciousness did not register anything except her need to be close to him. Slowly he bent down his head and kissed her. Desire blotted out her will to think, to remember. As they ended a prolonged, passionate kiss, his gaze touched her upturned face lightly, searchingly. Then, with sureness and slow deliberation, he slipped the gown from her shoulders.

Early morning light put gray shadowy ripples on the wallpaper. Lori lay contentedly in the circle of Bud's arm. Her body was satiated with love. As he gently smoothed some wayward strands of pale hair behind her ear, she sighed and stretched her smooth limbs against him. It was the familiar caress that made her murmur a protest. He was stroking her hair in a remembered way. But his voice was wrong. "You're some woman. You've been alone too long. Much too long."

His words brought her out of languidness, forcing her to acknowledge passion spent. If only he would stop talking, then she wouldn't wake up. "So soft and warm," he whispered against her ear, tipping it lightly with his tongue. "Like a purring kitten—"

Her contentment receded. Those were Kyle's words. They did not belong here. She was not ready to handle the betrayal of her only love. And then, because she was not fully alert, her old habit deceived her. Without realizing it, she muttered aloud, "I can't think of Kyle now."

Instantly Bud stiffened and pulled back. She knew what had happened! His anger was immediate. "Kyle! My God, you've got that sick-dog look even now! But it's a little late, isn't it?"

She protested, "Please, I'm sorry— I didn't mean—"

But there was no way to call back the insult. Her persuasive lover was gone. Cold fury had instantly replaced passion. "'I wish your Kyle could have seen you last night. Rose satin instead of sackcloth!" he sneered. "He wouldn't have recognized his insipid little Lori. Oh, I waited a long time for that!"

"A long time?" She drew away, cold.

"A long time. A very long time!" Bitterness coated his anger. "No man learns he's been cuckolded without it cutting deep, destroying something inside. Like being made a eunuch! Even with a wife like mine. But I should have known what was going on. The way Kyle—"

"Please, no!"

"That bastard! He should have been named Dorian, all young and handsome on the outside but underneath—"

"Stop it! I told you I was sorry. No need to—"

"What a night!" He gave an exaggerated sigh. "I'll remember every surrender, won't you? Where are you going?"

Without answering she stumbled through the shadowy room to the bathroom. Quickly she shut the door behind her and leaned up against its cold surface, trembling with an emotion that rent a strangled cry of pain from her. She hunched up, shivering. Hurt and humiliation tore at her insides. She put a clenched fist against her mouth. How had it happened? It couldn't be! No! No! But her sobbing denial was empty. There was nothing she could draw upon to lessen the shame, to change the truth that Bud had made love to her throughout the night not out of any deep feeling for her, but motivated by a revengeful hatred for Kyle!

# *Twenty*

Bud rented a car to take them back to Denver. Lori put Lang in the front with Bud and she sat in the back holding Kee. Since she had emerged from the bathroom dressed in her wrinkled, torn jumpsuit, she had not looked directly at Bud or spoken to him.

Once he had touched her arm and she had swung on him like a wildcat. "Don't touch me—ever!"

His eyes narrowed and lost their color to gray slate. He opened his mouth to say something and then clamped it shut. With controlled detachment, he organized their departure and limited his conversation to the children.

All the way back Lori stared without seeing the scenes that had given her pleasure such a short time ago. She would have to leave. It was all over. Even the children could not keep her in such an appalling situation. It was more than she could endure—for anyone! Even now, staring at the back of his head, she remembered how her hands had lain there, pressing him forward to meet her moist half-parted lips. She closed her eyes tightly to capture tears that sprang hotly under searing lids. She had to get away—far away!

When they reached 9801 Packard Road, they discovered a package waiting in the mailbox. A small box. In an innocuous brown wrapper. No postage. No markings.

"Is—is that 'it'?" she gasped as he pulled it out of the roadside box, addressing him directly for the first time.

"I don't know. Your name is on it. Let's go inside. Then we'll find out."

Please, let it be! The prayer was a continuous supplication as she bounded up the stairs, hurrying Lang Su along in front of her. Oh, please let it be! Some sanity would come back into her life if the pretense was over—and Kyle was safe!

When Bud thrust the package into her hands, she nearly dropped it. Then she handled it gingerly as if it were too precious or dangerous to open up in a normal fashion. "I can't!" She handed it back to him. "You—you open it."

Bud gave a snort of disgust, but she could tell from the way his hands tensed that he was not feeling as casual about the whole thing as he pretended. He pulled the paper away from an unmarked cardboard box and then opened it. "Damn it!" he swore, staring at the contents.

"What—what is it?"

"It's for you all right. It's your goddamn tape!" And with another curse, he tossed a cassette tape at her. "Your precious Kyle has sent you a message."

"From Kyle! This is really from Kyle?" Her mouth went dry.

"Have you forgotten the scene you threw about wanting a tape?" he asked sarcastically. "I told you I'd try. Well, here it is! I can imagine what kind of tender message Kyle has sent you." His mouth twisted in a sardonic curve. "Too bad, it's twenty-four hours late to be received with your usual dedication. Somehow I think last night's events may put an ironic twist on his remarks. Well, let's hear what he has to say." He took out the car key. "There's a tape deck in that rented car, we can—"

"No! It's mine!" She grabbed the car keys, and like a child trying to protect a present from a bully, she hugged the tape and fled down the back steps to the garage. As she locked the car doors, she gasped breathlessly and wondered if Bud was going to follow her. She waited but he did not appear. Then fumbling with nervous fingers, she turned the ignition and inserted the cassette tape. As she pushed the on button, he was there!

His voice was slightly distorted in the recording but it was clear enough. He spoke slowly and evenly, as if he knew the agitated state of her mind and wanted her to understand perfectly what he had to say. "By the time you receive this, I hope the authorities have accepted the truth—that I know nothing of Lois Brandon's illicit activities or her plans to continue her operations stateside. If such plans are delivered to you—in her name—you can free me! I hate to put you in this position, dear Lori. I gave you up once, because . . . because I loved you too much to drag you along through the muck of these war years. But now it looks as if I may make it . . . without having my brains shot away . . . or losing half of my body in a fox hole. We may have a future after all. Dear Lori, I must ask you to do this for me. Please get the evidence that will bring me back. I love you. I want you. I—" His voice broke then. With tears in her eyes, she waited for his next words but the tape ran out, making a clicking noise as it shut off. She stared at the silent tape deck for a long time. *Oh, Kyle. Kyle. You don't know what you're asking! Why didn't you send this sooner?*

Then leaning her head back against the seat, she closed her eyes and played the tape over and over. At last she took it out, slipped it into her pocket, and returned to the house.

Lang Su was waiting for her in the kitchen. "Lowie come back?" It was a question that asked for reassurance. The child stood motionless in the middle of the floor, her little arms and legs rigid.

"Yes, I'm back." She took her hand and they walked upstairs.

Bud was just coming out of the nursery bedroom. "Well?" he demanded abruptly as he confronted them on the balcony.

Lori gave him a direct stare that might have been interpreted as "Go to hell!"

"I supposed you believe every word he said. He's lying through his teeth and you know it!"

"Lowie back!" volunteered Lang, instinctively trying to stem heightened emotions swirling around her.

"For how long?" he snarled. A leathery expression contained no softness as he tried to stare her down.

"For as long as it takes—to prove Kyle's innocence." Her voice was so controlled it amazed her. But as she brushed by him, pulling Lang into their bedroom, she slammed the door in his face with all the force of uncontrollable hysterics. Damn him! Damn him!

They went back into the old routine, perfected during

their early antagonistic days. Lori stayed away from the kitchen, family room, and nursery whenever his presence was in evidence. She ate alone or with the children, refused to leave the house, and spent her time on the deck or in the solarium.

Bud continued his early morning golf games, and since Lori refused to leave the house, the grocery shopping fell to him. He was gone when the front doorbell chimed unexpectedly one morning, less than a week after their return from the mountains.

When Lori heard it, she felt a familiar surge of panic that drew all moisture from her throat. With Kee perched on one hip and Lang like a shadow at her side, she slipped back the night lock on the front door and opened it.

Two women stood there, perfectly recognizable from the photo in Bud's room.

"Hello. Is Buddy home?" The beautiful one addressed Lori with a smile. But Lori had the satisfaction of seeing Brandy's eyes narrow as her gaze flickered over the two children.

"He's out . . . playing golf."

Audrey gave a nervous laugh. "That's my brother. I think all doctors must pledge themselves to that little white ball when they take the Hippocratic oath." She held out her hand. "I'm Audrey Brandon. We thought it was about time to meet you, *Lois*. Bud has had you too long to himself."

"And I'm Brandy Bishop." Copper ringlets framed her petite face. "A friend of Bud's. It's nice to meet you."

"Brandy and I were planning a trip from the West Coast to New York when I received a brief postcard from my brother finally letting us know of his whereabouts. On the spur of the moment we decided to interrupt our flight in Denver and see if we could hunt him up."

"I'm not crazy about the East this time of year anyway," confessed Brandy with a suggestive smile that said New York could wait indefinitely. "I've been wanting to meet you, Lois, for a long time."

Audrey shifted her weight. "May we come in?"

# *Twenty-one*

Audrey's green-gray eyes matched Bud's in intensity, and Lori felt herself being peeled, layer by layer, down to her very deceitful soul. "Yes, come—come in," she stammered, thinking, Oh, my God! And the next second she wondered if she might have said it aloud in her usual unconscious manner.

She should have taken them upstairs to the lobbylike living room, but she was so utterly distracted that she had no purposeful thought in her head.

The family room was in its usual "pigpen" decor, and her visitors stepped around Kee's playpen and over the latest jumble of toys that Bud had bought or won at the amusement park.

"Won't you sit down?" suggested Lori with dry lips, flushing as Brandy's slender arm reached out and removed some rumpled baby clothes from the couch. Fortunately there were no wet diapers in the bunch.

"We didn't know about the children," said Audrey with sanguine sweetness, but her smile didn't reach her eyes as she looked at Kee. He had pulled himself to his feet and was grinning affably at everyone. A pearly edge of his first tooth was shining brightly.

Lang continued to finger Lori's pant-leg, peering around as if it were some kind of protective barrier. Lori patted her head reassuringly while she stilled an impulse to bound from the room.

"No, we hadn't heard," said Brandy with more open honesty. "Bud hasn't been much of a correspondent these last few years. I don't know why he wanted to keep you so much to himself. We were all hurt when we didn't get to meet you after the wedding—and now the children. Did you bring them back with you?"

175

Careful, now, cautioned an inner voice. Either one of these women were sharp enough to rend the charade to shreds. Why didn't Bud get here? Stay with the facts as much as possible and leave out the rest, ordered some rational part of her confused thinking. "This is Kee. He's nine months and very bright. We're sure he was saying Bud's name yesterday. Every time he came near, Kee would say, 'Buh, Buh.' " She smiled proudly as any ordinary parent might. "And this is Lang Su, also very precocious for a six-year-old. And very pretty, too," Lori winked at the little girl, who was well aware of the trembling in Lori's rigid body. The child was an excellent reader of body language, and Lori's smiles and nice words hadn't fooled her one bit. Lori didn't like these women and Lang knew it. Consequently, she gave them her flat, blank stare as they tried to draw her into some conversation.

"You should see Bud with them," babbled Lori, trying to rush into the pointed silence. "Talk about a proud father." She gave a high-pitched laugh and then gasped for breath. Damn, where was Bud?

Brandy and   udrey shot a quick look at each other. It was clearly readable—Is this the ninny Bud followed halfway around the world?

"I can't quite see Buddy in that role," responded Audrey, dryly. "But of course he was never predictable, was he, Brandy?"

"No." And for a moment a cloud dulled her beautiful blue eyes. "But he's always been good with children. I remember watching him in the pediatric wards."

"Are you a doctor, too?" Lori wasn't just keeping the conversation away from dangerous areas, but was under some kind of compulsion to find out everything she could about this woman who brought such a lover's gaze to Bud's eyes.

She *was* lovely. Her hair was that rich brown with reddish overtones—the kind expensive hair colorings promise but never deliver. Her features were petite and her figure small, but shapely. Lori felt colorless and gangling just looking at her.

"No, I dropped out of medical school after a couple of

years and went to Europe. I decided I really didn't like sick people and I thought . . ." Her voice trailed off.

Audrey's quick voice cut in. "She thought one doctor in a family was enough. You see, she was going to marry Buddy.'"

Lori had the satisfaction of saying, "Yes, I know. Perhaps things would have turned out differently if you had stayed and looked after—your interests." There was a feminine dig in the words.

Brandy's face reflected the critical implication and her laugh was superficial. "Yes, perhaps, but then, Lois, it might not have worked out so well for you."

"Please call me Marty. Bud does." It was foolish for Lori to feel like the antagonist in this situation. She had not married Bud. She had not run off to the Orient with him, taking him away from his sister and sweetheart . . . there was no reason to get her own emotions in the middle. Protection of the children was her only concern. Why should she bait Brandy or defend Bud's choice of a wife? It was his dirty puddle, let him lie in it. Damn him, where was he, anyway?

"I do hope it won't put you out if we stay with you and Bud a few days," Audrey was saying. "It's been ages since we've had a good visit with Buddy, and we do want to see some of this marvelous country. Maybe we could all take some camping trips—" Then her gaze slid to the children. "Someone could come in and care for Kee and Lang."

"That would be fun," lied Lori, knowing that the idea was utterly ridiculous. Most likely Bud would take off for the mountains and end up sharing a sleeping bag with the luscious Brandy while she stayed with the kids and waited for Lois's package to show up.

At that moment Kee came to her rescue by picking up his gourd rattle and banging it on his playpen with such force that further conversation was discouraged.

"Why don't you go up to the deck and enjoy the scenery?" yelled Lori over the banging. "I'll bring you up some coffee."

Both nodded in relief, glancing at the happy baby as if he were showing very bad manners and should be reprimanded. With a slight shrug of her shoulders Audrey seemed to dismiss the situation as another mess her baby brother had gotten himself into.

Lori took as long with the coffee as she could; anxious thoughts darted in and out with the speed of droning mosquitoes. What was this next complication going to demand? She knew she couldn't hold up before a constant audience, especially one that was as personally aggressive as these two women. The family unit they had been mimicking was not strong enough to withstand the kind of emotional pressure that live-in guests would bring to it. Bud would insist on maintaining the charade until he secured Kee's adoption, then he would be willing to tell all. Lori tried to visualize Brandy's face as she learned the truth. And a different kind of despair made her hands tremble and click the coffee mugs together. She knew that the beautiful Brandy would be willing to accept a ready-made family if Bud came with it.

"Lowie hurt?" asked Lang gravely, putting down the cookie she had been munching.

Easing her intense expression, Lori leaned down and kissed her forehead. "Lori's fine—just thinking."

"You don't like them."

Lori formed her lips to lie and then relaxed them into a smile. "Not much. But Bud does."

"Does what?" His voice made her jump, spilling the coffee.

"Oh, I didn't hear you come in. Thank God you finally came back."

He raised one eyebrow. "Finally? What are you talking about. I didn't go my usual eighteen holes." Then he reacted to the tenseness in her face. "What's up?"

"We have houseguests . . . your sister and Brandy."

All color drained from his face, leaving his tan complexion without a rosy undertone. "Brandy?"

Lori felt sick to her stomach. She deposited the tray in his hands. "They're up on the deck, waiting to say hello."

But she was wrong. Apparently they had seen Bud drive in and had come to greet him.

"Buddy!" squealed Audrey as she caught sight of her brother and grabbed him in a squeeze around the neck while he still held the full tray in front of him. "Let me look at you. What a rascal you are! Running off to Colorado after all those years out of the country!"

Bud shrugged with a half laugh. "You look great, Sis."

"Hello, Philip," Brandy said shyly, standing back, allowing him a full view of her loveliness and the tender, appealing expression on her face.

"Hello," Bud responded smoothly enough, but there was a tattletale betrayal in the slight clicking of the cups as his grip on the tray became less steady. Then he set it down and Lori knew he was going to take Brandy in his arms.

She turned away from the lovers' reunion, and with Lang's hand in her own, she went into the family room and took Kee from his playpen.

"Let's go take care of the plants," she said with a brittle brightness that threatened to crumple. It didn't take an expert in psychology to predict what was going to happen now that Brandy was back on the scene. There was no real wife standing between the sweethearts. Even if Brandy didn't realize it, Bud did. He would be more impatient than ever to end this charade.

"Well, so will I!" said Lori as she filled a watering can. "So will I!" But she sat down on the floor with the children and drew them both to her as she buried her head against them. Kee thought it was some kind of game of peekaboo and he began to giggle, putting his pudgy little hands on Lori's face and trying to raise it up. Lang's little body stiffened in the old familiar way, and with a wiseness beyond her years, she entreated, "Lowie stay. Lowie not go away."

"No, I won't go away," promised Lori, realizing that adults lie to children when the pain of reality becomes too great for the human spirit to withstand the truth. She gave them both a squeeze as if the whole matter had been settled. "Now, let's see what new flowers we can find today."

As they went through their morning ritual in the solarium, Lori chattered to Lang about removing dead leaves, shifting some pots into different light, and smelling all the fragrant blossoms.

They had almost finished when Bud came in and said he was taking the ladies into town for lunch. She just nodded without really looking at him. As Brandy appeared in the doorway, he came closer to Lori, bending his head so it looked as if he were planting a kiss somewhere near her ear.

"Move my stuff into your room," he whispered.

She jerked her face around to his, her eyes round and a retort lurching to her lips. But the words never came out. He kissed her soundly, effectively cutting off any protest she was about to make. He never quite closed his eyes for the kiss, and the message in them was quite readable—"Do it!"

After he released her, he bent down and scooped Kee up from the floor. His tummy and knees were black from scooting about under the tables. "Tell your mother you need a diaper change and some clean clothes." And then had the audacity to deposit him in her arms with a wide grin. He turned to Brandy, "Shall we go?"

With an affectionate ruffling of Lang's hair as he passed her, he left without another glance in Lori's direction, taking Brandy's arm as they disappeared through the doorway.

Furious, Lori reached for a flower pot and raised it in the air to hurl it through the doorway after them. Only a tiny gasp from Lang stayed her arm. Looking down at the frightened child, Lori set the plant down again. Neither of the lovers was worth any scene that would disturb Lang.

"It's all right, honey." She took the little hand. "I'm afraid your new father is something of an ass!"

"Ass?"

"Donkey—hee-haw—hee-haw."

Lang laughed at the funny noises and Lori let herself chuckle with her. Anger lessened in the joy of seeing the shine back in Lang's eyes. How dare he kiss her like that? Move his clothes, indeed! Wait until he got back!

"Let's go play in the sand pile," Lori said as she changed Kee's diaper but left on his soiled suit.

At the back of the house, behind and under the porch deck, some sandlike dirt had been left by the workmen, and in this small area, surrounded by large boulders, Lang spent many hours filling baby jars and building sand villages.

Kee sat alone easily, so after he had thoroughly tasted the dirt, he banged on some empty cans or emptied out Lang's jars, sometimes before she wanted his help.

Lori had a favorite spot where she sat and leaned her head back against a smooth rock. Daily sunbathing had tanned her face and brought golden sunstreaks to her hair. Soothing warm sunlight caressed her body and she felt her anger and anxiety slipping away. More than once she had given up trying to decide on a future course of action and had allowed herself to be manipulated by events. Today seemed to be another one of those times. What could she do about the intrusion of Bud's womenfolk into this explosive situation? She was caught in an impersonation that continued to carry her along toward destruction. If the children hadn't come between her and the memories of Kyle, she could anticipate the end of the charade with some hope in her heart that the past would be renewed when he gained his safety. Even though she could not trust Bud and his accusations against Kyle, he had managed to fade her water-colored memories of her love affair, and she was afraid the Kyle she had known and loved was not the same one who had followed at Lois's heels.

Leaning back against the boulder with her eyes closed, she might have momentarily dozed for she did not hear footsteps upon the back stairs. It was an inner sense that made her open her eyes with a start and look up at the railing.

The blond ski bum grinned down at her. "Hi," said Rex. "May I play in the sand pile, too?"

Without waiting for an answer, he quickly walked around the corner of the porch and came along the rough path to where she sat.

"What are you delivering today?" she demanded without smiling, trying to still the spurt of panic that his presence had brought. So he had come at last. The moment that she had imagined was to be enacted. It felt like blows beating on the inside of her. She braced against the truth —that her time with the children was up. It couldn't be. Her hands dug into the dirt at her side.

He still did not look like the law. He wore faded jeans

and a blue work shirt. His tight pants showed no bulges of a gun, or the handcuffs she expected to see.

Casually he sat down on the ground beside Lang and made some appreciative remarks about her mud pies. Then his clear blue eyes looked up at Lori. "And how's the orchid lady today?"

It took real effort to make her stiff lips say, "Fine."

He cocked his handsome head to one side. "You wouldn't lie to the King, would you?"

Then instead of answering, she made a pretense of piling up some cans for Kee to knock over. She'd be damned if he was going to lead her into any open-ended questions. "What do you want?" She was too uptight to play games with him. "I know you're a detective."

"Relax, pretty lady. I just came to pay a social call—and find out who your visitors were this morning."

She studied him then, wanting to ask if he had observed every move she and Bud had made the past week. For some reason the thought disconcerted her as much as the discovery of someone peeping in her window. He must have witnessed their family scenes at the parks and zoos. She wondered if she had appeared as foolish to him as she now felt. What a laugh he must have had over her playing the role of motherhood.

"Ouch," he said. "Those dagger looks of yours are cutting me to shreds. I just want to know who the two women are who arrived in a taxi this morning."

"Bud's sister and an old friend of the family, Brandy Bishop."

"An old girl friend, I take it."

"How do you know?"

"I saw the way she was hanging on him when they left."

"Don't you have something better to do with your time like—like—" and a mocking voice inside completed the sentence, "like pulling dead women out of rivers?"

"It wasn't a river."

Horrified she realized she had said the words aloud.

He reached out and touched her hand. "You look like a doe facing a man with a shotgun. Why don't we talk this thing out? Maybe I can help you—Lori."

Her mouth went dry and she tried to swallow the thick

lump in her throat. "You knew—you knew that first day—" She jutted out her chin as angry tears threatened to fill her eyes. "I hope you enjoyed your fun and games. You must have had a good laugh over my bungling impersonation. What did you want to find out anyway—you already knew I wasn't Mrs. Brandon."

"We weren't certain Dr. Brandon had convinced you to carry out the impersonation. It was important to be sure in case the information we want came into your hands."

"Well, it hasn't!" she flared. "I'm beginning to think there never was a package in the first place. Jade! Smuggling ring! I think Mrs. Brandon was leading all of you around by the nose. She probably never got anything out of the country after all."

"We're positive she did. She wasn't the kind to let a lucrative business like hers disintegrate just because she had to move her location of operation. She was ready to leave the country, and we know she wouldn't try to take that kind of damaging evidence out with her. If she had not been killed, we could have stuck to her like a coat of glue until she had her new operations set up. Now we'll have to settle for a list of her associates and contacts. I'm convinced that the information has already arrived in Denver. Now where is it, Lori?"

She just glared at him as if the question were an accusation she refused to deny.

"Have you and the good doctor decided to inherit the business and rake in a few million for your own high living?"

"Of course we have. Don't you think I'd make a good Mata Hari?"

He laughed openly at that. "You're right. I don't think you're quite the type. I'm surprised that you were persuaded to go along with this in the first place. You must love Kyle very much."

"Is he really alive?" She was surprised to find the question on her lips. Somewhere deep inside her she did not really believe that Bud had told her the truth.

"As far as I know," said Rex evasively. "But they don't tell us lowly detectives everything."

The same runaround, she thought. There wasn't anyone she could depend on to tell her the complete truth. She was still running blindly in a maze with dead ends facing her in every direction.

Rex reached out and took her hand, holding it firmly. "You have that terrified look in your eyes again. I wish there were some other way, but this is terribly important to a lot of people. Do you think that Brandon's sister and lady friend believe you?"

She shrugged. "I guess so. They didn't like the real Mrs. Brandon even though they had never met her and they didn't like me when they met me, so you might say they're convinced."

"How long are they going to stay?"

"I have no idea. Audrey said they wanted to take some trips into the mountains. In fact, she asked me to come along—suggested we find a baby-sitter for the kids. How would you like a job? You seem to have a different one every time I see you." A wan smile turned up her lips.

"I have a better idea. Let's get the doctor to baby-sit and we'll go to the mountains." His smile was disarming and youthful.

"Really—and me a married woman, too!" Her false indignation melted into a companionable laughter and suddenly she felt refreshed. The tension she felt eased away in the banter of a light flirtation. It was nice to have someone looking at her with such appreciation. In another setting it might have been fun to find out what kind of line he used in his romancing.

As if Lang wanted to join in the merriment of the moment, she squealed and pointed to a deep tunnel she had made in the sand.

"Is that a cave or a tunnel?" asked Rex with the proper amount of appreciation in his tone.

Lang cocked her head to one side in puzzlement. Then Rex repeated the question, only this time he easily used some Vietnamese words for cave and tunnel.

The smile froze on Lori's face. She knew that thousands of American servicemen had served overseas and had picked up a smattering of the language, but in this bizarre situation the coincidence that Rex had the words so readily on his lips was not believable. In an instant the whole picture changed in her mind like a kaleidoscope. What if Rex had been one of the disgruntled young men whom Lois had taken in tow and used in her blackmarketing and smuggling? He could have made it back to the States before her and waited for her to arrive in Denver in some kind of plan to get operations going from here. Then, with her unexpected death, he could have purposefully gotten himself into a position where he could legally be on the premises when the incriminating evidence arrived. Every police force was desperate for young, intelligent men like Rex, and they never had enough undercover men to go around. His dedication to an assignment like this would not be questioned.

If Rex's name was on Lois's list of associates, his protection was going to be as deadly as a black widow spider's web.

As the summer sun overhead slipped behind the blanket of a cloud, the sandbox was bathed in a shadow that matched the one that had suddenly chilled her to the bone.

# Twenty-two

Rex thought moving Bud's things into her room was a good idea. "Give the appearance of true marital bliss," he said.

"And what kind of bliss is it supposed to give me?"

"Come on, Pretty Lady, you don't really object to having a prince charming share quarters with you."

"When I want a man to share my bedroom, I'll do the inviting," she spat.

"I thought, perhaps, that you had already done the inviting . . ." He left the sentence hanging.

There was no way he could have known, but even as mental reassurances came to mind, something denied it. He knew everything else! Nothing seemed to have slipped by his surveillance. Their every move had been monitored. He probably knew every detail of their two-day picnic. A searing hot flush rose in her neck and cheeks. Then she lashed out at him as her discomfort brought a roaring to her ears. "If you followed us to Estes, you were probably the one who ran us off the road!" Hearing the accusation out loud gave it credence. "You were the one in that four-wheel drive! Don't shake your head at me. It could have been you. Someone ran us off the road. If you were sneaking around, trying to find an opportunity to kill us—" she was talking wildly.

"Take it easy! I wasn't accusing you of anything. And I certainly didn't have anything to do with that incident. In fact, we didn't know where you had gone. I had my buns in the fire for letting you get out of town without my knowing it. Believe me, I was mighty glad to see you come back." He slipped his arm around her shoulders. "Please, don't look so upset. I was only joking. I didn't realize—"

"Realize what?"

"Nothing! Nothing! I was out of line." Then he cleared his throat in a businesslike manner. "But I think you'd better put up appearances for your houseguests."

She felt foolish for having reacted so emotionally. "You're right, and for the great cause I'll let Bud move into my bedroom, while I share the nursery bed with Lang."

Rex grinned. "I think that will be satisfactory to everyone—except Bud, perhaps."

"Don't worry about him. Most likely he'll be in someone else's most of the night anyway." She hoped the words sounded casual and not vindictive.

Then she discovered why Rex had volunteered to help move Bud's things. It was an easy way for him to search every personal item. Quickly and efficiently Bud's coats, shirts, hair brushes, and toiletries went under close scrutiny.

"Would you like to examine all my things too?" asked Lori caustically.

"Not a bad idea," responded Rex and immediately ran his fingers around in a box of dusting powder.

"Is it something that small?" asked Lori, surprised.

"Could be. It doesn't take much paper to list names and addresses, passwords, pick-up point, and the like." But his professional efforts didn't turn up anything—except Lang's adoption papers. Bud had put them back in the battered suitcase, either because he didn't care if Lori saw them or because he thought she wouldn't be looking there again.

Rex scrutinized the papers carefully. Lori swallowed nervously. Would he spot it for the forgery it was? She hoped Sister Marie Elena's talents ran along forgery lines, and the Brandons' signatures looked authentic.

"That's funny."

"What?" asked Lori, her chest burning because she was holding her breath.

"The two kids! We didn't know the Brandons had adopted *two* children. The Thai officials told us they had adopted a baby boy."

"Oh, yes. Both of them had the same mother," volunteered Lori quickly, perhaps too quickly.

Rex raised his gaze from the paper and studied her. "Mela Phamn?"

Lori nodded, feeling as if his stare were some kind of lie detector gauge that could register the honesty of her answers.

"Who took her out of Saigon?"

"Mela's sister, Mrs. Holmes."

"Was that why she was here that day?"

Lori felt the gauge waver as she lied, "I really don't know what she and Bud talked about that day. I know Lang was afraid of her." She added that bit of truth, hoping to get him off the track. She wondered how firmly the sister would protect Lang's adoption if Rex decided to pursue its authenticity. If he proved the papers false, Lang could be taken away immediately and given to someone else through legal channels. What the new uprooting would do to a sensitive child like Lang, Lori did not want to think about. It was better that she remain here and get used to a new mother—like Brandy—than be sent to another institution until placement was made.

Her eyes must have shown a new hardness because Rex looked away from her and said casually, "Too bad Mrs. Holmes got herself killed before I could talk to her."

"Was it an accident—or did someone—?" Why did she ask that, she thought horrified. It was an answer she really didn't want to know. "Never mind," she added hurriedly. "It's really no concern of mine."

Rex was studying her with a quizzical expression and a hint of amusement on his lips. "Oh, your precious doctor is safe enough. I guess if anyone killed her, it was me."

"You?"

"It sometimes happens in the line of—business. That afternoon I saw her leave here and decided to stop her for questioning. My unmarked car must have frightened her, or she had good reason for not wanting to be questioned by the police. Anyway, she tried to outrun me in a speed chase. It was raining hard, and slippery—" He shrugged. "She missed a curve and went right into the creek."

"That's why you were there—in the picture."

"I was so busy trying to get her out I didn't notice that

photographer when I showed my ID to a state patrolman. If I had, I would have smashed his camera and his nose for blowing my cover."

"Did you find anything—in the car?"

Rex laughed openly. "You're one hell of an actress, Lori. If you mean your purse, no. We found it in her apartment. We'll save it for you—if you ever decide you want to go back to being a Kansas City teacher."

"It's my property and I'll thank you to return it to me now."

" 'Fraid we can't. It's incriminating evidence."

"Of what?" Her ears roared with a thumping that suddenly made her heart sound like a bass drum. "If what you and Bud say is true, the authorities have been in on this charade from the first. I am cooperating with the law."

"Let's say we will have to reserve final judgment about your cooperation until this thing is finished. *If* the information about Lois's business has not arrived, and *if* you turn it over to me when it does, you may have your purse back. Then you can become Lori Martin, if you want to."

"Of course I want to!" Her words were almost a shout. "I'm not going to be Lois Brandon forever."

"Then you and the good doc better come up fast with what we want or we'll throw the book at you as accessories." Although his tone was apologetic, there was a firmness in it that was underlined with cords of steel. "Kyle swears that what we want is here."

"Then why don't you bring Kyle here and let him find it?"

"You would like that wouldn't you?"

Why her lips wouldn't move in a quick affirmative, she couldn't understand. It took real effort to say, "Of course I would but . . ."

Rex waited, leaning back against the dresser in his usual lounging fashion. "Yes?"

"If everything I've heard about him is true, then he's not the same person I loved. But everyone"—and her direct gaze included the blond detective—"everyone may be lying to me. He may only have been working with Lois because it was his job. Not—not anything more. He sent me a tape, you know?" The question was only perfunctory. Rex knew everything that came or went in this house. "He says he's innocent and he's depending upon me to handle the evidence."

"And if he's clean and he hasn't changed, then what?"

"Then I want—to be with him again." And at last, the old familiar flood of affection swept over her. Oh, Kyle, I need you! How I need you!

"If he's freed before Lois's package is found, do you think you could persuade him to track down the information?"

"Probably not," she said honestly. She had never had that kind of control over Kyle.

"But you'd be willing to carry through?"

"Of course," she snapped. "But I'll be out of here in a minute as soon as this fiasco is over."

"You didn't leave when Bud left you free those few days."

"Well, you ought to know, sneaking around outside watching my every move." And then the truth of her words hit her. "You were the one who scared me to death sneaking around the house when he was gone."

His sheepish look confirmed it.

"And the telephone, too!" She was angry now. "Why you—"

"Sorry, but I didn't know where the good doctor had gone. I didn't know whether you were going to take off after him . . . or stay."

"If the King is so smart, he should have known that I wasn't going to abandon the kids," she said with some acidity. "Once they are secure with Bud, I'll be on the next plane back to Kansas City, with my house-sitting membership card torn in shreds. As I understand it, once the authorities get the goods on Lois's operations, Bud's adoption of the children will be finalized."

"That's the deal."

"And Kyle will be freed!"

"If his name isn't on that list—as he claims. Of course, he's not quite clear with the army either. Although he was on an assignment, no one seems to be quite certain just how much leeway he was supposed to have in associating himself with Lois. A lot of his activities don't make sense.

Anyway, he seems to have found better things to do than fight a war."

"Lots of young men felt that way."

"But some of us fought in it, anyway," he countered.

Now was the time for her to ask him some questions to prove her suspicion that he was one of Lois's disgruntled GIs who liked money better than they did playing soldier.

He must have sensed which direction the conversation was heading because he quickly said, "I guess I'd better get out of your bedroom before your houseguests and husband return to find you entertaining a gentleman caller."

Her retort was swallowed as they both heard voices below in the hall.

"Too late, it seems." He straightened up. "Shall we compromise your reputation, Mrs. Brandon?"

"No!" And the whisper contained a new kind of panic. How could she ever face the disgust in Brandy's eyes if such a sordid affair seemed to be taking place right under Bud's nose. "What'll we do? They can't find us here."

Since her bedroom door was clearly visible from the family room below, there was no way for him to reach either of the doors on the ground floor. "You'll have to go out on the deck and down the outside staircase."

"All right, but how do I get there without being seen leaving this room?" He was whispering too, standing close to her, and he casually put his arm around her shoulders. "Quit trembling. They're not the firing squad, you know."

"You haven't seen Bud when he's angry. He'll be furious. Why did I ever let you in the house!"

"Maybe you didn't have a choice." A quiet firmness accented the truth of the statement.

"Well, I have a choice now," she flared. "If you embarrass Bud or me like this, you'll never get what you want from either of us!"

He tightened his arm around her. "Why don't you trust me, Lori? I'm not going to let you get hurt. Relax, there's no reason to panic. They won't find me in your bedroom."

"You've probably had a lot of practice in situations like this," she couldn't refrain from saying.

He laughed quietly at that. "Now you know what I'm king of."

Her nerves were stretched too taut for such light banter. "What are we going to do?" She could tell from the volume of voices that everyone was in the family room, right below her door. They might all troop upstairs any minute, to visit the nursery, or to get settled in their bedrooms.

"Go down and invite them into the solarium, to see something special. I'll slip outside and wait until they leave the solarium before I go by the solarium windows on the outside balcony. Understand?"

She nodded and he gave her a quick squeeze. "Hang in there, Pretty Lady. One of these days we'll be home free."

As she stepped out onto the balcony, three pairs of eyes looked up. She hoped to heaven that Rex was out of view.

"Oh, hello, honey," called Bud. "Are the kids down for their nap?"

She nodded. "Yes, but—there's something I want you to see." And as she quickly went down the circular steps, she searched frantically for some idea of what that "something" might be.

They all looked at her expectantly as she came into the family room. Bud's eyes went quickly to her empty hands, obviously expecting her to be holding the "something." Irritation mingled instantly with disappointment as he saw they were empty. "Well, what is it? What has put all that excitement into your voice?" Maybe he hoped the mysterious delivery had been made while they were gone to lunch.

"It's—it's out in the solarium. Come on, I'll show you."

With a little laugh from Brandy and a shrug of Audrey's shoulders, they trooped after her.

Her eyes frantically swept around the room. "Now where is it?" she babbled, knowing she must look like a stupid fool. "Oh, yes, here it is." She made a dive for the same plant that Rex had taken the orchid from that first day. Despite the rough handling, the plant had continued to thrive and had produced another pink-tinged white orchid, smaller than the first one, but lovely nonetheless.

Lori plucked the blossom and quickly held it out to Brandy. "It just opened up this morning. Lang wanted you to have it. She thinks you're very pretty," Lori gushed.

Bud's eyebrows went up. "How very thoughtful of Lang," he said dryly, while Brandy murmured all the polite responses.

Audrey obviously thought this ado about a flower was ridiculous, and her opinion of her brother's wife reached a new low.

Lori didn't care what Audrey was thinking. She just hoped that Rex had been able to make his escape outside by now, and could go by the solarium windows as soon as they went into one of the other rooms. Audrey helped achieve this.

"If you'll show us what rooms are ours, Buddy, we'll freshen up," she said, addressing her brother as if his wife were too unreliable to handle any social graces.

'Sure, Sis. You can take the hall bedrooms. We are using the balcony ones for the nursery and our room." His glance caught Lori's for affirmation. She nodded slightly. "I'll bring up your things while Marty shows you the way."

As if Brandy had sensed Bud's presence in his old room, she chose that one, while Audrey settled in the unused bedroom across the hall.

As quickly as she could, Lori returned to her bedroom and breathed an audible sigh of relief when she found it empty.

Bud came in right behind her and shut the door. "What in the hell is going on?"

# Twenty-three

"What—what do you mean?" she stammered.

"Marty, you are the world's worst actress. I can't imagine anyone else who could make such an idiotic production out of a flower."

"Then why didn't you choose someone else for this farce?" she lashed back and started to flounce away.

He grabbed her hand and swung her back. "It's too late to change the casting. Now what's up? What was that little melodrama about?"

There was no reason to be afraid of telling Bud the truth. They had talked about Rex when Lori showed him the newspaper article about Mrs. Holmes's death. Bud had said that he hadn't known Rex was a detective the day he delivered the plants. Bud would be interested to know how close a watch Rex had been keeping on their activities.

For some cautious reason, Lori wanted to keep him in the dark about it, just in case she might have to draw on that protection. So she jutted out her chin and said flatly, "That detective Rex was here searching the house. I didn't think your houseguests would be too impressed, so I made a fool of myself while he got away."

"Searching the house?" Bud's eyes had that cold gray sheen to them, and she instinctively backed away as his gaze cut into hers.

"They—he thinks that we're trying to double-cross the authorities," she said hastily, "and keep Lois's lucrative business for ourselves." Then the next question rushed out of its own volition. "Did you ever see Rex in Vietnam?"

He looked at her as if she had gone daffy. "No, why?"

Her speculations were too vague to parade in front of

Bud's cold logic. She shrugged. "I don't know. Everybody else seems to have some connection over there. Anyway, he helped put your things in here. And I moved some of mine into the nursery. I think you'll find my bed quite comfy . . . and your lady friend won't suspect a lack of conjugal rights."

"I'm sorry, Marty," he finally had the decency to say. "I didn't invite them. It's a hell of a time for them to show up. If it weren't for the kids—"

"Yes?"

"I've had enough of this damn charade and I'm ready to clear the air with the truth, but—"

"But you're afraid Brandy might not want to go along with it."

"She hasn't had a chance to know the children yet. I know this isn't easy for you, but I can depend on you to wait it out."

She wished she could deny it. Pride made her want to throw a denial in his face. How dare he take her for granted? And it was this bitterness that made her say, "For the children and Kyle, I'll put up with the situation for a little longer."

And with that parting thrust, she banged shut the connecting door between them and promptly paid for this bit of childish tantrum as two pairs of dark eyes flipped open and she was a mother again.

That evening Bud informed her that they would be dressing for dinner. He had spent most of the afternoon working his culinary artistry.

"I think I can find something suitable for the occasion," she retorted.

"Wear your long white jersey," he ordered. "It shows off your figure and coloring, but you really need a decent string of pearls to wear with it."

"I wouldn't dare wear my real jewels. There are too many thieves about these days."

Perhaps as a gesture of defiance when eight o'clock arrived she still hadn't dressed. She had fed the children early and taken them up to the nursery. Bud had been giving the children their nightly bath and bedtime romp. After a day playing outside Lori had been exhausted and only too willing to start this new nightly tradition.

But tonight he had not shown up in the nursery even for a good-night kiss. She doubted if Kee was aware of his absence but perceptive little Lang was.

"Where's Bud?" she asked as Lori tucked her in the big nursery bed with the promise that she would sleep there with her.

"He's busy with the two ladies," explained Lori, trying to keep the gravel out of her voice. "He'll be up later," she promised, and vowed silently to make him fulfill the promise.

As a defiant gesture she put on a long blue cotton skirt and red peasant blouse. He needn't think he could dictate what clothes she was going to wear. She certainly didn't feel like white jersey and pearls—real or otherwise.

As she descended the stairs, delicious aromas greeted her nostrils. Bud was certainly rising to the occasion, she thought with a bitter twist to her lips.

Drinks and hors d'oeuvres had been set out in the dining room, and Lori could see Brandy through the arched doorway as she finished setting a modernistic glass-top table. This would be the first time that they had used the large room. Apparently the long buffet contained a set of chartreuse dishes and some silverware. A brown tablecloth with multicolored napkins matched the splashes of color in the surrealistic wall hangings.

Brandy looked up as Lori came in. "This is a lovely room, Marty, and the table service is just perfect." Brandy was smiling warmly, looking gorgeous in a green hostess pantsuit.

The compliment reached Lori as an insult to her own good taste because such choices were not in line with her preferences. She would have chosen an ivory damask cloth, white china, and a traditional pattern of silverware, but she smiled her "thank you." Then she returned the social amenities by complimenting Brandy on her appearance.

Audrey was in the kitchen with Bud, and they could hear her voice raised in protest about the lack of help. "It's ridiculous that you haven't found someone to do the work."

"Help is hard to get," responded Bud. "Besides, no

one can cook like your kid brother. Come on. Everything is ready."

Lori was certain the food was excellent but she didn't taste any of it. Sitting at the foot of the table, she was slightly out of the circle of conversation as both women turned toward the head of the table where Bud was looking perfectly at ease and handsome in a white dinner jacket. His quick appraisal of Lori's outfit had brought a lift of his eyebrow and a mocking, "You look bright and cheery this evening, Marty."

If they had completely ignored her, she would have been more at ease, but the minute she began to relax, one of the women always turned and fired a quick question at her. It was usually something referring to Lois's past and not her own. As a result her replies were stumbling and so vague that Audrey and Brandy exchanged glances that openly dismissed her as a fool.

Bud ignored the blazing looks she sent him. Fortunately, he did monopolize most of the conversation, which seemed agreeable to everyone. Brandy hung on his every word and gave him the kind of undivided attention that expands every male's chest.

"Do you remember when . . ." was the line used most often, and Lori's stomach tightened against food and wine as she listened to reminiscences about a happy past that openly revealed overtones of regret about the present and future.

Just as she was about to slip into a reverie of her own, Lori was jerked back into the conversation again. "Do you have many friends in Denver, Marty?" asked Brandy, tipping her auburn tresses in Lori's direction.

Lori hastily set down her wineglass, sloshing some of the red liquid over the rim onto the chartreuse cloth. "No —not yet."

"Who was that good-looking fellow waiting outside the solarium this afternoon? He must be special if you don't want to share him with us." A narrowing of her eyes denied the innocence of her question.

Bud stopped with a fork halfway to his mouth and for once the poised Dr. Brandon seemed speechless. Lori rather enjoyed the look on his face and decided to wait out the silence until he found something to say. "Who —who was it, honey?" he stammered.

Wait until he brought up her acting ability again, she thought smugly as she smiled brightly back at him. "Oh, she must have seen Rex." She swung her gaze to Brandy's challenging expression. "He's the one who delivered all of our plants. Some of them haven't done very well." She let her gaze slide back to Bud. "I don't know why, but they had a setback just after we got them. Didn't they, darling?"

He looked ready to choke her, but now that the spotlight was fully on her, she realized that three glasses of wine had given her the courage she needed to do a little manipulating of her own. She turned to Brandy. "If you like his looks we can invite him back and introduce you. Would you like that?"

It was Brandy's turn to flush and stutter, "Oh, no— I—"

Audrey jumped quickly to her defense. "Of course not."

"I'm sorry," apologized Lori, still smiling brightly. "I thought that since she was so interested, maybe—"

Abruptly Bud took the conversation back to "remember when," and shot a demanding look at Lori that she get the smirk off her face.

Maybe it was the wine, or the way Brandy bent her ample bosom in Bud's direction, that brought Lori's mood to a combustion point. She got to her feet before the others had quite finished. She walked down to Bud's end of the table, perhaps swaying just slightly but feeling very light on her feet.

She eased herself down on the arm of his chair and bent over him, giving a gentle caress to a wave of hair that was just long enough to fall over his forehead. "While our guests finish, darling, let's slip up to the nursery. The children missed their bedtime with you. They couldn't understand why you couldn't play with them tonight." She spoke softly enough to sound intimate, but clearly enough to be heard. "I told them you couldn't help it."

Audrey's face registered the implied criticism and

Brandy said stiffly, "I'm sorry, Philip. We didn't intend to keep you from your children."

"It's perfectly all right," said Bud stiffly as he maneuvered Lori off his chair and to her feet and stood up beside her. "They are used to changes in their routine. Aren't they, darling?" And the arm he put around her waist was as rigid as his voice.

His face didn't quite come into focus, so she giggled, letting herself lean up against him. "He's such a good father—and husband."

"Please excuse us for a few minutes. Marty isn't what you would call an experienced drinker. I'm afraid the wine has made her a little light-headed." He gave a little laugh that was supposed to pass for amusement, but Lori felt the barbs underneath it, and as he propelled her out of the room, her giggles died inside her throat.

Even before they were up the stairs, he began to lash out at her. "What in the hell are you trying to do?" Then as she stumbled, he caught her against him. "Why do you drink if you can't handle it?"

"Because there's nothing else to do at a dinner party where I'm treated like—like a piece of furniture. Besides I'm not li—li—drunk!"

A deep chuckle matched the sudden amusement in his eyes. "Try smashed. Well, I guess it's my turn to tuck you in. I'm sorry you didn't enjoy my dinner. I tried to keep the chitchat going at my end of the table. You looked like a trapped fawn every time someone looked at you. I know my sister. If she gets a scent of something false, she'll pry until the whole thing blows."

He maneuvered her into her bedroom, which was no longer hers, and she plopped down on the bed without remembering. The whole room was reeling like a surfboard.

"It's your fault!" she lashed out, sitting up and waving an accusing finger at him. "The way you've been behaving makes me sick!" And once the word was out, Lori realized that was exactly what she was about to be.

She closeted herself in the bathroom until she got rid of the alcohol which her system would not tolerate. Pale and drained, she showered and then made her way quickly into the nursery bedroom. There was no sign of

Bud. He had undoubtedy returned to his guests while she was miserably sick in the bathroom.

She eased herself into bed and gathered Lang into the crook of her body, laying her head against the warm child. Lang stirred and snuggled in closer like a contented puppy.

Sleep evaded her completely, and she heard dance music floating up from the room below. She had no trouble picturing the couple who moved together to the romantically persuasive rhythms.

# Twenty-four

Although Bud tried to keep the two women away from the house as much as possible, their intrusion was a constant burden. Everything had to revolve around their plans and their presence in the house. As in the early days alone with Bud, Lori tried to keep herself and the children in one part of the house while Bud entertained his guests in another, but it was impossible to avoid confrontations that had become openly antagonistic.

Even though Lori knew Brandy was going to be in the winner's circle as soon as Bud satisfied the authorities, Lori determined she would not tolerate their open contempt of Bud's wife and her peculiarities.

The whole situation might have exploded in a real feminine "knock-down-drag-out" if the end of the whole affair had not come as suddenly as it had begun. It was a telephone call that brought the news.

Bud had gotten into the habit of calling her from different excursion points. He might say, "We're in Colorado Springs and will be touring the Air Force Academy this afternoon. Is everything under control?"

She always reassured him with some barbed remark to let him know how nice it was to have the house to herself. "Don't hurry back" was her habitual good-bye, as she tried not to remember what companionship they had once enjoyed.

On this particular outing the trio had gone to Central City with plans to stay and see the opera that was presented in a famous old opera house during the summer. Lori had already put the children down and was restlessly wandering around the house, keeping one eye on a television program that really didn't have her interest. When the telephone rang, she grabbed it with open resentment. If he was calling to tell her what a glorious time they were having, she was going to make it a little less pleasant. But it wasn't Bud. It was Rex.

"Hello, Pretty Lady."

"Oh, Rex," she said eagerly, admitting for the first time how desperately lonely she was. "I'm glad you called."

"Anything wrong?"

"Nothing, and everything!" She gave a thin laugh. "Bud is squiring around his lady friends, and I'm experiencing the 'poor wife left at home with the kids' syndrome."

"They've been hitting the tourist scene pretty steadily, haven't they?"

"You should know if you've been keeping up your snooping act," she countered, but lightly and without vindictiveness. Somehow she liked the idea of someone being that close. "You really aren't as good as you think. Brandy saw you the other day and tried to drop the bombshell at dinner."

"Wow! I bet that was a scene."

"Not really. I just suggested that if she went for your looks, I might be able to arrange an introduction."

"Hey, all right. She looks like a passionate little bundle the King might like to—"

"Down, boy! You'll have to stand in line." This time the levity was coated with bitterness.

Rex picked it up. "Hey, cheer up. Your lonely days are over. Just heard something and called to let you in on it. Kyle will be arriving in Denver in about five hours."

At first her brain refused to take in the words. She heard them but they had no meaning for her, and then when they finally did, her reaction was like that of someone suddenly plunged into shock. Her mouth wouldn't work and her heart seemed to suspend its action.

She must have gasped, for Rex said, "Lori? Lori, are you all right?" He raised his voice to a near yell. Although the words roared in her ears, her response came out as a near whisper, "Kyle?"

"Listen, gal, get ahold of yourself. Do you hear me?"

Her stiff lips were getting back some feeling. "Yes. I I'm just—surprised."

"I shouldn't have told you over the phone. I didn't realize it was going to be such a shock. Are you sure you're all right?"

"I'm fine." Now that the first thrust of the shock was over, all kinds of emotions began surging through her —joy, fear, anticipation, anxiety, and relief. And with the emotions came a myriad of questions.

"Is—is he free? I don't understand. We still don't know where Lois's things are. What—"

"Whoa! I don't know how he worked it, but the Thai officials let him go and the Army guys have withdrawn their charges against him. He is going to be discharged —honorably—at the end of a thirty-day leave. He lost no time buying a ticket to Denver."

"Then everything is settled."

"Not quite. Dr. Brandon is still holding the bag for his wife's illegal affairs. But that needn't concern you or Kyle. You can go back to being Lori Martin now."

"But what about the children? Will they let Bud keep them?"

"If he can come up with the right kind of proof or the evidence the government wants. But it's not your worry anymore. You've done more than enough as it is. How about it? Do you want to meet the returning warrior when he steps off the plane at two forty-five this morning?"

That was like asking if she wanted her favorite dream to come true. Did she want to feel those caressing arms around her again, to feel loved, protected, and wanted? Tears began to bubble down her cheeks. Kyle. Kyle. But would he want her again? Why hadn't he contacted her immediately? "Why didn't he let me know?"

"Maybe he wants to surprise you. I just thought it might be better for you to meet him somewhere else besides that house."

"Yes. Yes, thank you." She didn't want to be Lois Brandon when Kyle walked back into her life. "I would like to go to the airport. Bud should be back by then to stay with the children."

"Good. I'll pick you up about one o'clock. And, Lori . . ."

"Yes?"

"Don't be frightened."

She nodded mechanically as if simple agreement could chase away the flutterings of panic that were already contracting her stomach into a hard knot. After she had put down the receiver, she stared at it for a few moments without moving. When she did, it was like someone sleepwalking. Slowly she went up the circular stairs and mechanically walked out on the deck into a summer's night.

Crisp breezes fresh from the mountains lifted her hair and bathed her flushed face. She leaned against the railing and stared into purple darkness.

Far away patches of city lights stretched along the horizon, and a smattering of stars lent twinkling illumination to the heavens. The flashing red light of a jet airplane drew her eyes to the sky, and she tried to visualize Kyle sitting in a plane only a few hours away. Would he look the same? Of course not, scolded a rational, inner voice. And he won't be the same, it added, as if pleased to add to her mounting apprehension. "But if he still loves me, it won't matter." She voiced the words into the night, and somehow hearing them added strength to their truth. "We can get to know each other again, and we can recover what we once had." Other people had been through the same kind of thing, she rationalized. Every couple separated by war were strangers for a while, but if love remained they brought their lives together again and their relationship became stronger for it. It would be that way for her and Kyle. She tried to visualize the future, and as she wrestled with immediate problems and feelings, a plan began to form. Her tense muscles began to relax. She had been a pawn in this situation long enough. Allowing herself to be exploited for an end that would only benefit someone else was pure idiocy. It was time she made some demands of her own.

By the time Bud's bronze Matador pulled into the driveway, she was ready. She went inside to greet him with a new inner confidence that made her step firm and her body held in a stiff carriage that would have made Aunt Adele proud.

# Twenty-five

Bud came into the house by himself. It was a bit of luck Lori hadn't planned on. In answer to her questions he explained that Audrey and Brandy had decided to stay in Central City for a few days and take in an art fair.

"I'm glad," said Lori smiling broadly.

"What's going on?" demanded Bud suspiciously. "You look as if you have the world by the tail with a downhill swing."

"Kyle's back!"

His face blanched. At first she thought he was going to cram the words back down her throat, but he only stiffened and then uttered one word, "No!"

"Rex called. Kyle's coming in on a flight in a few hours," she insisted. "I'm going to meet his plane."

Without responding, he turned away and said nothing as he fixed himself a drink—a double scotch and soda. As he took a swig of the fiery liquid, he glared at her over the rim of his glass. When he lowered his drink, there was a mocking derision in the twist of his lips. "So, your beloved Kyle is back. I wonder how he managed to pull himself out of this one."

"Apparently somebody believed the truth! He's clear with everyone—including the Army. I think you let your jealousy cloud your judgment about him and Lois." She tossed her head. "Anyway, it doesn't matter. He's home safe—and my part of the bargain is over."

"But what about Kee and Lang?" This time he did take a step toward her. "I thought you were going to stick it out until we made sure they could stay." His eyes turned cold gray. "You lying bitch! I thought you really cared—"

207

"Just a minute—Doctor!" The blaze in her eyes matched the angry flush along her neck and face. "Before you flaunt that holier-than-thou routine in front of me, let's set this straight. I haven't been lying to anyone —I love those kids!"

She dared him to deny it, leveling her eyes at him. He looked away and nodded. "I know you do, Marty. I'm sorry. I—"

"Save your apologies. I'm not nearly through. This is a different ball game now and I'm willing to continue— only the terms are going to be a little different. I'll stay and try to recover the evidence you need to clear yourself and keep Kee—on one condition. I want Lang."

Her words seemed to hit him like a full blow to the stomach. He even wavered as if he had been struck physically. "You—"

"Wait a minute. Listen. You love the kids too, right? And you want what's best for them. Lang loves me. If we transfer her now to someone else, the upheaval may be very tragic. She is just now coming out of her shell. The next time, she might not. Kee is different. He will respond to a new mother—like Brandy." She might as well say it. "Kee is your son. He belongs with you, but Lang is as much mine as yours—maybe even more because right now she means more to me than anyone else in this whole world."

"Even more than Kyle?" he taunted.

"Yes—but I don't have to choose between them. If Kyle and I still care for each other then we can properly adopt Lang."

"If not—?"

"If not, I'll raise her myself. Single adoptive parents are not unusual these days."

"You have thought this all out very neatly, but what if I say, no—to hell with you and Kyle!"

For some reason his anger only made her calmer, as if his lack of control assured her that she was in the driver's seat. Her smile was even condescending. "If only Lois can receive the evidence needed to clear you, you really have no choice. No more than you had in the very beginning."

"I'll find a new Lois. You're not irreplaceable, you

know. Someone else can handle the impersonation—probably better."

"Not if I cry from the rooftops that it *is* an impersonation. Who is going to deliver the goods to a fraud?"

"If you do that, you'll lose Lang."

"No," she corrected patiently. "Lang was never legally adopted by you. Your signature on her papers is a forgery. I can prove that and probably adopt Lang without your help, but if the truth comes out, you might lose Kee." Her manner softened and she had to resist the impulse to touch a soothing hand to his furrowed forehead. "So you see, we all win. You and Brandy keep Kee and I get Lang—and Kyle."

And then, because victory had been such a long time coming, and she knew from the tired way he sat down in his chair that she had won, she said, "I believe, Dr. Brandon, that this is checkmate." And she waited with a smile for him to deny it.

## Twenty-six

Kyle's plane was twenty minutes late. As they waited, the unreality of the situation grew for Lori. Maybe it was the nighttime hours, the enveloping darkness outside, and the muffled sounds within the huge terminal that created the eerie mood. The coffee that Rex brought her was bitter and lukewarm, as if even the vending machines were suspended in some kind of holding operation.

In her mind she went over worn-out memories, already made threadbare during the years she had been clinging to them. Their ability to arouse emotions in her had been depleted. She couldn't draw on them at this tense moment to create the warmth and desire they had so often cued for her.

"Because I'm scared," she said aloud.

Rex covered her hand with his. "No need to be. You look great in that sweater outfit," he said as if he knew a woman's appearance was an important prop for her self-image. "He'll take one look at you and zingo!"

"Zingo—right back on the plane, you mean," she said dryly, trying to laugh. "I hope he isn't angry about my coming."

"Don't worry about it. Never fear—the King is here! And don't you forget it, Pretty Lady." He winked at her.

But she did forget it. From the moment the plane taxied up to the concourse and emptied its passengers, she had no perception of anything or anyone except the tall, rather pale Kyle, who sauntered off the plane as if he were returning from something as inconsequential as a business conference.

She gasped when she first saw him and was unable to move. He might have walked right by her, out of her life again, and she would have been so mesmerized that she would have let him go. It was Kyle who covered the space between them.

"Lori!" He tossed a coat he had been carrying on a nearby bench and took her in his arms. The kiss he gave her was swift and demanding. If memories hadn't been able to generate weak knees and an exciting breathlessness, reliving them did!

As Kyle set her away to look at her, she wanted to laugh with relief. Why had she been so terrified? "You look about the same," she said with an air of disbelief.

"I can't believe you're here. Who told you I was coming in?"

Only then did Lori remember Rex and turned around to find him, searching in the groups of milling passengers until she saw him near the tunnel entrance, where he had probably been when Kyle entered the waiting room. Lori motioned for him to come over.

"Who's that?" asked Kyle, stiffening.

"Rex—he brought me. This is Kyle," Lori made the needless introduction and glanced quickly from one to the other. If they had known each other before, it was not discernible.

"Hello, Kyle." Rex stuck out his hand.

"How did you know I was on this flight?" Kyle asked again as they shook.

"Our office was notified. I've been assigned to the Brandon case."

"I thought that had been settled when they released me."

"Nope. We still don't have the goods on that smuggling operation. I thought maybe you could tell me something about it that we don't know."

"The officials finally believed what I had been saying all along. I was trying to crack the organization, not join it. Anyway, I'm sorry I ever got Lori into this mess. From the way Lois talked, the last shipment of jade and a list of her business connections would be delivered to her here in Denver. I thought it would be a simple matter for someone like Lori, who resembled her slightly, to receive it. I guess I was wrong."

"Or maybe it hasn't been delivered yet."

It was difficult to tell whether this was a casual repartee or some kind of unspoken tug-of-war.

Lori's elation of a moment ago was fast disintegrating. She felt like a pawn between the two men. Now that she looked closer at Kyle, she could see a guarded weariness in his stance and a rigidity in his jaw and neck muscles. "You're tired," she said. "All of this can wait. You've been through enough." She was angry and let down that this long-dreamed-of reunion was being ruined by Rex and the same old unanswered questions.

Kyle nodded agreement. "Are you still at the Brandons?"

"I've decided to stay and see this through. I'll tell you about it as soon as we have a chance to talk." And she threw an accusing look at Rex.

He had the audacity to grin before he responded. "The lady's right. There's a new motel, the Packard Inn, not far from the Brandon house. If you like, Kyle, we can drop you off there. After you both have had a few hours' sleep, you can get reacquainted."

Kyle agreed and Lori couldn't find any objection to it, except that Rex had presented it in such a way that there was no question of Lori remaining at the motel with Kyle. Even though she probably would have rejected the idea since she wasn't ready for such intimate surroundings just yet, she still bristled silently that she hadn't been given a choice in the matter. She felt herself being deftly managed.

When they reached the motel, Kyle kissed her again, more lingeringly this time. "I'll see you soon," he whispered. Then he slipped out of the car and was gone into the shadows again.

Lori stifled an impulse to call him back, as if it might be another five years before she saw him again. But Rex had already backed away from the line of motel units and had turned the car onto the winding road that led back to the sprawling house, perched grotesquely against a rim of rocky bluffs.

"Tired?" he asked.

"No. Not at all! I guess I'm too keyed up. It will probably hit me all at once and I'll drop in my tracks." Then she felt guilty for thinking of Rex as an intruder at the airport. "Thank you for taking me tonight."

"Glad to be a part of the happy reunion. I hope things work out the way you want. I am surprised you are going on with the impersonation." He glanced at her quizzically. "Care to tell me why?"

"Oh, you'll figure it out," she parried. "You ought to be glad. When I turn over the delivery to you, you'll probably get a promotion."

"I'd rather have something else." He looked quite serious. "It might be fun to know you better."

"I'm flattered, but you can't make a conquest out of me."

"Why not?"

"I'm in love with someone else." She said it frankly, with a kind of purr of happiness.

He saw her to the door of the house, and with only a quick good night went back down the steps to his car.

Bud was waiting for her in the family room. At first she thought he had been drinking all the time she had been gone. He was stretched out in his TV chair, with his legs out in front and his head resting back against the headrest. Only the tenseness in his hands, which clenched the armrests, denied the casualness of his position. He looked at her with clear and cold eyes.

"Where is the conquering hero?"

"Down the road. At the Packard Inn."

"Well, how did the passionate reunion go?"

"Nicely," she replied evenly, deciding to ignore the overtones of mockery in his voice. "He looks about the same—a little thinner, but—"

"But still as handsome and debonair as always?"

"I think so and—and I think we can put it back together again—this time for good." There was deep satisfaction in her words, and her face reflected an inner glow of anticipated happiness.

He was looking at her now with his head slightly raised and his body erect as he leaned toward her. "He's a sonofabitch! A goddamn lying bastard!"

Frozen by the onslaught of foul words, she stared at him. Then every ounce of protest she could muster came pouring out with the same level of verbal abuse that his foul words had laid on her.

"And who left his wife to shack up with a Vietnamese prostitute?"

He was on his feet while she was trying to verbalize the next insult. "You're the whore lover," she spat. "Not Kyle!"

He slapped her hard and then pinned her arms behind her. "You'll not speak of Mela like that," he said in that even, cold tone that was more frightening than his bellowing anger.

Tears of fright and shame made her turn her head away. "Please—please let me go."

"Why should I? This is the kind of man you like. I was wrong about ice in your veins. That first time, when I forced you to kiss me, you almost had me seduced. And then there was that night in Estes—"

Savagely she buried her head into his neck and bit into the soft flesh. His cry of pain only increased the pressure of his hold, and he pulled her so close her body arched backward.

"You're mad," she sobbed.

"Kyle told me you were a wildcat when you were aroused. He even told me where you like to be kissed—"

"No, no!" she protested.

"Oh, yes. All those little intimate, soft places. You haven't forgotten the ritual, the buildup that drove you out of your mind. Remember how—"

"Please—" she sobbed. "Don't—don't—let me go."

But his words flowed out, making the intimacies between her and Kyle sordid and dirty. The descriptions were pure degradation, and she stopped struggling, as if nothing that could happen to her physically could defile her more than his words. He described moments of ecstasy she had forgotten, and she tried to close her ears against them as he laid his head against hers and poured them into her ears.

It was her passiveness that finally staunched his flow of words. But as he grew silent, he did not release her. Then with a cry that seemed to be torn out of his guts, he buried his head against her.

She stood rigidly in his arms. When he raised his head

to look at her, her gaze was like that of one who has been hurt to the point of insensibility. He pulled his arms away from her, and she continued to stand there in front of him, like something shattered that has not yet crumbled to the floor.

"I—I—" he stammered in a hoarse whisper. "You—you had to know—to know Kyle for what he is. My wife told me those things. She taunted me with them. How she loved describing their orgies. Kyle told her all about you . . . made comparisons that caused Lois to speak scornfully of you. He's filth. Marty. I can't let you throw yourself away." He ran an agitated hand through his hair as if to clarify his thoughts. "I know you hate me now —but I had to destroy him for you because I love you, Marty. At first I thought you were another one of Kyle's women and I couldn't stand the sight of you. But the children knew the truth about you before I did. Your love for Kyle isn't the cheap, ugly, destroying kind . . . you were willing to sacrifice yourself for it. But he's not worth it!" He reached out and shook her. "Don't you understand? He's not worth it!"

But the eyes she leveled at him revealed no understanding; they only reflected a shattering within that had rent apart the foundations of her being.

"I should have told you another way," he said simply. "If I hadn't been so desperate—so emotionally involved—"

A mental shield shut out his words of contrition, and an overpowering urge to suppress the torturous moment dispelled her lethargy. An instinct to run caused her to bolt from the room and stumble up the circular staircase. But at the top she paused, as if physically lost. Then she turned and in measured steps went out into the protective darkness of the deck.

# Twenty-seven

Faraway strips of city lights were fuzzy in her vision, and she clutched the railing as if to orient herself with something firm and solid. There was no grayness in the shadows about her, only blackness, as if to deny the truth that a new dawn was only a few hours away. It could have been midnight with the earth shrouded in darkness forever. And yet, a thin edge of light, barely perceptible, would soon etch the horizon in pinkness. If there had been time, she might have responded to its growing promise and found some hope in the emotional wreckage that lay so darkly within. But immediately she heard Bud's footsteps going down the back stairs and then the motor of his car as he started it up. It roared around the driveway below her, its headlights slicing the darkness. With a squeal of tires the car turned west, toward the mountains . . . and Brandy!

The thought tore a protesting cry from her. "Bud! Come back, Bud! Please!" But there was no time to analyze the new loss she felt, one that was biting into her with new urgency. She stiffened as she heard a movement behind her.

Jerking around, she tried to focus in the darkness as a hand descended upon her mouth and her arms were pinned to her sides with a crushing grip.

The deck's railing was less than waist-high, and in an instant she was pushed up against it. Strips of wood cut into her stomach as her assailant tried to shove her over it. The large hand that held her mouth was closing off the end of her nose so that her chest began to burn and every muscle in her body lost its strength. Only an undefeatable instinct for self-preservation kept her clawing, biting, and kicking until all strength was gone.

It was the child's scream that saved her. A high-pitched frantic cry of horror distracted him for a moment and gave Lori the chance to bury her teeth into the hand he pressed against her mouth.

In the instant that he loosened his grip to bring his hand away from her vicious teeth, she was away, grabbing one of the deck chairs. With strength born out of desperation, she lifted it up and hurled it against him.

As he staggered against the blow, she lurched to the open glass door where Lang stood. "Run!" she screamed, grabbing the child's hand and jerking her along through the living room, and down the short hall to the nursery bedroom.

Once inside, Lori slammed the door shut and turned the lock on the door knob. She knew she had gained a few seconds on him because he had stumbled against some furniture in the shadowy living room while she and Lang had sped easily through the familiar room.

Now she ran through the dark bedroom to the bathroom and locked that door, just as she had done that first night, fearing Bud's amorous advances. The same thought she had entertained then darted back—Would such feeble precautions keep anyone out if they really wanted in?

The answer came almost instantaneously as the balcony door splintered and a muscular hand reached through the opening and deftly turned the lock. Then the door flung open, and Lori put the child behind her as she stiffened to meet a new attack.

But this time the assailant leaned casually against the door frame and then reached out and flipped on the light switch.

"Shall we have a little light on the subject?" asked Kyle tritely.

There was no spurt of surprise anywhere in her. From the moment he had touched her on the deck, some inner awareness had known who it was.

"Why do you want to kill me?" She stared at him steadily, amazed at the firm fiber in her voice.

"I overheard a little of that scene with the Doctor. And the way you called his name. There's no trusting you anymore, my dear little Lori. Your feelings for the

Doctor have gotten in the way. I had to depend upon you to take care of any evidence you found that might do me harm. That's why I persuaded them to try this little farce. But now . . ." He shrugged.

"You were pretty sure of me."

"I knew you'd never hang a noose around my neck. And I was right, wasn't I?"

She wished she could have denied it, but they both knew her too well.

At that moment Kee made a disgruntled cry from the crib and began to protest loudly this early morning intrusion. Without waiting to see what Kyle was going to do, she grabbed the baby out of the crib and backed away. With Lang still cowering at her side, Lori's eyes were fixed steadily on Kyle's face, as if she could anticipate any move he might make.

"Quite the mother lioness, aren't you? Christ, what a laugh! I knew you'd be good at the part—anything for dear old Kyle. Right, honey?" He gave that deep laugh of his. "But you were too stupid to figure things out. Despite the brilliancy of my plan, it never came off because you never found Lois's things. Luckily they let me go so I can do the job myself."

"What—job?" Lori was trying to shush Kee by holding him over her shoulder and patting his rump. The effort was mechanical, and she brought every ounce of concentration to bear on what Kyle was saying.

"Getting this." He walked over to Kee's crib. With a quick movement he picked up Kee's gourd rattle and brought it crashing down on the end post of the baby bed. As the gourd shattered, pieces of it and jade stones flew in every direction. A small plastic cylinder containing a tightly rolled-up piece of paper landed nearly at Lori's feet. She didn't need to look at it to know whose name would be first on Lois's list of associates.

Kyle spread his mouth in a broad laugh. "I'll be damned! She sent out the jade, too. What luck! With the ransom the Doctor will pay to get his brats back, I'll be solvent until I get Lois's business back into operation."

"Ransom?" she gasped. "You're not going to touch either of these children."

"Grow up, Lori," he snapped. "I saw whole villages

of slant-eyed kids like these lying dead on the ground. I'm not about to be squeamish about a couple more." He bent down to pick up the pieces of jade.

As he stooped to retrieve one that was nearly under her dresser, Lori grabbed Lang's hand and bounded toward the hall door.

Kyle swore as he straightened up. "You dumb broad—"

Lori didn't wait. She jerked Lang down the hall in a run and down the stairs, automatically dismissing the deck and stairs as an avenue of escape. With the wriggling Kee she couldn't travel fast and still keep her balance. The back door seemed nearest. But even as they bounded into the family room, Lori realized they wouldn't make it before Kyle overtook them.

She heard Kyle round the last of the stairs. Panic-stricken, she flung Kee down on the couch. Her movements were frenzied. There was just time enough for her to unhook one of the heavy chains from the wall and let it go as he came through the doorway.

The mammoth planter might have missed him entirely if he hadn't paused just then, trying to grasp the reason Lori was standing there, facing the doorway with rounded, expectant eyes. But if a flicker of understanding came, it was a second too late. The planter caught him squarely on the back of the neck and splintering bone was heard as he fell.

She just had time to collect the children in her arms again when Bud came racing in through the back door with Rex at his heels.

Somehow Bud's arms stretched wide enough to circle all three of them, and Lori let her head rest against the firmness of his shoulder as Kee and Lang snuggled in close enough to make one compact unit.

She buried her head against his neck and shoulder. "I had to do it," she sobbed. "He was going—to take them —for money. I had to do it. I—"

"It's all right, darling. It's all right." His touch was tender and caressing. "It's over now. It's over." She felt his loving protection encircling her and she knew, in that bittersweet moment, that there was much that had just begun. She lifted her face to his. He kissed her and her lips responded with a warmth that confirmed the love between them.

Rex was contritely apologetic, embarrassed about his "never fear, the King is here" routine. He had gone back to the motel to keep a surveillance on Kyle, since it had been his idea to release Kyle so he could lead them to the cache. But Kyle hadn't even registered at the Packard Inn and had hitched a ride to the house only a few minutes after Rex and Lori drove off.

When Bud arrived at the motel to have it out with Kyle, Rex had just discovered Kyle's absence. By the time the two men got back to the house, the drama had already been acted out.

A few days later Mrs. Wallace of the House-Sitters Association received a brief and puzzling letter. She frowned as she read it over twice. Lori Martin was no longer on her assignment in Denver, Colorado. She had moved into a new mountain home just bought by Dr. Brandon in Evergreen, Colorado. At the moment, she and Philip Brandon were on their honeymoon, accompanied by two Oriental children.

The tone of the letter was ecstatic, rather than apologetic, and this caused Mrs. Wallace to push her black frame glasses higher on her nose in irritation. None of it made any sense at all!

She sighed as she put down the letter. It certainly was difficult these days to find good help to carry out a simple job like house-sitting.

A STUNNING AND PROPHETIC THRILLER
OF INNOCENT PEOPLE CAUGHT IN A
WEB OF INTERNATIONAL SUSPENSE

# CANNIBALS AND MISSIONARIES

# MARY McCARTHY

## author of THE GROUP

"PURE PLEASURE . . .
A TENSE, INTELLIGENT ENTERTAINMENT."
*Chicago Tribune*

"FASCINATING . . . A KIND OF
CANTERBURY PILGRIMAGE WITH MACHINE GUNS."
*Mary Gordon, The New York Times Book Review*

"Mary McCarthy turns her keen mind and brilliant
style to the subject of terrorism and an airplane
hijacking . . . a tale psychologically astute, ironic
and ultimately heartbreaking . . . superb."
*Publishers Weekly*

"A return to the wicked brilliance of her early
work . . . sheer pleasure to read."
*Quest*

 AVON   50690/$2.75

CAN 9-80

# AVON ⬡ THE BEST IN
# BESTSELLING ENTERTAINMENT

- [ ] **The Black Lyon** Jude Deveraux — 75911 — $2.50
- [ ] **Fires of Winter** Johanna Lindsey — 75747 — $2.50
- [ ] **The Jade Unicorn** Jay Hulpern — 50708 — $2.50
- [ ] **Chance the Winds of Fortune**
  Laurie McBain — 75796 — $2.95
- [ ] **The Heirs of Love** Barbara Ferry Johnson — 75739 — $2.95
- [ ] **Golden Opportunity** Edith Begner — 75085 — $2.50
- [ ] **Sally Hemings** Barbara Chase-Riboud — 48686 — $2.75
- [ ] **A Woman of Substance**
  Barbara Taylor Bradford — 49163 — $2.95
- [ ] **Sacajawea** Anna Lee Waldo — 75606 — $3.95
- [ ] **Passage West** Henry Dallas Miller — 50278 — $2.75
- [ ] **The Firecloud** Kenneth McKennay — 50054 — $2.50
- [ ] **Pulling Your Own Strings**
  Dr. Wayne W. Dyer — 44388 — $2.75
- [ ] **The Helper** Catherine Marshall — 45583 — $2.25
- [ ] **Bethany's Sin** Robert R. McCammon — 47712 — $2.50
- [ ] **Summer Lightning** Judith Richards — 42960 — $2.50
- [ ] **Cold Moon Over Babylon**
  Michael McDowell — 48660 — $2.50
- [ ] **The Moonchild** Kenneth McKenney — 41483 — $2.50
- [ ] **Homeward Winds the River**
  Barbara Ferry Johnson — 42952 — $2.50
- [ ] **Tears of Gold** Laurie McBain — 41475 — $2.50
- [ ] **Monty: A Biography of Montgomery Cliff**
  Robert LaGuardia — 49528 — $2.50
- [ ] **Sweet Savage Love** Rosemary Rogers — 47324 — $2.50
- [ ] **ALIVE: The Story of the Andes Survivors**
  Piers Paul Read — 39164 — $2.25
- [ ] **The Flame and the Flower**
  Kathleen E. Woodiwiss — 46276 — $2.50
- [ ] **I'm OK—You're OK**
  Thomas A. Harris, M.D. — 46268 — $2.50

Available at better bookstores everywhere, or order direct from the publisher.

In the deadly world of international espionage,
love is the total risk . . .

# THE
# HUMAN
# FACTOR

# GRAHAM
# GREENE

"Probably the best espionage novel ever written."

*United Press International*

**SIX MONTHS ON THE N.Y. TIMES
BESTSELLER LIST!**

**NOW A MAJOR MOTION PICTURE**

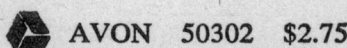 AVON   50302   $2.75

HF 5-80